Tunnel Vision

Brenda Adcock

Quest Books

Port Arthur, Texas

ISBN 978-1-935053-19-4
1-935053-19-1

First Printing 2009

9 8 7 6 5 4 3 2 1

Cover design by Donna Pawlowski

Published by:

Regal Crest Enterprises, LLC
4700 Hwy 365, Suite A, PMB 210
Port Arthur, Texas 7764

Find us on the World Wide Web at
http://www.regalcrest.biz

Printed in the United States of America

Acknowledgments

There are always too many people to thank by the time an author types the words "The End." It's an unusual way to end a story because it's really only the beginning. This story is partially based on a murder that occurred while I was an undergraduate, and I was never able to shake it. I hope I've done it some justice in the end.

By the time I completed the original manuscript I was indebted to many friends. I'll always be grateful for the support of my reading group in Austin, Texas. They have certainly broadened my horizons. Gail Robinson, one of our members, beta read this manuscript for me and added valuable insights. Carol Poynter became another beta reader and pointed out all kinds of errors. My buddy, Ron Whiteis, spent a couple of long nights commenting on the big picture and helped me see the overall story much more clearly. He's truly my flashlight in the dark. Donna Pawlowski created yet another great cover and I am always amazed. A former beta reader and good friend, Ruta Skujins, was my editor for this project and asked way too many questions, but they needed to be asked. Thank you is not a strong enough phrase for my publisher, Cathy LeNoir. She took a chance on me and I will never forget that. Lastly, a special hug for my partner, Cheryl. She's always there for me and I couldn't ask for more.

For Ron Whiteis
for being my best friend when I needed one.

Chapter One

AN ACRID TASTE rose in her throat as the scream erupted from her mouth with the first flash of gunfire. "No!" A second flash, followed by searing pain, dropped her to her knees. She raised her revolver and squeezed off two quick rounds before crawling toward the prone body near her on the damp grass. Wetness soaked through the knees of her uniform pants and her vision was blurred by the tears forming in her eyes. She couldn't cry. Wheeler needed her.

She didn't remember hearing the back-up cars sliding to a halt nearby or the shouts of other officers running toward her as she reached out and rolled her partner and friend onto his back, yanking at the Velcro of the bulletproof vest that hadn't protected his neck and head. She could barely bring herself to look at him. She had to concentrate. What she did was a matter of life and death, now more than it ever had been. Ignoring the throbbing in her leg, she began chest compressions and leaned over his body to breathe air into him. As she returned to the compressions, she glanced quickly at his neck and watched frothy red bubbles oozing from the black hole torn in his throat.

"You'll be okay, Stan," she whispered over and over as she pushed on his chest, creating a mantra to guide the rhythm of her movements. She breathed air into his lungs once more and saw a burst of red flow from the neck wound. As she turned to resume compressions, a hand grabbed her wrist. She tried to push it away, but it was too strong. "You're killing him!" she said as she struggled. The hand squeezed her wrist tightly and she looked down to see a blood-covered hand. Flashing her eyes to Wheeler's face, she tried to remain calm. She brought her face closer to his and managed to say, "You're gonna be okay, Stan. I promise."

The look on his face twisted into a frown and his head moved slowly from side to side, his lips moved, but no sound escaped. "What? What are you trying to tell me?" she asked as she leaned closer to hear. In a rush of unexpected air and sound, she heard him. "Your fault, Brodie. This is your fault."

Trying to get away from the accusation in his voice and the dimming light in his eyes, she fought against the steel grip. "I'll always be inside you," he whispered, his lips curling into a cruel grin. "I'm taking part of you with me." She watched in horror when his eyes refused to show any sign of forgiveness as a dull, milky film clouded them and the final air escaped from his lungs. She could hear him inside her mind already, accusing her.

"No!" she screamed, sitting up abruptly and sucking in air through her mouth in short, panicked gasps. Her eyes frantically searched the blackness surrounding her and she begged for one small flicker of light to prove the persistent nightmare was finally over. That she was still alive. Her clothing was wet with perspiration. Small droplets of sweat ran between her breasts and trickled down her neck and along the hollow of her spine. She drew her knees up to her chest and wrapped her arms around them tightly until she could stop shaking. As her breathing became more controlled, she lowered her forehead to her knees and squeezed her eyes closed, pushing away the face in her dream. It was always the same. *Is this what happens when you die unexpectedly? You crawl inside someone else's mind and make their life hell?* Why did Wheeler have to stare at her like that as he exhaled his last harsh metallic breath into her?

She shivered from the sweaty clothing sticking to her damp skin. She was pulling the wet t-shirt over her head and leaning down to pull a dry shirt from the nightstand drawer, when the sudden, explosive sound of gunfire made her bolt from the bed, plunging her back into the nightmare. She grabbed her service revolver and flashlight from the nightstand. She crouched and made her way to the bedroom window, looking carefully outside as she pulled an old heather-gray t-shirt over her head. Through a slit in the Venetian blinds she saw a car parked on the shoulder of the road in front of her house. Its hood was up and a figure leaned into the engine compartment. She moved quietly into the living room and opened the front door, shining the beam of the flashlight on the car, her revolver following the shaft of light. A man turned his head toward the glare and waved. Relaxing slightly, but still wary, she lowered the revolver and walked toward the car.

"Didn't mean to disturb you, ma'am," the man said.

She glanced around the car and then shined the light into the vehicle. An old woman with mussed white hair sat behind the wheel, looking like a deer frozen in the headlights of a Mack truck. She raised an arm to shield her eyes from the flashlight beam. The man under the hood was considerably younger than the woman and his shaggy hair kept falling in his face. Brodie clicked the safety on her revolver and stuck it in the back waistband of her shorts before moving to the front of the vehicle.

"Car trouble?"

"Yeah. I keep telling her she needs a new fuckin' car, but noooo, she's bound and determined to hang onto this one until they both croak," the man said in a low voice.

He tinkered under the hood a little longer and finally stuck his head out from under one side of the hood. "Try it now, Grandma, and remember, just pump the gas pedal one time."

The woman didn't reply, but Royce Brodie heard the clicking sound as she pumped the gas pedal and turned the key in the ignition. The engine sputtered a few times and sounded as if it might die again until the man reached under the hood and grabbed the throttle rod to keep it going.

"It just has to idle a few minutes and then it should at least get us to a gas station," he said, glancing at her. "Probably just a clogged fuel line. She won't buy nothin' but that cheap shit and it keeps fouling the engine."

The man slowly released the gas pedal and the engine grumbled, but continued idling. He slammed the hood down and walked to the driver's side of the vehicle.

"Scoot over, Grandma. Better let me drive in case she dies again," he said as he opened the door.

"Just don't you speed in my car, Billy," the old woman said as she slid across the seat.

Smiling at Brodie, he shrugged and said, "Not much chance of that."

She stepped out of the way and watched as the car began to crawl away. As she walked back toward her house, the car began to sputter. Suddenly, a series of backfires poured out of the car's exhaust, a flash accompanying each sound. It was the same sound she had heard the night her life changed forever and the nightmares began. The night Stan Wheeler found his way inside her mind and soul to torment her. Then there had been someone to hold her and soothe the nightmares away. Now there was no one. Wheeler had died because of her, and she had killed the love that might have saved her. Rubbing a hand across her face and through her damp hair, she stepped into her house but knew she wouldn't sleep again that night. The shrill ring of her phone kept her from having to worry about it.

FROM A DISTANCE, the activity in the field off the steep westbound lane of the main highway into Cedar Springs, Texas looked like a convention of fireflies on a humid summer night. Patrol units blocked the divided highway at the top of the hill above the accident site to make room for emergency vehicles, their red and blue lights cutting through the darkness. Brodie yawned and squeezed her eyes shut, shoving a finger under her wire-rimmed glasses to rub the pre-dawn blurriness away. Exhaustion would eventually give her the nightmare-free sleep her body craved, if only for a couple of hours. She barely remembered groping for her jeans and boots in the dim light of her bedroom. She hadn't been in a hurry to reach the scene. Once a victim was dead there wasn't a helluva lot she could do for them. She nosed her vintage 1969 Olympic Gold Camaro along the shoulder of the eastbound lanes, past a line of slow-moving vehicles obviously hoping to get a better look at the accident. She shook her head and ran a hand through her short, dark, but graying hair. Everyone talked about how horrible accidents like this were, all the while busting a gut hoping to catch even a glimpse of a bloodied and mangled body.

Halfway up the hill, she swung the Camaro onto the grassy, sloping median separating west and eastbound lanes. Before she could extract the wallet holding her detective's badge from her waistband, a flashlight-waving patrolman in the median signaled her to stop. She didn't recognize him and concluded he was one of the new eager-beaver types the department had recently hired to beef up its ranks in response to the rising crime rate that accompanied the rising population rate of Cedar Springs. The small town she escaped to nearly eight years earlier was being slowly but steadily gobbled up by Austin's relentless urban sprawl. And no matter how hard people tried to get away from them, every time they moved, the cockroaches managed to tag along. Brodie rolled the window down as the officer, dressed in brand-spanking new dark-blue pants and gray shirt, approached. He leaned down to the driver's side window with a frown and began the speech he had probably already repeated dozens of times, all the while ogling the car's immaculately restored interior.

"There's been an accident, ma'am," he droned as he reached into his shirt pocket. "I'm issuing a citation for illegally crossing the median and obstructing the right-of-way for emergency vehicles."

"Don't think so," Brodie said matter-of-factly, holding her detective's shield up for the officer to see.

"Oh, I'm sorry, ma'am. I didn't know detectives came out for traffic accidents."

She was becoming mildly annoyed at being referred to as 'ma'am'. At fifty she already felt old enough without being reminded of it multiple times by some kid barely out of puberty. Forcing a smile, she focused on the officer's nametag and shrugged. "What can I say, Underwood, it was a dull night and I've already used up my departmental quota of sleep. Is Ramirez at the scene?"

"Uh, I don't know Ramirez, Detective. This is my first day."

Brodie nodded as she surveyed the scene. Finally she turned her attention back to the officer. "Well, listen, another detective named

Nicholls will be showing up in a little while. You can't miss him. Blond, surfer-looking type. Tell him I'm here somewhere."

"Yes, ma'am. Will do."

She would have sworn the patrolman was going to salute as she struggled to look serious, hoping she hadn't looked that innocent twenty-five years earlier when she began her first day as a patrol officer.

She continued across the median and recognized an officer standing in the westbound lane. She pulled her car over, leaning partway out the window as she approached.

"Hey, Southard! Seen Ramirez?"

"That you, Brodie? What the hell you doin' out here this late?"

"Not sure yet."

"Ramirez should be somewhere down by the fire trucks." He looked appreciatively at the Camaro. "Let me know when you're ready to sell that baby," he said.

"Won't be in your lifetime," she replied with a smile.

Waving a hand at Southard, she let her vehicle roll closer to the scene before braking and turning off the ignition. Getting out of the car and stretching the kinks out of her thin five-ten frame, she reached into the back seat and retrieved her police jacket. By the time she arrived the area was well lit by emergency vehicles. She surveyed the ground leading to the still smoldering vehicle as she walked toward it. An ambulance was backed onto the grass near the site, and she finally spotted Patrol Officer Eduardo Ramirez interviewing a fireman near the rear of the ambulance. Ramirez was an experienced patrol officer who, in her opinion, should have been moved up to detective years ago. He was writing in a small notebook as she shoved her hands into her jeans' pockets and sauntered up to the men.

"Ramirez."

The stout Hispanic officer turned his head toward her and continued writing. "Just a sec, Lieutenant."

She nodded and moved toward the burned car. Apparently the fire had spread into the heavy bushes and overgrown grasses surrounding the area, and three or four firemen were pulling at the underbrush with long poles, looking for potential hot spots. Ramirez joined her and looked around.

"Messy, huh," he said.

"Yeah. So why'd you feel the need to drag my happy ass out of bed for a fucking traffic accident? Even a messy one," she asked as she lit a cigarette, flipped her lighter shut with a metallic click and took a deep drag.

"Didn't look right somehow. Come on," Ramirez motioned.

As Brodie followed him, Ramirez began to point out things

around the vehicle.

"No plates, front or rear," Ramirez said shining his flashlight on the plate holder below the vehicle trunk.

He moved to the front of the vehicle and stopped again. "What do you see?" he asked.

She walked around the front end of the car before answering. "Hood's up and the engine appears to have been the source of the initial fire. Was there an explosion?"

"Yep, but not from the gas tank or the engine."

She squatted down and looked at the front of the car. "What's the scenario?"

"Driver speeds down the hill, loses control, vehicle leaves the road, strikes these trees, catches fire and explodes."

"It doesn't look like there's much damage to the front end from the impact, certainly not enough to cause an explosion unless it's a very touchy vehicle."

"That's what I thought. There's barely a dent in the front end. And look over here, Brodie."

Putting her hands on her knees, she pushed herself up slowly, grimacing as her knees crackled, and followed Ramirez.

"I didn't notice this until the fire was out." Ramirez shined his flashlight on a semi-circular burned area a few feet from the car. "See how round this area is? Looks like someone was throwing something onto the fire. You know, keeping it going."

"Sounds like a stretch to me, buddy."

"There are footprints just outside the burned area."

"Hell, Ramirez, there were a dozen people wandering around in here putting the fire out."

"But they all wear the rubber boots the Fire Department issues. Pretty distinctive tread. These are different."

Brodie walked over to the circular area and ran the beam from her police flashlight around the edges of the burned grass. She squatted down again and adjusted her glasses to see the faint indentations in the grass and dirt.

"Anyone else been around here?" she asked without looking back at Ramirez.

"Just me and the fireboys. The witness said he wasn't on this side of the car."

She stood up and turned around. "What witness?"

"Well, he's not really a witness. He came up on the scene after the explosion. Some college kid comin' home for spring break. Name's Jeff Quincy."

"You've already questioned him?"

"Just preliminary stuff. I told him to wait for you. He's up by the highway, probably still shakin'. He was pretty spooked when I got here."

"Cordon off this area until we can get a better look at it in the daylight. Good job, Ramirez."

"Thanks, RB."

"So when you moving to detectives? We'll have a vacancy soon," Brodie asked with a smile, already knowing the answer.

"Never."

"And miss playing Sherlock Holmes?"

"I still do that and don't have to wear no stinkin' coat and tie. And I never get called out in the middle of the night unless it's my shift."

"So, where's this semi-witness?" she asked.

Ramirez pointed to an older-model Toyota parked on the shoulder of the highway. "I assigned a patrol officer to stay with him until you got here so he wouldn't wander off."

"Okay. Make sure you put everything you've noticed out here in your report. And that includes anything you think is suspicious. Thanks, Ramirez."

ALMOST TWO HOURS had passed since he called 9-1-1 and his bladder was telling him he shouldn't have Super-Sized that last soft drink. He glanced at his watch. It was nearly one-thirty. As he looked up again, he saw a thin middle-aged woman in jeans and a police windbreaker walking along the shoulder.

"You the one who called this in?" the woman asked as she strode toward him.

He nodded as he slid off the hood of the Toyota. "Yes, ma'am."

"Lieutenant Brodie," she said casually, field stripping her cigarette and stuffing the remaining filter in the pocket of her jeans. "Cedar Springs PD." Glancing at the patrol officer, who looked bored, she said, "Thanks for keeping an eye on Mr. Quincy until I got here, officer. You can return to your patrol duties now."

"Yes, ma'am," the officer nodded.

Returning her attention to the nervous-looking teenager, she leaned against the side of his car. "Why don't you tell me what you saw?"

"I really didn't see anything. I saw a flash ahead of me and after I came over the hill I saw there had been an accident and the car over there was on fire."

"Is that when you called in the accident report?"

"No. I thought someone might have been thrown from the car, so I ran down there to check."

"Did you find anyone?" she asked as she looked toward the vehicle.

Jeff shook his head. "No, I didn't see anyone. At least not on this side of the car. Before I could look too closely, I smelled this...this..."

"Yeah, I get the picture."

"Then I ran back and called for help. I guess nobody can help whoever was in there now, can they?"

"Doesn't look like it," she said. "Let me get an address and phone number for you in case we have more questions later. We'll need you to come in tomorrow and make a statement, just for the record."

She handed him a small notebook and he wrote down his name, his parent's address and phone number.

Glancing at the notebook, she said, "Thanks for your help, Mr. Quincy. We'll be in touch."

"Um, how do you think it happened, Ms. Brodie?"

"Lieutenant," she corrected him. "Hard to tell at night. Was he going very fast when he passed you?"

"He didn't pass me. I never even saw his tail lights ahead of me."

"You didn't see his tail lights at any time?"

He shook his head. "No, ma'am. No tail lights and no one passed me. I just saw the flash ahead of me."

"It could have been a delayed explosion after the car hit the trees. We'll know more when it's light."

As he began slowly pulling away, a half-smile crossed Brodie's lips. Like others who happened upon an accident or some other tragedy, he seemed reluctant to leave. Hell, he'll probably envision a career in law enforcement because of this, she thought. She began walking toward the wreckage again when another vehicle pulled off the road and came to a grinding stop near her, throwing up a small cloud of dust. Squinting into the headlights, she recognized the silhouette of her partner, Curtis Nicholls. He exited the car quickly and strode toward her, still adjusting his tie and finger-combing his thick blond hair.

"What've we got, RB?"

"Probably just a traffic accident. Fell asleep at the wheel or drunk. Hope it didn't interrupt your evening," she said.

"The lady was leaving anyway," he said with a boyish grin.

Since Curtis Nicholls had joined the Cedar Springs PD and become her partner, Brodie had found him to be occasionally intolerant and a shameless womanizer. She couldn't fault him for the womanizing part, having been accused of the same thing herself a few times by women who had been in a position to know.

As they reached the vehicle, firemen at the scene were making their first attempt at pulling the driver's side door open. Heat vapors drifted off the wet metal as the men worked cautiously to avoid making contact with the hot car. Brodie moved around the vehicle, jotting down notes in a worn black notebook she carried in the breast pocket of her jacket.

From what little was left of the car it appeared to be an older model Mercedes Benz. As she pondered the age of the vehicle, a loud piercing scream of metal scraping against metal split the quiet. She winced as every filling in her mouth responded to the sound. The two detectives returned to the driver's side of the vehicle as firemen were finally successful in prying the door open. Inside they saw the remains of what had once been a person, but were unable to determine whether it had been a man or a woman. To Brodie the head resembled pictures she had seen of desiccated Egyptian mummies after they had been unwrapped. The blackened cheeks were sunken in and the jaw had dropped. It seemed that the unrecognizable face was laughing at her and even though it presented a scene of horror, she was compellingly drawn to stare at the remains.

"When will you get the body out?" she asked a fireman standing nearby.

The fireman shook his head. "Probably have to wait for things to cool down a little more. Hell of a mess, ain't it?"

"Yeah. Let us know when you can remove it. We'll keep routing traffic and sightseers around the area until then."

"It'll probably be another hour or two." Motioning toward the car with his chin, he added, "It won't take the crispy critter there nearly as long to cool down as the vehicle itself. They may not be able to tow this heap away until after dawn."

"When you get the body out transfer it to the Travis County Medical Examiner for autopsy." Brodie turned to Nicholls and said. "We might be able to trace the car through DMV, but the driver might not be the owner."

"I'll check on the VIN after it cools down," Nicholls said. "At least it's a starting place."

"Let's see where the vehicle left the road."

Uniformed officers were still cordoning off the area as Brodie and Nicholls cast flashlight beams across the grass leading to the road. On the highway itself, they looked for skid marks, which might indicate speed and abrupt braking.

Nicholls shined his light up and down the road. "I don't see a damn thing, RB. Looks like he didn't bother to use the brakes. Maybe he fell asleep at the wheel and just left the road."

"Could be," she said. "Judging from the final position of the vehicle it's a straight line from the road to where the vehicle struck the trees. There was minimal damage, at best, to the front end so there couldn't have been much of an impact."

"Did you notice that area back there?" Nicholls says, shining his light along the presumed path of the vehicle.

"Yeah. What do you make of that?"

"Well, the ground is pretty chopped up and dippy. If the car hit it doing any speed at all, it should have awakened a dead man. Maybe the driver had a heart attack or something."

"The kid who called it in said no one passed him and swears he didn't see any tail lights before he saw the explosion."

"What are you thinking?"

"Might be a torch job. Ramirez was suspicious enough to call us in and he's pretty thorough at working scenes. He pointed out an area near the vehicle where someone could have been standing, but it's hard to tell much in the dark. We'll have to wait until the ME hands down his ruling from atop Mount Sinai to determine if it's an accident or not."

Brodie rubbed her eyes and shined her flashlight on her wristwatch. Two forty-five. "Shit," she muttered to herself.

"You look beat. Go home and get some rest." Nicholls looked back at the car. "The paperwork can wait a few hours and Charcoal Bill back there's not going anywhere for a while."

"Yeah, you're right. You gonna stick around?"

"I'll wait until they remove the remains and take the pictures. The crime scene boys can take care of the rest of it."

SHE TRIED TO get back to sleep when she got home, but no matter how hard she concentrated on sleeping, it refused to come again. After two hours of tossing and turning, she gave up. Lighting a cigarette, she went into the kitchen, made a pot of coffee, and watched the hot, brown liquid trickle slowly into the waiting pot. As she turned to get a cup out of the dish drainer, she tripped over a furry, black heap lying on the floor near her feet.

"Goddammit, Max. Where did you come from?"

The big Lab looked up at her with lazy brown eyes, his tail sweeping the floor behind him as it moved. She opened the kitchen door for the dog, who went outside quickly. Returning to the coffee maker, she poured a cup and carried it onto the back deck and watched the first pink and gray hints of morning intrude into the black night sky. The wood on the deck felt damp under her bare feet. She inhaled deeply to clear her head, but it didn't help as she stifled a yawn.

She knew she wasn't getting any younger. When she had been twenty-five she could have worked all night and still been ready to party, but it was a different story now that she was twice as old. She still enjoyed going to the clubs and watching the women, but she was beginning to suspect she was getting too damn old to continue the social life she had always enjoyed. Regardless of her age, the sight of beautiful women still took her breath away and made her long to hold and touch them, taking them high slowly, and feeling them come down even more slowly. But in over thirty years of what her friends referred to as "leching around" she had found only one she had been willing to give up other women for. Now she knew she would never give up her freedom and her heart that way again. It hurt too goddamn much when it ended.

Growing older was a bitch, she thought, swallowing the last of her coffee. Maybe she'd get lucky and not feel as tired later as she did right now. After all, Thomas Edison slept only three or four hours a night even when he was an old man and look what he accomplished. As she turned to re-enter the kitchen, she wondered who the hell she thought she was kidding.

SHE POURED ANOTHER cup of coffee, adding sugar and powdered creamer and could feel the need for an antacid tablet from the smell of the black liquid. Police coffee was possibly the worst substance on the planet. As she stirred in the powdered creamer, she stared at the contents of her mug and shook her head. Nicholls walked up next to her and grabbed the coffee carafe.

"I wouldn't drink that if I were you, unless you've just had a bottle of antacids," she warned.

"Why?"

"I put a shitload of creamer in mine and the stuff never even changed color." Brodie looked around the squad room. "Hey, Carelli! Who made the coffee this morning?"

Carelli, a slightly overweight officer in his late fifties, was looking through a stack of paperwork. He picked up his coffee cup and took a sip.

"Tastes like Harlan got here first," he answered without looking up.

Shaking her head she muttered to herself. "Harlan should have stayed in the Marines. No wonder they're so damn mean. Probably from drinkin' his fuckin' coffee."

Returning to her desk she opened a manila folder and began reading the contents.

"That the prelim on Charcoal Bill?" Nicholls asked as he flipped on the computer terminal on his desk.

"Yeah," she grunted. "Guess what? Vehicle burned, victim died."

Nicholls chuckled to himself. "Who wrote that astute observation?"

"Patrol Officer Allen Underwood. First shift on the job."

"Well, you always told me to keep my reports simple and to the point."

Before she could respond someone tapped her on the shoulder. She looked up and saw Captain Fred Donaldson standing over her, wearing his customary white shirt with light blue stripes and rolled up shirtsleeves.

"How's your workload, Brodie?"

She shrugged. "Depends on what the ME tells us about that TA last night. Pretty light other than that. A couple of burglaries."

"Good. I need a Field Training Officer."

"I did the last one. Use Carelli."

Donaldson shook his head. "Come to my office."

Donaldson walked away from the desk and Brodie cursed under her breath as she got up and followed him to his office at the back of the squad room. Blinds on the glass windows facing the squad room were still closed when she entered the cluttered room. That was never a good sign.

"Close the door behind you," Donaldson ordered as he dropped into his chair. The office was sparsely furnished with an old wooden desk he had salvaged from property disposal because he claimed it had character and a couple of straight back wooden chairs which were definitely not built for comfort. If an officer was called before Captain Donaldson, he wanted to make sure they were not comfortable while he chewed their asses off. She had known Donaldson for more than ten years and considered him to be a fair man. Hell, she owed her job to him. When she resigned from the Austin PD under less than auspicious circumstances, he hired her despite a barely adequate proficiency report in which her watch commander questioned her competency. She had been determined Donaldson would never regret hiring her. But that didn't mean she always liked his decisions.

"We have a new detective coming on board from Austin PD," Donaldson said. "She passed the exam about a month ago and I'm going to put her with you and Nicholls until she learns the way we do things around here."

"She?"

"You got a problem with that?"

"Why isn't she training with Austin PD?" Brodie asked.

"Because there's at least a six month waiting list before she could be placed in a position in Austin and we have a slot opening here when Harlan retires next month."

"And after we do all the hard work is she planning to move back to a higher paying position when one comes open in Austin?"

"Says she doesn't have any plans to move back to Austin."

"Who're you gonna partner her up with after her training is over?"

"I'll worry about that when the time comes."

"You should worry about it now, Fred. Look what's left out there. Carelli hasn't been ten feet from his desk in months waiting for retirement. Shit, he was on the job here when this place didn't even have paved roads."

"There is Romero, but the department and the city council can't afford a sexual harassment lawsuit and he couldn't keep his dick in his pants long enough to train a flea," Donaldson said with a smirk.

Brodie laughed out loud. "Cap, you know as well as I do that the minute there's an opening in Austin, she's gonna rabbit outta here. We'll be footing the training bill for a detective we might never get to use."

"I don't think so. Said she wants something less political than Austin PD. That political bullshit was part of what brought you here, wasn't it?" he asked, hitting a nerve.

"You know why I'm here." Chuckling to herself she asked, "Who did she have to sleep with to get hired anyway?"

Donaldson leaned forward on his desk. "Let me tell you something, Brodie. I'm the one who interviewed her for the opening here and fuckin' her wasn't part of my interview process. I'm a happily married man getting more than my fair share of pussy at home. So get your ass out there, grab Mr. Hollywood and get ready to train her. She starts bright and early Monday."

"Can I assume Mr. Hollywood and I will both be her training officers?"

"I don't give a shit what you assume. Whatever rotates your rudder. Just make sure Nicholls doesn't turn into another Romero and chase her skirt around all fuckin' day. No matter how much you object, I know you'll train her right. You did a helluva job getting Nicholls in line. He's one of my best detectives now and if this woman turns out half as good I won't give a shit who she's sleeping with. Questions?"

She opened her mouth to say something, but before she had time to get it out Donaldson said, "Good! Get out!"

She pushed her body up from the chair and walked out of the office. It might be a weekend, but she already had the feeling it wasn't going to be a memorable one. By the time she reached her desk, mild depression had begun to settle in. She sat down and picked up her cold cup of coffee, glancing at it for a moment before thinking better of it. Nicholls was on the phone and furiously scribbling down whatever he was hearing. Finally, he tossed his pencil onto his desk. "Look, why don't we just come down there? It'd be faster than me playing stenographer," he said. After a few uh huhs, yeps and nopes, he finally hung up.

"Anything enlightening?" she asked.

"That was some egghead from the ME's office. Must have just graduated from college and is still enamored with polysyllabic words. Feel like taking a run over there and see if we can find someone who speaks generic English?"

"Why not? An autopsy couldn't possibly depress me any more than I already am," she said with a shrug. "But before we head into the big city, I want to stop by the scene of last night's TA and see it in the daylight."

THEY DUCKED UNDER the yellow tape cordoning off the area around the accident scene and stood looking around for a few minutes. Calvin Davis, a technician with Cedar Springs' two-man forensics department, was guiding a wrecker up to what remained of the vehicle as they approached.

"What brings you two out here again?" he asked as the detectives approached him.

"Just wanted to see if we missed anything last night," Brodie said. "How long do you think it'll be before we get a report on the vehicle?"

"Couple of days. We're not too backed up. Cedar Springs isn't the crime capital of America or anything."

Brodie walked to the far side of the vehicle looking for the place Ramirez had pointed out the night before. She squatted down when she finally saw the footprint impressions. There wasn't much of an impression left, but what remained was definitely distinctive. She stood up and looked to see if there were other footprints leading toward or away from the vehicle.

"What're you looking for?" Nicholls asked.

"What size shoe you think made these prints?" she asked, squatting down again.

"Hmm. Could be a ten or eleven" he answered as he placed his shoe next to the impression. "Kinda hard to tell."

"Hey, Davis!" She motioned for the technician to join her and waited as he jogged over.

"You think you can get a decent cast of these shoe impressions?"

Davis looked at the prints and shook his head. "Not much to work with. There's a pretty distinctive pattern on the bottom of the shoe, but I doubt I could pick it up with plaster. Too much grass. Pictures might be better."

"Did anyone take pictures last night?" she asked.

"Probably, but I couldn't swear to it."

"Got your camera?"

"Always."

"Then take some shots of these prints and get as close as you can. The pattern on the soles might be useful. Even if they did take pictures earlier, a second set won't hurt," she said as she walked away from the vehicle.

"Now what?" Nicholls asked.

"Trying to see if we can pick up those prints again. Look over that way," she said.

They searched through the grass for half an hour before giving up. "Guess either the guy flew in and then flew out or any other prints were goobered up while they were working on the fire," Nicholls said when he rejoined her.

"Looks like," she said absently. "Let's get to the ME's office so we can miss the lunch hour rush."

FORTY MINUTES LATER, Nicholls was guiding their car skillfully through Austin traffic. It seemed to Brodie that no matter what time of day or night you hit the Austin freeways there was always a traffic jam. She had lived in the city for years and never figured out where everyone was always going in such a God-awful rush. Even little, blue-haired old ladies who could barely see over the steering wheel somehow managed to do seventy on the way to the beauty shop for their weekly appointments. She had once stopped an old lady for speeding, but when she approached the car she thought it was empty. The woman was a bag of wrinkles, so shrunken she was barely tall enough to see out the side window. Without a periscope there was no way in hell she could have seen what was around her, but there she was, clipping along at seventy-five.

She smiled as she gazed out the window at the cars passing them. She knew Nicholls was speeding. He always did, claiming it was the only real perk being a police officer offered. But cars were rushing by them on both sides as if they were standing still. When she had been a patrol officer on these very freeways she enjoyed driving forty-five in a sixty zone for no other reason than to see how many motorists would be afraid to pass her for fear of getting a ticket. Locals would stream by her and only the tourists would faithfully follow her until she turned off. It had been her own informal experiment in human behavior to convince herself her degree in psychology hadn't been a total waste of time and money. Not that it had ever helped her solve the complexities of her own life.

"You're pretty quiet, RB. Not happy about the new trainee?" Nicholls asked, interrupting her thoughts.

Squinting, she looked at her partner. "It's a woman."

"So what's the problem?" he grinned. "You like women."

Yeah, I do, she thought. *On the dance floor, in the kitchen, or on their backs in bed.* Although Nicholls was aware of her sexual preference he wasn't particularly comfortable with it. It was a non-topic between them despite the fact she was usually forced to listen to stories of his sexual exploits on a daily basis. Hell, if she were his age again she would probably be doing the same thing. She smiled to herself.

"Did you turn it down?" Nicholls asked.

"What? Oh, no. Didn't get a chance to, but it's not all bad. You get to be the unofficial official assistant training officer," she said.

"I'm sure she'll be all right, RB. What's her name?"

"Don't know. Didn't get that far before Donaldson told me to haul my ass out of his office."

Nicholls' face took on a serious expression. "You're not gonna show her any slack, are you?"

Watching the seemingly endless line of cars and trucks in front of them, she said, "Nope. A woman has to cope the same as a man."

They remained silent the remainder of the drive deep into the city. Nicholls finally found a parking place halfway between the Travis County Medical Examiner's Office and the Austin city limits. It was apparently a busy week for the Medical Examiner. As they rode the elevator to the basement of the county office building Brodie could smell the formaldehyde and other chemicals from the morgue and autopsy rooms before the elevator doors opened.

The Medical Examiner's section was surprising bright. Someone, obviously someone with a sense of humor, had placed cheerful posters of children and wildflowers along the corridor walls in an attempt to counteract the nature of the work taking place inside the basement autopsy rooms. They stopped at the receptionist's desk halfway down the corridor. The woman behind the desk was typing furiously and appeared to be in a trance. She was wearing headphones attached to a cassette player on her desk and didn't seem to notice the two visitors until Brodie reached over the counter and tapped her on the shoulder. Startled, the woman ripped the headphones off and glared at the detective. She appeared to be in her mid-twenties and Brodie noticed she had been a little heavy-handed with her make-up that morning. She smiled to disarm the fuse she lit by surprising the woman.

"Hi. You must be new to be so jumpy."

"I'm sorry, but this is kind of a spooky place. I was concentrating on the report on the recorder. One of our doctors doesn't speak English too well. Can I help you?"

"I'm Detective Royce Brodie and this is Detective Curtis Nicholls from Cedar Springs. We're here about a victim from a traffic accident in our jurisdiction last night."

"Name."

"We don't exactly know that yet. Probably came in as a John Doe."

"Do you know how many John Does we get in here?"

"I'm sure it's a bunch, sweetheart, but it should be the only one from Cedar Springs." Turning to her partner, Brodie asked, "Who did you talk to?"

Pulling a notebook from his inside jacket pocket, he grinned at the receptionist as he looked through it.

"Dr. Harrald."

Brodie looked hopefully at the secretary, who was rewinding the tape in her cassette player.

"I think he's in Room Six. End of the hall."

The detectives moved down the hall, stopping to knock on the door to Room Six. No one answered, but they could hear voices inside. Brodie pushed the door partway open and stuck her head in. Two men, dressed in green hospital scrubs, were standing over an autopsy table. Seemed like everyone in the building was pre-occupied.

"Dr. Harrald?" she asked loudly.

"Yeah, come in," one of the men said. Both wore masks over their faces and she wasn't sure which one had answered, but she pushed the door open farther and led Nicholls into the room.

"You here about the burn victim?" the voice said.

"Yeah. Brodie and Nicholls from Cedar Springs," she answered.

"Well, Brodie and Nicholls, come over here. This is a very interesting case."

They moved to the foot of the table, and Brodie couldn't help but notice that the victim took up surprisingly little room on the polished steel table. She had lain under glaring lights on a similar table eight years earlier. She had survived. Remembering how cold the metal had felt through her uniform sent a shiver down her spine.

"Short little fella," Nicholls commented.

One of the men looked up at them and then back down at his work.

"Shrinkage. Like putting half a pound of hamburger on the grill and removing a quarter pounder when it's done cooking"

Smile lines formed around the eyes of the second man.

"Let's flip him over, Les," the first man said.

The second man nodded and moved a few instruments out of the way. The first man looked at Brodie, pulled his mask down and said, "Frank Harrald, Deputy Medical Examiner. My assistant here is Les Phillips. I'd offer to shake hands, but..."

She looked at the gloved hand and said, "Royce Brodie. This is Curtis Nicholls. What have we got, doc?"

"One white male, well-done. The initial report said it was a traffic accident."

"There's some preliminary evidence it may not have been an accident."

"Do you have an I.D. on him yet?"

"No. We're hoping there might be dental records or some other anomaly about him to help us out."

"He's ready, Dr. Harrald," Phillips said.

Harrald pulled the mask back up over his face and returned to the body which was now lying on its stomach.

"Well, at least there's some meat left on the backside. If it wasn't an accident someone probably hoped the whole body would be burned. Almost never works that way. There's always something left."

Brodie pulled her notebook out and waited.

"Okay," Harrald began. "We've got a white male. From the measurements we've already taken, I'd place his height at about five-five or six, below average height. If I had to make a guess, and I suppose I'll have to, I'd say he weighed anywhere from 150 to 200 pounds. There's some hair remaining here on the back of the head."

Harrald used tweezers to pull a small clump of singed hair from what remained of the scalp and held it out to Brodie. "What color would you guess?"

Adjusting her glasses, she looked closely at the hair. "Could be brown, but some of it looks gray."

"Sounds right to me," the doctor said. "So it looks like he was probably older."

"What about the teeth?" Nicholls asked.

"There weren't any."

Brodie looked up quizically.

"They were knocked out, but the roots were all in place. Probably a hammer or some other blunt object. He may have had a partial plate on top. There was a space, about an inch on each side, with no roots."

"Well, now that we know he didn't just keel over from a heart attack, I guess we can assume that he was dead before the fire," she said.

"Absolutely. I didn't detect any evidence of smoke in what was left of the lungs. And there are a couple of other things, too. Roll him back over, Les."

The lab assistant rolled the remains over and repositioned the man on his back. Harrald leaned down closer to the corpse and looked at Brodie. "Look at this," he said pointing to the victim's head with the tip of his scalpel. "See this discoloration here on the bone just above the forehead?"

"Yeah. What is that?"

"It's not from the fire. May have happened earlier, but it's recent. See how the bone of the skull is pitted? Looks like damage from some type of acid. But, of course, I'll have to run more tests to determine that for sure. We had a body in here a few weeks ago. Chemical accident of some kind and he had similar pitting and discoloration on his skull, ulna and radius. Just a guess, but I'll check on it. The body also has a peculiar odor about it, don't you think?"

"How the hell can you tell?" Nicholls wrinkled his nose. "Burnt skin's not exactly Chanel Number Five."

"It's not the skin. More like kerosene. Again I'll test for it, but it looks like this poor fellow was the victim of two kinds of burns, chemical and combustible."

"Overkill, isn't it?" she asked.

Harrald shrugged. "Dead's dead. He wasn't alive when either kind of burn occurred."

"Want to hazard a cause of death?" she inquired.

"Nope. Not ready to jump out on that limb yet. I haven't found any evidence he was shot or stabbed, but I feel confident that this death was not the result of natural causes."

After an hour with the Medical Examiner, the two detectives headed back to Cedar Springs.

"How about some lunch?" Nicholls asked as they entered the Cedar Springs city limits.

"You can eat after seeing that mess in Austin?"

"Sure," he grinned, "as long as it's not too well done."

She groaned as he slowed down to turn into a fast food joint. When their food arrived, they ate in silence for a few minutes.

"Got big plans for the weekend, RB?" Nicholls asked.

She wiped her mouth and shook her head. "Nothing special. You still after that jail bait I saw you with a couple of weeks ago?"

"She's legal," Nicholls said with a grin. "I did a record search."

"Lucky you."

"Damn straight and you're just jealous," Nicholls chuckled.

"I do okay."

Although she had been dating Dr. Camille Jacobs off-and-on for nearly six years, a lifetime in the lesbian scene around Austin, Brodie hadn't spoken to her in several days. The last time they had been together Camille made no secret of the fact she wasn't completely happy with the way their relationship was progressing. Or not progressing, as Camille had put it, none too subtly. Brodie enjoyed spending time with Camille, and God knew the sex was above average, but she wasn't willing to risk full time with anyone no matter how good they were in the sack. She'd been burned the only time she'd had a permanent relationship. To set herself up for a repeat performance would be nothing short of plain old stupid. Better to go home alone at the end of an evening, leaving them smiling and satisfied. If they expected more than that, they would have to hunt elsewhere.

"When will the report on John Doe's vehicle be ready?" she asked, dragging her thoughts back to the business at hand.

"Probably Monday after lunch, but Calvin said it was definitely a torch job. He was all worked up on the phone. Said he finally got a challenge to work on."

"How's that?"

"No plates and no VIN. Said he would try to track down the part numbers on the computer."

"When we get back to the office, check the stolen car list and missing person reports."

"Probably won't be anything from missing persons unless the guy's been missing for a couple of days. Hell, maybe his old lady whacked him and will never report it."

"At least we can say we've covered all the bases. Wouldn't want Donaldson to think we're doing half-ass work."

"You gonna get your new trainee involved on this one?"

"*Our* trainee, partner. Why not? Anyone can do paperwork and unless we suddenly get lucky that may be all we ever have. We're not even sure the vic is from Cedar Springs. Could've been driven here from Louisiana for all we know. That reminds me, let's check the missing persons list for the surrounding states too."

Nicholls nodded as he pushed the remainder of his burger into his mouth.

Chapter
Two

BRODIE PULLED THE day's mail from her mailbox, unlocked the front door to her house and kicked it shut behind her. Her house was small, but more than roomy enough for a single woman who didn't own much and craved solitude. She wouldn't have considered buying the old fixer-upper if it hadn't been for the ten acres surrounding it. The way Austin was growing it would have been only a matter of time before she found herself in the middle of yet another yuppie subdivision if she hadn't purchased the whole package. It had taken her nearly three years to complete the upgrades to the house, and everything was where she wanted it at last.

She tossed a handful of file folders onto the coffee table and draped her jacket over the back of her recliner as she stripped off the shoulder harness holding her service revolver. Max nuzzled against her leg and she absently petted the Lab's head as she began unbuttoning her shirt while glancing through the mail. Most of it was junk. If she won all the millions they promised she sure as hell wouldn't be standing in Cedar fuckin' Springs, Texas at that moment. She dropped the mail on the coffee table next to her work folders before starting toward the kitchen and a cold beer. The sharp ring of her phone stopped her.

"Brodie," she snapped as she quickly stopped the ringing.

"Hey, RB," a familiar honey-warm voice drawled. "How are you?"

A smile came to Brodie's lips as she pictured the blonde psychologist's face in her mind. "Better now," she said.

"Have you had the nightmare again?"

"Couple of nights ago," she admitted.

"You should have called me, sweetie. We could have talked about it."

"We've already talked the fuckin' thing to death, Camille, and, as good as you are, it hasn't helped."

Camille paused a moment before continuing. "I thought I might pick up a couple of thick juicy steaks and toss them on the grill at your place this evening. Unless, of course, you've already made other plans."

"You know I don't make plans."

"I'm leaving work now, so give me an hour or so. I'll see you soon."

"I'll be ready and waiting."

Camille laughed lightly. "Is that a promise?"

"Well, you never know."

Replacing the receiver, she went into the kitchen and opened the back door for Max. She grabbed a beer from the refrigerator before she returned to the living room and flopped onto the couch, propping her feet on the coffee table. The truth was each time she had the damn nightmare it took her longer to shove it away, leaving her moderately depressed for two or three days afterward. Maybe the feel of Camille's warm body against hers would improve her mood.

She shuffled through the stack of file folders on the coffee table and opened the top one. She had been backing out of her parking slot at work when Nicholls came running out of the building waving the folder. Donaldson wanted her to look over the personnel file on the new trainee before Monday. She had been in a hurry to get home and tossed it on the car seat beside her. With an hour to kill and the need to unwind before Camille arrived, she decided to bite the bullet and get it over with.

A deep frown creased her forehead as she read the first line. *Name: Weston, Margaret A.* She hoped she was wrong, but what she read halfway down the page had the same effect as a slap in the face. *Emergency Notification: Timothy Weston.*

"Fuck!" She threw the file across the living room.

Lighting a cigarette and inhaling as much smoke as her lungs could handle and holding it as long as possible before finally expelling a gauzy, blue-gray cloud, she watched the smoke curl through the late afternoon sunlight filtering into her living room through half-opened Venetian blinds. Her mind refused to allow her to push the painful memories away and she absently rubbed the scar on her thigh, a visible reminder of the night Stan Wheeler died. His accusing eyes floated past her, gradually fading into the soft, inviting eyes of her former lover, bringing more painful memories. The metallic smell of blood and death was obliterated by the memory of the musky scent of arousal and passion as she lost herself in Maggie Weston's willing body.

She stood and went into her bedroom, trying to shake the memories from her head loose. But they refused to loosen their grip on her mind. She quickly stripped off her clothes and stepped under a hot shower in an effort to burn the memories from her body, but nothing worked. She felt her body react as it remembered the way Maggie touched her. The sound of her laughter, the way she gave herself, seemingly submissive while still in control. She remembered it all in a rush that forced her to her knees as tears streamed down her face. She was responsible for her partner's death and hadn't had the guts to fight for the woman she loved. She *was* the coward Tim Weston had accused her of being.

DRESSED IN BAGGY faded jeans, flip-flops, and a white t-shirt, and following her physically and emotionally draining trip down memory lane, Brodie sipped another beer while she ran a wire brush over the grill on her deck. She heard the French doors to the patio open and couldn't suppress a smile when she saw Camille. The light inside the kitchen shone through her hair giving it a soft, yellow glow against a dark-chocolate linen blouse. The top two buttons were open, revealing an alluring cleavage. She wanted Camille's body the moment she saw her. She needed to lose herself in it to drive away her demons. As soon as she was close enough to touch her, she slid a hand around Camille's waist and pulled the five-five woman closer, kissing her deeply.

"I guess this means you've missed me," Camille said as she savored Brodie's exploration. "The steaks..."

"Can wait," Brodie whispered. "The only thing I'm hungry for right now is you, baby."

A SHAFT OF annoying sunlight across her face woke Brodie the next morning. For a moment she wasn't sure the night before hadn't been another dream. She rolled over and buried her face in the pillow next to her, inhaling the scent of the woman whose body had given her a safe haven from the nightmares that haunted her. She got out of bed and pulled on gray shorts and an old t-shirt before wandering into the bathroom to brush her teeth and throw water on her face. As she walked barefoot down the hall she didn't hear anyone else in the house.

"Camille?" she called, but there was no answer.

In the kitchen she was grateful to find fresh coffee in the coffee maker. Pouring a cup, she saw Camille on the back deck, drinking coffee and scratching Max's ears. All she wore were bikini briefs and one of Brodie's t-shirts. She stood at the kitchen window watching the woman for a few minutes, knowing she had used her to forget the past the night before.

"Good morning," Camille said when she heard the back door open.

Brodie leaned down and kissed her. "You're up early."

"Max woke me. Guess he'd kept his legs crossed as long as he could stand it and you were dead to the world. Coffee okay?"

"It's great, hon."

"Ready for breakfast?"

"Sounds like a winner to me. I'm starving."

Camille glanced at her over her coffee cup. "I thought you might be." Standing, she stroked Brodie's face on her way to the kitchen. "You were certainly a woman on a mission last night."

"Was I successful?"

Camille looked down at Max and stroked his head. "I suppose that depends on what your mission was and your definition of successful," she answered.

Brodie watched her go, then looked at Max, thinking about her lover's cryptic statement. "Houston, I think I may have a problem."

Camille was standing at the sink beating what appeared to be half a dozen eggs as Brodie refilled her coffee cup. She moved behind her and ran her hands around Camille's waist and under the t-shirt, feeling the soft weight of her breasts fill her hands. She was everything Brodie should have wanted in a woman. Sensual…giving… understanding…willing. Why wasn't it enough?

"I thought you were hungry, RB."

"Starving," she said as her body responded again to the feel of Camille's warmth against her.

Turning to face her, Camille's hands wandered down the back of Brodie's shorts as they kissed. "Breakfast first, darlin'," Camille finally whispered. "I wouldn't want you to run out of strength."

Brodie smiled and released her with a quick kiss. Maybe the niggling feeling that something was wrong was nothing more than a remnant of a long week. While she waited for Camille to finish the eggs she went into the living room and opened the front door to retrieve the morning paper. By the time she returned, a steaming plate of scrambled eggs was next to her coffee cup and Camille was buttering toast.

"Anything worthwhile in the news today?" she asked.

"Are you kidding? This is the *Cedar Springs Journal*, not the *New York Times*," Brodie chuckled.

"Not much news?"

"Nicholls and I are working a case we caught a couple of nights ago. I wanted to see if the local reporters know something we don't. Like who the guy was."

"What kind of case is it?"

"Looked like a simple traffic accident at first, but now it looks like it might have been a homicide. We've just started our investigation. Maybe we'll be able to ID the guy Monday, if we get lucky."

Camille sat down across from her and picked up a forkful of

eggs. "How do you feel about working with Maggie again?" she asked, her tone casual.

Brodie's toast stopped halfway to her mouth and she looked up at her quickly. "How do you know that?"

"After I let Max out this morning I was in the living room and saw a folder on the floor, so I picked it up. I wasn't trying to be nosey, but I did see the first page."

They ate in silence until both had finished their breakfast. "Well?" Camille asked.

"Well what?" Brodie replied with noticeable irritation in her voice.

Camille appeared calm as she spoke, "I'd imagine you might be a little...concerned...about working with her. Does Donaldson know about your relationship with her and the problems between you and Tim?"

"I don't know. It's never been a topic of discussion. It was a long time ago and I've gotten over it," Brodie answered, her voice beginning to show her annoyance with the conversation.

"Have you?"

Standing abruptly, she glared at Camille. "Yes, I have, goddammit! And I don't need you to remind me of it again. You may have been my shrink eight years ago, but I don't need you crawlin' around inside my fuckin' head now!"

"Is that why you called out her name in your sleep after we made love last night?" Camille asked. The question stunned Brodie. The hurt she saw in Camille's eyes was obvious. She had no answer and left the room.

As she left the kitchen, she felt the beginnings of a migraine start to pound in her temples. *I haven't even seen her yet and already the shit starts,* she thought. She shut herself in the bathroom to splash cold water on her face and calm down. By the time she reemerged Camille was gone.

A LIGHT DRIZZLE fell from heavy gray skies Monday morning as Brodie walked into the squad room. Somehow the weather seemed perfect for her mood. Her anticipated weekend with Camille had ended abruptly in less than stellar fashion, and she had spent most of Sunday alone, ridding herself of a fucking migraine. She glanced around the room as she brushed wet spots from the arms of her jacket. The fluorescent lighting cast a pale yellow tint over everything in the room, but it wasn't a cheerful yellow. Nicholls' jacket hung from the back of his chair and other officers were beginning to filter in for the day. She saw light behind the blinds of Donaldson's office. Taking a deep breath, she strode to his door and knocked.

"It's open," his gruff voice rumbled.

Donaldson had already begun plowing through a stack of paperwork on his desk. He leaned back in his chair when he saw her head and looked at his watch.

"You're in early, Brodie," he said. "Got a big day planned?"

"Just running down some leads, Cap, but I needed to ask you a question."

"Shoot."

Stepping toward his desk, she placed Maggie Weston's personnel folder in front of him. He glanced at the folder and back at her.

"Did you read it?" he asked.

"Yes. Her qualifications seem above average."

"So what's your question?"

"Does Detective Weston know I'll be her training officer?"

Donaldson leaned back in his chair. "Yes, she does. She told me there had been a problem between you and her old man a few years back, but didn't go into any details."

"It could be a problem, Fred." As much as she hated having her personal life become a part of her work, she knew she owed it to the man who had taken a chance by hiring her to be honest. Clearing her throat, she couldn't think of a way to make what she was going to say less potentially damaging. "The problems I had with Commander Weston were because of her. She and I, we were...um...personally involved at the time." Looking down at her hands she didn't know what else she could say that wouldn't make it worse. "You took a chance on me, Fred. I thought I owed you the truth."

Donaldson leaned farther back in his chair and laced his fingers behind his head, staring at the ceiling for a few moments before dropping his eyes to her.

"I appreciate your honesty, Brodie. I know that wasn't easy for you. But I also know you're the best I have in this department. Can you put whatever happened eight years ago behind you and train Weston effectively?"

"I think so."

"Then I'm leaving you as her FTO for now. If you feel, later, that it isn't working out, for whatever reason, I want you to come to me. Understand?"

She nodded and stood to leave the office. "Thank you, Captain."

"And Brodie," Donaldson said.

She turned her head toward Donaldson with a questioning look.

"I made the coffee this morning, so you better grab a cup before it's all gone," he grinned.

"MORNING," NICHOLLS SAID as Brodie picked up her coffee cup. "Your trainee's here."

Suddenly the promise of decent coffee lost its appeal. "Where?"

"I left her back in booking. I guess Levinson's giving her the grand tour of our state-of-the-art facilities," he shrugged.

"What's your first impression?" she asked as she leaned a hip against her desk.

"I wouldn't kick her out of bed."

Brodie was pouring coffee into her cup when she saw Maggie Weston walk into the squad room accompanied by the jailer, Sergeant Levinson. He was bending her ear about something and she was struggling to look interested in whatever he was telling her. Her five-six body looked exactly the way Brodie remembered, although her auburn hair was now shoulder length and brushed behind her ears. Most regrettably for her, she found the older, more mature Maggie even more annoyingly attractive than the woman she had known eight years before. She was wearing a white Oxford shirt tucked neatly into khaki slacks that rested easily on her hips. Brodie could see her service revolver under her brown tweed jacket as she crossed her arms in front of her and nodded to Levinson. Her smile seemed to waver perceptively as she glanced around the squad room and saw Royce Brodie watching her. Unfolding her arms, she touched Levinson on the shoulder, giving him a dazzling smile as she spoke to him briefly before walking toward Brodie's desk. She was wearing very little make-up and Brodie noticed there was no polish on her fingernails and no jewelry adorned her fingers.

MAGGIE HAD SPENT the last three days getting settled into her new home in Cedar Springs, emotionally fluctuating between excitement over beginning the next step in her career and more than a little trepidation over the idea of facing the glare she knew she would see in Royce Brodie's eyes. It had been years since Maggie had last seen her, but she had no doubt the older woman would be less than thrilled to have her as a trainee, possibly even hostile, considering the angry words that had passed between them the last time they had been together.

Brodie's feet seemed to be glued to the floor as she watched Maggie make her way across the squad room toward her. Each time she blinked another slide from her memory bank flashed behind her eyes. The defiance in Maggie's eyes the first time she saw her. The teasing half smile at the corners of her mouth that promised so much. Her musical laughter. Her surprisingly aggressive passion mixed with innocent tenderness. The memory of everything Brodie had found irresistible.

"Lieutenant Brodie. It's good to see you again," Maggie said as she extended her hand.

Brodie hesitated before taking Maggie's hand, forcing herself to look at her former lover. She should have been drawn to the expressive hazel eyes, but the faded scar on Maggie's forehead was the first thing she saw. Dropping her eyes to avoid seeing the reminder of their volatile last meeting, she accepted Maggie's hand. The firmness of her trainee's grasp brought her back to the present, shutting down memories of what had been. Clearing her throat she said, "I guess Nicholls has shown you everything there is to see around here."

"Yes, Curtis has been very helpful," Maggie said with a smile at Nicholls.

"Curtis?" Brodie repeated, looking at him.

"You two already know each other?" he asked, ignoring Brodie's question.

"Lieutenant Brodie was with the Austin PD when I was a rookie," Maggie answered, relieving Brodie of thinking up a quick response.

"Ever work together before?"

Maggie glanced briefly at her before answering, "No, we never worked together."

Brodie pushed herself away from her desk and looked around the squad room.

"Help me move a desk over here for Weston."

They managed to wrestle an old wooden desk against the sides of their desks, placing Maggie between them. Brodie picked up the phone from her desk and set it in front of Maggie with a thud.

"One of your duties will be answering the phone," she said, clearing her throat again, working hard to achieve a middle ground between blatant hostility and don't-give-a-shit.

"RB hates phones," Nicholls explained as he returned to his paperwork.

He no sooner finished his explanation than the telephone rang and Maggie looked at Brodie.

"Just pick it up and say Cedar Springs Police Department, Detective Weston speaking," Brodie instructed as she sat in the old wooden rolling chair behind her desk.

Maggie did as she was told and listened to the voice on the other end carefully. Brodie picked up a stack of stolen vehicle reports from her desk and began the boring and tedious task of thumbing through them looking for a Mercedes-Benz. Suddenly Maggie's hand reached in front of her as she grabbed a notepad and a pen and began writing. Brodie caught a faint but familiar scent of vanilla wafting from her trainee and inhaled it deeply.

"Which building? Secure the area and don't touch anything. We'll be there in fifteen," Brodie heard her say before she hung up the phone.

"Well?" she asked.

"There's been a homicide at the university," Maggie answered without looking at her.

"How do they know it was a homicide?" Nicholls asked.

"They only found the victim's head. The responding officers seemed pretty certain it didn't part with the rest of the body voluntarily," she responded.

The two veteran detectives were on their feet before their trainee could finish her sentence. "Uniforms already there?" Brodie asked over her shoulder as she and Nicholls walked briskly toward the front door.

"Yes," Maggie replied as she trotted to keep up. "They have the biology lab cordoned off."

THE DRIVE TO the campus of the University of the Southwest was short and, as far as Brodie was concerned, blessedly devoid of needless, inane small talk. Once or twice she caught a brief glimpse of Maggie in the rearview mirror and looked away when Maggie seemed to be looking back. The morning drizzle had stopped by the time they arrived at the university. A patrol officer directed them toward the Biology Building, one of three four-story buildings that formed the Science Quadrangle. She parked their car near the front entrance of the building and got further directions to the crime scene from two officers guarding the front doors of the building. They took the stairs to the second floor two at a time. As soon as they reached the second floor hallway Brodie paused, stopping Maggie as she joined them.

"When we get in there, interview the officers who responded to the initial call and find out what they observed. I don't care how trivial the information seems to be. Write it all down. You got a notebook?"

Maggie pulled a small black notebook from her jacket pocket. Brodie nodded at her and they proceeded down the hallway. It was easy to find the crime scene. A small cluster of students and older adults, who looked like graduate instructors, stood at one end of the hall, craning their necks to see what all the excitement was about. A uniformed officer was guarding a set of double doors with opaque windows. He moved the curiosity seekers out of the way when he saw the detectives approaching. Brodie motioned to Nicholls, who began politely dispersing the on-lookers.

"Okay, folks. Go on about your business. There's nothing for you to see here," he said without smiling.

A young woman in the group spoke up. "We have a class in that lab," she said.

He looked at her and said with a slight smile, "Class has been canceled for today, ma'am. You might want to call your TA later to find out when it will meet again. Now go on home."

The students began shuffling away, looking back over their shoulders and wondering what was going on. When most of them had dispersed, Brodie and Nicholls pushed open the frosted glass double doors. Before Maggie could follow them, a uniformed officer stopped her. Pausing, Brodie walked back to the door. "She's with us, Ted."

"Sorry, Brodie. Trainee?" the officer asked.

She nodded as she held the door open for Maggie. "You've got a shield, Weston. Use the damn thing," she snapped. Maggie stiffened slightly and gave Brodie a curt nod.

The room was a standard biology lab with long black Formica-topped tables in rows. Spaced along the tables were what Brodie assumed were dissection trays with cheap scalpels, boxes of latex gloves, plastic goggles, and an assortment of other metal instruments. The air in the room was heavy with formaldehyde and reminded her of the ME's autopsy room. Aquariums filled with formaldehyde and specimens lined one wall. There were five sinks at various locations around the room. The remains of a dissected frog covered with liquid sat on the lab table at the front of the room. The frog had been cut open and there were pins inserted into its major organs with a small colored flag attached to each pin. She wondered if she should salute the little critter that had given its life to educate future scientists.

A young man with thick glasses and curly black hair sat at a lab table and looked as gray-green as the preserved frog. She estimated his age at no more than twenty-two or -three. Nicholls was squatting next to the man, asking him questions slowly and writing down his responses as she walked over to them and sat on one of the lab tables.

"He found the victim," Nicholls said as he wrote in his notebook. "This is Kevin Larson, biology TA."

"When did you find the victim, Kevin?" she asked.

When the young man finally looked up at her, his eyes seemed to be in constant motion. "This morning. I came in early to get the lab set up for today's dissection. Jellyfish."

"What time did you get here?" she continued.

"About six-thirty, I think. Class starts at eight-thirty."

"How long were you here before you found it?" Nicholls inquired.

The lab assistant shrugged, "I don't know for sure. Maybe ten minutes. We don't need much equipment for jellyfish so I just threw it all on the tables and went to make sure there were enough jellyfish."

"Were there?" Brodie asked.

The man looked sharply at her. "I don't fucking know! My count was interrupted. It's not like I thought 'Oh goodie, we have twenty jellyfish and one human head'."

Nicholls patted the lab assistant on the shoulder and said, "It's okay, Kevin, just try to take it easy."

"How can I take it easy, man? Another forty-five minutes and there would've been twenty kids in here. Do you know what would have happened if one of them had found...it."

"They're lucky you got here first, Kevin," Nicholls said to comfort him. His hands were still shaking and he held them clasped tightly together, hoping no one would notice.

"Did you recognize the victim, Kevin?" Brodie asked.

"To tell you the truth, ma'am, I didn't look at him long enough to know."

"But you know it's a man," Nicholls said.

"Well...I mean...I guess I just supposed it. I can't imagine anyone doing something like that to a woman," Kevin said with an incredulous look on his face.

Brodie gave her partner a 'you wouldn't believe what people can do to each other' look and he smiled. She hopped off the lab table and spoke quietly to Nicholls. "Make sure you have his name and address. As soon as they get his prints for comparison let him go on home to lie down."

Nicholls began taking down information about Kevin Larson while Brodie walked across the room to where her trainee was interviewing a police officer. Maggie finished speaking to the officer just as she got there. The officer nodded to Brodie as he turned to leave.

"What's his story?" Brodie asked.

"He and his partner took the call at six-fifty. When they arrived, the kid over there was semi-hysterical."

Brodie smiled at Maggie's reference to the lab assistant as "kid". She had been about the same age when Brodie first met her and it wasn't a word she would have used to describe the young woman.

"Officer Corcoran inspected the tank and determined there was indeed a head in it, but says they didn't touch the tank or anything else in the room, with the exception of the doors," she continued. "He remained here while his partner called it in. The crime scene people haven't arrived yet, but should be here any minute."

"Good. Have you inspected the tank yet?"

"No. I didn't think I should touch it until the lab techs finish their thing."

"That's right, Weston. Cedar Springs may not be as sophisticated as Austin, but the same rules apply."

"I'm aware of that, Royce," Maggie frowned.

"That's *Lieutenant Brodie* to you, Detective," she stated, shifting a cold glare toward her. Other than her family, she had never allowed anyone to use her first name...except Maggie. That had been in a different lifetime and a familiarity she wouldn't tolerate now.

Maggie looked at the woman glaring at her. "I'm sorry. I'll remember that, Lieutenant." Her former lover wasn't going to make her training period easy and Maggie wasn't sure she could blame her.

Brodie walked away from her and went to the aquarium. Nicholls joined her and the two detectives bent down slightly to look into the mass of jellyfish.

"What do you think, RB?" he asked.

"Well, this obviously isn't where the guy was killed. No discernible blood in the tank. No mess in the lab anywhere, and to decapitate someone would have made one helluva mess."

"It doesn't seem likely the killer would have stuck around and cleaned up after himself either. Where do you think we'll find the rest of him?"

"I'm sure it will turn up in the worst possible place," she said as she stood again and stretched her back.

The doors to the lab opened as three lab technicians, a photo tech, and two paramedics with a gurney entered the room. A man in his mid-thirties with long brown hair pulled back into a ponytail walked toward the detectives. He was wearing bright yellow coveralls and worked at pulling on a pair of latex gloves.

"Sorry we're a little late, *chica*. Car trouble. The city council better get off its dead ass and vote us a new van soon. Where's the body?" the technician asked, looking around.

"Can't tell you that, Frank. But part of him is in there," she said pointing at the aquarium.

"You won't be needing that gurney either," Nicholls added. "A bowling bag should do it."

The technician's eyes widened, "No shit! Cool."

"We'll be downstairs while you work. Let us know what you find. Enjoy," she said as she and Nicholls turned to leave the room.

Maggie was waiting in the hallway. Brodie stopped and seemed to be thinking. Then she turned to her.

"Take a couple of uniforms and go through the rest of the building. Make sure there aren't more body parts waiting around for some unsuspecting coed in any of the other labs. Grab a walkie-talkie from the car in case you come across something. Nicholls, you and I will take a few officers and canvass the area around the building. Before we split up, tell Gus the Ghoul in there that I want a preliminary report on my desk this afternoon. And none of that bullshit about the victim was decapitated. I want something more concrete than that this time."

Nicholls re-entered the lab while Brodie and Maggie went to the car for the walkie-talkies. As they retrieved them from the trunk and checked them, Maggie leaned against the vehicle. The sun was out in full force, driving the humidity to an uncomfortably sticky level. Brodie watched Maggie slip on a pair of aviator-style sunglasses. She silently chastised herself for thinking Maggie couldn't look any sexier than she did at that moment. What did she expect? That Maggie would have turned into the same kind of bitter woman Brodie had become inside?

"Do you think it could be a random act?" Maggie asked.

"Nope," said Brodie, startled from her thoughts. "I don't believe in random acts. I've never seen a single case where there wasn't some kind of motive involved."

"What could be the motive for decapitating someone? Seems a little over the top."

"Who knows? Maybe the vic made a smart ass remark to the killer's girlfriend or bumped into him in the hallway the wrong way. I didn't say it had to be a good motive, or even a logical one," Brodie said, looking at her. "People do irrational and unexpected things when you least expect it all the time. You should know something about that, Detective," she added, the words falling unbidden from her mouth before she could stop them.

Maggie removed her sunglasses and looked at her, revealing fiery hazel eyes. "Why am I getting the distinct impression you're not thrilled to have me here, *Lieutenant Brodie*?" she asked with a touch of irritation in her voice.

"Probably because you've always been very perceptive," Brodie answered flatly. "But whether or not I'm excited about it is irrelevant. If you want another training officer, I won't oppose the request." Taking a step closer to Maggie, her eyes hard, she lowered her voice, "Why the fuck are you here? Tim could have gotten you on in Austin and we both know it."

"Leave him out of this. He doesn't make decisions for me," Maggie said, raising her voice a notch.

"Well, he sure as shit did eight years ago," Brodie seethed, immediately regretting reopening the old wound, but unable to stop.

"And you let yourself get out of control," Maggie said, her voice becoming less confrontational. "Just let it go. It's already cost us both too much."

"What the hell does that mean?" Brodie demanded, her closeness to Maggie suddenly becoming uncomfortable.

Maggie knew she had been at least partially responsible for Brodie's resignation from the Austin PD. Now fate had put her on a collision course with her former lover. She didn't doubt her own abilities to become a good investigator. She just had to convince everyone else, and she couldn't do it without going through the woman now standing in front of her. Pushing away from the car, she cleared her throat, unable to look into Brodie's eyes any longer. "Nothing, Lieutenant. Should I meet you and Detective Nicholls back here?"

"In an hour," Brodie snapped, stepping away from her. "We'll contact you if we find anything and you do the same."

Maggie walked away from the car and pointed at two officers standing near the steps leading into the building. "You two, come with me," she ordered in a firm voice.

As she watched Maggie and the two officers re-enter the building, Brodie saw self-confidence and assertiveness she hadn't seen in a younger Maggie Weston.

THE DETECTIVES, ACCOMPANIED by a dozen uniformed officers, combed the grounds around the Biology Building, as well as the other buildings in the Science Quadrangle for the better part of an hour. Nothing seemed out of place. Brodie spoke to a number of students, none of whom seemed aware of anything unusual happening over the weekend. The campus was spread out over a large area, giving the appearance of spaciousness. None of the buildings, other than the dormitories, was over four stories. The grass and gardens around each of the Spanish-style buildings were immaculate and she figured that it must take a battalion of groundskeepers to keep everything mowed and trimmed. The university had been in Cedar Springs for more than fifty years, but hadn't caught on with people outside the county until ten years earlier. Then, like everything else in Cedar Springs, it experienced a sudden rapid growth cycle.

She looked at the buildings around her, and everything looked perfect. She had taken a few graduate classes in American Lit in a building across the long grassy mall from the Science Quad. There didn't seem to be as many students around as usual, but the university was preparing for its spring break.

"Find anything?" she asked when they met Maggie and her team making their way down the front steps of the Biology Building.

"Nothing," she answered. "We've been through every lab, storage closet, toilet, and office in there and didn't find a thing."

"Looks like our forensic friends have finished up," Brodie said, nodding toward the building.

As the lab team exited the building, the man in yellow coveralls stopped and spoke to the other members of the team and then bounced down the steps to speak to the detectives. He smiled as he reached them.

"Who's the fox, Brodie?" he asked, looking over his glasses appreciatively at Maggie.

"Maggie Weston, trainee," Brodie answered. "Detective Weston, meet Frank Cardona, head ghoul. What'd you find, Frank?"

"About what you'd expect for a classroom. Got fingerprints from every damn person in the state. So, needless to say, it will take a month, minimum, to match them all up to their owners."

"What about the victim?" she continued.

"Male. Hispanic. I'd guess around thirty or thirty-five years old, but it's hard to tell with Hispanics. We age well, you know," he said, waggling his eyebrows at Maggie. "Full set of teeth with no apparent dental work. Probably gnawed on a few thousand tortillas over the years. Hard to tell anything about his height and weight considering that he's now a shadow of his former self. I'll know more when you locate the other three-fourths of him."

"How long has he been dead?" Nicholls asked.

"Who the fuck knows? Coulda been in there a week or an hour before he was found. Formaldehyde is a great preservative, you know. His companions in the aquarium are in pristine condition and they've been toast for months. Find me a body to work with and if it hasn't already been pickled, too, I can be more specific unless, of course...."

"Enough of the anatomy lesson, Frank. We get the idea." Brodie said.

"Tell you one thing though. This wasn't some quickie slice and dice. Whoever separated our friend from his body did some pretty neat work. Maybe not a Harvard- trained brain surgeon, but definitely not the butcher at the local A & P."

"Okay. Let me know if you come up with anything else we should know."

Cardona shook hands with Brodie and Nicholls, but when he got to Maggie he raised her hand to his lips and kissed it. He winked and jogged back to the lab van as a pink blush began to spread up her neck.

"Now what?" Nicholls asked as they walked across the grassy area in front of the building toward their car.

"Punt, I guess," Brodie said.

Following a few feet behind them, Maggie glanced through the notes she had taken and looked at the diagram she had drawn of the scene. Her foot sank unexpectedly into a depression in the grass and she was barely able to catch herself before falling down. "What the hell?" she muttered to herself.

"You coming, Weston?" Brodie called out when she and Nicholls reached their car. Maggie was on her hands and knees, shining a small flashlight on something on the ground.

Squinting, she answered, "Yeah! Hey, what's under this grate?" She looked around until she spotted an older man wearing the blue denim workshirt of a university employee. She motioned him toward her and dusted grass from her slacks.

The man walked up to her and rested on the rake in his hands. "What's this grate for?" she asked again.

Brodie sighed as she and Nicholls strolled back to where Maggie was kneeling. "What's the problem?" Brodie asked shortly when she and Nicholls rejoined Maggie.

"I asked what this grate is for," Maggie repeated as she leaned closer to the grate and cupped her hands around her eyes to see into the darkness below.

"Oh, that's part of the old tunnel system the university tried when it first opened," the man explained. "There's a vent about every couple hundred yards. It was supposed to let students get from one building to another in bad weather. I think they were used as shelters in case of tornadoes too."

"Are they under every building?" she asked, still straining to see what her limited light illuminated.

"Just the original four or five buildings," he answered. "They turned out to be better suited for muggings and lover's lanes than anything else so the university sealed them off."

"Is the Biology Building one of the original buildings?" Maggie asked.

"Yep."

"But all the exterior entrances are padlocked," Nicholls said. "We checked them out while we were combing the grounds."

Standing up and brushing the grass from her hands and knees, Maggie looked around again. "Who has keys for the padlocks?"

"Security should, ma'am," the maintenance worker said.

"Get in touch with security and have them bring their keys, Nicholls," Brodie said.

A SHORT FLIGHT of narrow concrete steps led to the basement of the Biology Building. Brodie turned the key in the padlock and slowly pushed the door open, drawing her weapon as she reached inside and felt along the wall. Finding a light switch, she flipped it on and a series of dim overhead fluorescent lights flickered on. The room smelled dank and moldy and dust particles floated through the glow cast by the overhead lights. There were no windows along the walls and a dark green mold appeared to run down the wall from cracks in the mortar. "Clear," she said as she looked around and re-holstered her gun. Assorted desks and file cabinets were stacked against one wall. Other equipment she was unfamiliar with was pushed into piles along the other walls. Nicholls and Weston followed her down the steps before separating to comb the room.

"Jesus, smells like my grandmother's root cellar in here," Nicholls mumbled as he glanced around.

"Hope no one's allergic to mold and mildew," Maggie added.

"Look around and see if the dust on this crap looks like it's been disturbed," Brodie ordered as she pulled a pair of latex gloves from her pocket.

Brodie poked through some of the junk and began moving file cabinets away from the wall to clear a path between cabinets.

"Found a door," she called from behind the cabinets.

Nicholls and Maggie joined her and moved the rusting cabinets farther away. A large padlock secured the damp wooden door from the outside and Brodie began going through the keys they had gotten from campus security one by one. She looked over her shoulder at the other detectives. "Looks like no one's been down here in a long, long time and this mother is eat up with rust."

"I didn't see anything that looked out of place or had been dusted recently," Nicholls said while Brodie tried another key.

"Got it!" Brodie said.

She leaned against the old wooden door and pushed it open with her shoulder. She flipped on her flashlight and shined it into what was obviously a tunnel of some type. Moisture from rain earlier in the morning pooled in small puddles along the floor and the walls glistened with a dewy wetness.

"Where's it go?" Nicholls asked.

"Your guess is as good as mine," Brodie said with a shrug. "Any other exits?"

"Didn't find any," Maggie answered.

"Nick, check with maintenance to see if they have blueprints for this tunnel system while Weston and I see if this hole goes anywhere interesting. The dust on the cabinets and other junk in front of this door didn't appear to have been disturbed, but you never know."

Nicholls nodded and made his way back to the basement entrance as the beam from Maggie's flashlight joined Brodie's. Brodie drew her gun again and stepped into the tunnel. Sweeping the beams from their flashlights around, they moved cautiously.

"This tunnel probably hasn't been used since Custer was a corporal," Maggie said. She could feel the mold and dust spores attacking her sinuses and couldn't suppress a sneeze that had been building since they entered the dank basement. "Both the outside doors were locked, so this is probably a wild goose chase," Maggie observed. "We didn't find any doors inside the building itself that would lead down here."

"Let's talk to the janitors in the building who worked over the weekend," Brodie said. "See if they noticed anyone unusual in and out of the building after dark."

The tunnel curved slightly about a hundred yards from the entrance. The beams from their flashlights cut through the darkness like a knife as they stepped forward. Brodie stopped so abruptly that Maggie bumped into her. "Jesus fuckin' H. Christ," she breathed.

Maggie gripped Brodie's arm tightly and felt a wave of nausea rush over her. "Oh, my God," she said when she saw the scene in front of them.

"Looks like we found what we were looking for," Brodie said quietly. Their lights moved over what could have been a slaughterhouse floor. Semi-dried sticky black pools of blood covered the floor and apparent bloodstains had run down the walls.

"Let's get the lab guys back here and hope we haven't fucked up too much evidence in the process," Brodie said as they began to back away from the area. "Organize search teams as soon as we can get back in here. I want to know where these tunnels go."

THE WAITRESS IN the restaurant's smoking section, a college age girl with short blonde hair, cleared the plates from in front of the three detectives. As she lit a cigarette Brodie noticed the girl smiling at Nicholls and batting her eyelashes at him like a fan on a hot night. She smiled to herself as he winked back at the girl and asked for a refill, using his softest drawl. Within moments the waitress was back with the coffee pot.

"It's a fresh pot," she said while pouring.

"Thank you, sweetheart. I appreciate that," he said.

When the waitress finally left the table, Brodie asked, "Adding another one to your already long list of Barbies?"

"The list can never be too long," he laughed as he brought his cup to his lips. Maggie wasn't a part of their conversation and didn't ask any questions. She had been generally silent throughout the meal, a fact not lost on Brodie.

"When did you start smoking again?" Maggie asked, realizing her mistake as Brodie's eyes flew up to meet hers.

Nicholls didn't seem to notice Maggie's slip. "I've been trying to convince her to quit, but she's being stubborn about it."

Brodie took a deep breath and flicked ashes into the ashtray.

"You know, she's been dead for a while now, but if memory serves me right, neither one of you looks a fuckin' thing like my mother," she said tightly.

"Jesus, you're touchy today, Brodie. Strike out last weekend?" Nicholls asked.

"My personal life isn't any of your goddamn business, Nicholls. Remember that!" she snapped.

Surprised by the sudden irritation in his partner's voice, Nicholls narrowed his eyes. "What the fuck's wrong with you?"

Mashing out her unfinished cigarette, Brodie quickly changed the subject. "Nothing," she said, looking at Maggie. "What do you think our next step should be, Weston?"

Grateful to be on a safer topic, Maggie pulled her notebook from her pocket and glanced through it for a minute before answering. "If we make a few assumptions, and I suppose we'll have to for now, the victim was probably killed over the weekend and there might be a missing person report. Since the head was left on the campus he could have been a student or a university employee. I think we should check with personnel first to see if anyone has been absent from work today. Cardona said he looked to be at least thirty, so we might speculate he wasn't a student."

"Why?" Brodie challenged. "People over thirty have been known to attend college."

"I know, but universities don't keep attendance records the way public schools do. It would be easier to eliminate employees first."

"The vic could have come from anywhere," Nicholls said.

"True," said Maggie leaning slightly forward, "but why would anyone carry around a head and decide to dump it at the university here? He, or she, could have dumped it in a field somewhere in the boonies and it wouldn't have been found for weeks or months, if then. Besides, considering the head showed no signs of decomposition, I don't think the perp kept it around very long. Maybe a few hours at most."

"She's right," Nicholls nodded.

Emboldened by his agreement, she continued, "Decapitation is pretty extreme for a beginner or an impulse killer. Something like that would take some advanced planning. He could have done something similar before and gotten away with it. Perhaps not as flashy as this, but now he's willing to take more risks."

"Maybe he doesn't like Hispanics," Brodie said.

"Maybe he's just a fuckin' whacko," Nicholls added.

Brodie leaned her head back in thought. "We need to find how our perp got the victim into those tunnels. We've spent hours searching every one only to run into a brick wall, literally. I want to see the earliest floor plans for the Biology Building and examine the inside again at the exact original entrance location. He didn't get the victim down there by wiggling his nose and there's no evidence he used the outside basement entrance."

"My team and I checked that building thoroughly, Lieutenant," Maggie said defensively.

"I'm not saying you weren't thorough, Detective. But now I want that building torn apart. We have to have missed something. It's a good idea to check out the university employees. Make a few calls when we get back to the office. See what you can find out about the floor plans, too. In the meantime, Nicholls, you and I will check to see if there's anything new on our Thursday John Doe. I'll check the missing person reports and you go over the stolen car lists. Oh, and see if the lab was able to trace any part numbers on the car. Looks like it's time to let our fingers do the walking for a while."

THE DAY WAS shot and all Brodie had to show for it was another body, or at least part of one, and a throbbing headache. The good news was that the second victim at least had a face. She rubbed her forehead with her thumb and forefinger as she made notes to herself along with a list of questions that needed to be answered. She noticed Maggie and Nicholls seemed to be getting along and worked well together, bouncing ideas off one another. Occasionally, her train of thought would be broken by the sound of Maggie's laughter. She had an easy, infectious laugh that made everyone around her feel good. Frowning, she tried to shut the sound out. She didn't want to feel good about having Maggie around.

By five she felt like she was going cross-eyed from reading reports. Any time she had to stay at her desk for more than an hour she felt as if she was smothering. Flipping shut the folder she was reading, she stood and stretched as she pulled her jacket on. Too many thoughts and questions were shoving their way around in her mind looking for a way to connect. She had more questions than answers and needed something to distract her from her private thoughts.

"Don't think I can stand any more excitement for today, Nicholls. Everybody go home and get a good night's sleep. Hopefully tomorrow we'll have a few more reports in and can start to piece this thing together."

"I think I'll just run over my notes one more time," Maggie said.

Nicholls leaned down next to her as he slipped his jacket on. "Brown noser," he whispered.

"Whatever works," she said, smiling up at him.

Chapter
Three

JUST AFTER LUNCH Tuesday, Brodie was bravely pouring another cup of coffee when the telephone on Maggie's vacant desk rang. After a few phone calls, Maggie had driven to the university to pick up blueprints of the Biology Building and the other nearby buildings. Taking a few steps across the room, Brodie grabbed the phone quickly and sat down.

"Lieutenant Brodie," she said.

"Hey! Guess what we got?" Frank Cardona's voice boomed over the handset.

"What?" she asked.

"The other three-fourths of the man from Aquarius!"

Sitting up abruptly in her chair, she waved at Nicholls to pick up his phone.

"Where, Frank?" she asked, grabbing a pad.

"In a dumpster across town. You know where that new apartment complex is going up near Manchester? Behind that," Cardona said. "Found a little while ago by a troop of Boy Scouts out scavenging for aluminum cans. Can you believe that shit?"

"We'll be there in a few minutes," she said.

"No hurry. The body's pretty mushy. Between that and about four hundred shitty diapers, the smell's enough to gag a maggot, which are also plentiful. Bring Lysol, babe."

Frank Cardona was nothing if not vividly descriptive and suddenly the barbecue sandwich she had eaten for lunch was having second thoughts. She hung up the phone and grabbed her jacket from the back of her chair. Nicholls was already ahead of her.

"Let's go, Maggie," he called as he spotted their trainee entering the building with an armful of papers. "Looks like we're finally gonna get a height and weight on the Headless Horseman."

BRODIE STOPPED THEIR car near the flimsy boundary created by yellow police tape strung around the parking lot. She was ahead of Nicholls and Weston as she flashed her badge to the officer manning the perimeter of the scene. It was easy to spot Cardona in his bright yellow coveralls. He was directing the men with him in removing the headless body through the opening on the side of the rusty dumpster. Everyone working at the scene wore a filtered mask to avoid the smell, except Frank. Brodie often thought he must have been born without olfactory nerves. Otherwise, no one could have stood the smells associated with his work. She was grateful for the slight breeze that seemed to be blowing the odor from the body and the dumpster away from them. Frank smiled when he saw her.

"Great afternoon, huh, Brodie?"

"Delightful, Frank. How's it going?"

"He's about ready to come out of hiding," he said, looking behind her as he spoke. "Glad to see you brought the fox with you. Single?"

"I have no idea, but since she's still alive and kickin' I don't think she's your type."

"Ah, yes. But hope springs eternal."

"Maria would deep-fry your *cojones* for lunch if she knew you were even looking," she said.

"Which reminds me. Farmed the kiddies out to grandmacita for a coupla days and Maria and I have made big plans that don't involved a deep-fryer," Frank said with a wide smile.

"No plans until I get my report, Frank."

"Don't worry, I'll give you a complete report on the Headless Horseman before the close of business today. You want me to send him over to Travis County?"

"Yeah. I'm sure they'll be thrilled to get another John Doe from us."

She looked around to see what had happened to Nicholls and Maggie. Nicholls was talking to a uniformed officer whom she assumed had been the first on the scene. Maggie was squatted down next to two boys who looked about twelve or thirteen years old. One of the boys was doing all the talking, using his hands like a hyperactive Italian. The second boy was sweating profusely and appeared to be on the verge of fainting. Maggie patted the boy's shoulder and handed him a tissue from her jacket pocket.

"Hey! You! Shit for brains! I know the guy's already dead, but try not to mutilate him any further," she heard Frank yell. One man climbed out of the dumpster and was holding onto one end of a stretcher. He had to stand in an awkward position to raise the stretcher through the opening which was an inch or two narrower than the stretcher. Frank trotted over to help his men turn the stretcher just enough to get it out. The black body bag strapped to the stretcher glistened as sunlight struck its vinyl exterior. Nicholls and Maggie joined her as she watched the men work.

"Think it's the rest of our victim?" Nicholls asked.

"I sure hope so, or we'll be hunting for body parts again. What did you two find out?"

"The uniform didn't know much. Checked the dumpster and lost his lunch," he said.

"I'm sure those kids found that extremely helpful," she said.

"The kids appear to be okay," Maggie said. "Their parents have been notified and I had a unit transport them to the hospital."

"Were they hurt?"

"Not really. One of them may be suffering from shock, but he wasn't the one who found the vic. The second boy was in the dumpster. When he found the body it startled him. Scratched his arm on the dumpster, so I thought someone should look at it. Might need a tetanus shot or something."

Brodie looked at her and smiled. "Good thinking. We can get a statement from them tomorrow. Give them a chance to calm down a little." Remembering a time they had discussed having one or two of their own, Brodie's smile faded away as quickly as it had appeared.

"The Scoutmaster said they've been collecting aluminum cans for recycling and received a phone call this morning telling them to check out the dumpsters around here," Maggie added, looking over her notes.

"Did he get the name of the caller?" Brodie asked.

"No."

"Who the hell calls in a tip for aluminum cans?" Nicholls asked.

"Maybe the perp figured we needed a little help locating the body," Brodie said.

"Well, there's no way in hell we'll get any useable prints off that dumpster," Nicholls observed.

"Probably right," she agreed as Cardona re-approached them, pulling gloves from his hands.

"Okay, ladies and gent, scribble this down. The remains are the second installment of your find yesterday morning. No question in my mind. He's a mess, but the cuts are as precise as the first. No blood around anywhere. Still a Hispanic male. I'd say about five eight and one ninety. Hadn't missed too many tacos. Fully clothed in some kind of uniform, also sans blood. Must have been dissected and then redressed. No I.D. on the body or the clothes. It's been warmer than usual the last few days and the heat can really build up in these metal dumpsters. From the degree of decomposition, I'd guess that the time of death was three to five days ago. The maggots are pretty advanced so they've been at it for a while. That's about what you'll be getting in my report, Brodie, but I'll put it in writing and send it over."

"Thanks, Frank. Go home and get lucky. Give my regards to Maria," she said patting the man on the back.

"You, my friend, will be the last topic of conversation tonight," he laughed and then jogged away and jumped into the forensics van.

"We'll need to get some people into that dumpster," Nicholls sighed. "A wallet could have fallen out of the vic's pocket."

"We could always call Romero," Brodie said with a chuckle.

Nicholls snorted loudly. "Hell, you couldn't get Romero in there unless you promised him Weston was in there buck naked and willing." Realizing what he had said, Nicholls shot a looked at Maggie. "Jesus, I'm so sorry, Maggie. I shouldn't have said that," he apologized.

"No need to apologize," she said. "I have four brothers."

Brodie turned and looked at Maggie as Nicholls walked away shaking his head. "There's never been another female detective in Cedar Springs except me," she said. "They're used to saying whatever they think, so if you have a problem with it you can report it to Captain Donaldson."

"I know how cops talk. You don't have to explain things to me, Lieutenant," Maggie said as they began walking toward the car. "By the way, I may have an ID on our victim."

Brodie stopped and looked sharply at her. "Were you planning to keep that *your* little secret?"

"No. I planned to tell you when I got back to the station, but we got the call to come here. The supervisor of janitorial services reported that one of his men hasn't come to work for the last few days."

She pulled her notebook from her jacket pocket and flipped a few pages before continuing. "The man's name is Cruz Garcia. Very reliable worker. Never sick. He doesn't have a telephone so the supervisor wasn't able to check on him. I was going to run by the address he gave me, but we were interrupted."

"What's the address?" Brodie asked as they resumed walking.

"1229 Val Verde in Southeast Austin. It's in the last area I worked on patrol. Not exactly the high rent district. Lots of gangs, lots of problems."

"I'll go with you after we drop Nicholls back at the station. He's checking on another suspicious death from last Thursday night anyway."

Brodie chose her Camaro over the department issued Crown Victoria and accelerated onto the highway ramp toward Austin, hoping the trip would go quickly. They drove along in silence for what seemed like an eternity, before Maggie broke the silence.

"Is this the same Camaro you were working on while you were in Austin?"

Brodie hesitated before answering. Why revisit old times? But it wasn't going to be possible to work every day with Maggie and not speak to her. She supposed they had to talk about something and her car seemed like a harmless enough topic. "Yeah, finally finished it a couple of years ago. Didn't have much else to do in my spare time."

"It looks great."

"Thanks."

"Nicholls seems like a good detective. How long has he been your partner?"

"Three or four years. Since he finished his training."

"Were you his training officer?"

"Yeah."

"Sort of unusual for a TO to become the trainee's partner, isn't it?"

"You ask too many fuckin' questions, Weston."

"I'm a detective," Maggie quipped. "It's what I get paid to do."

Brodie smiled slightly and then said, "Well, the truth is, Detective, Curtis Nicholls is a semi-racist, homophobic hot-dogger with a tendency to believe he's God's gift to women and the police department. I got stuck with him because no one else wanted to work with him."

"Does he know you're gay?"

Brodie glanced across the car at her. "Yes. But he doesn't know you are and if you're smart it will remain that way."

BRODIE EXITED THE Interstate onto Cesar Chavez Boulevard and turned into an older, run-down neighborhood within sight of the freeway. The majority of the houses were in need of paint, which gave them the overall appearance of weathered gray wood. Occasionally, someone had made an attempt to beautify their property, but the effort had obviously been hampered by a lack of money or a lack of interest. What once passed for grass was generally dying from a scarcity of water. Periodic green patches appeared to have been mowed but not edged, leaving long tendril of grass crawling across the cracked sidewalks. She followed Maggie's directions through a series of turns that carried them deeper into economic depression. Brown faces stared at the Camaro as it moved slowly through the area, searching for a house number. It didn't help that the many of the street signs were missing. The city had replaced them for years before finally giving up. Although she never caught them doing it, she suspected local gang kids or illegals removed them to confuse the authorities.

Eventually, she was forced to stop and ask directions from a juvenile who was walking lazily up the street. The kid looked about fourteen years old and was dressed in baggy tan work pants that fell across the tops of expensive looking tennis shoes in multiple folds virtually obscuring his feet. A white t-shirt, and long-sleeved blue and black plaid shirt buttoned only at the neck completed his gang-banger attire. The boy's hair was wavy and neatly trimmed, held in place by a hairnet which was pulled together in a small knot in the middle of his forehead. The beginnings of a skimpy moustache sprouted along his upper lip. He stared appreciatively at the car as it pulled to the curb next to him. Brodie rolled the window down and motioned for the boy to approach the car. He sauntered over to the car and rested his hands on the window frame.

"I'm lookin' for Val Verde," she said.

"What for?" the boy asked.

"Well, if I wanted you to know that, I'd have told you," she said.

"You a cop, right?"

"And you're an upstanding citizen who's always happy to help out the police," she answered with a grin.

The boy chuckled and looked into the car at Maggie. Then he looked back at Brodie. "She a cop, too?"

"Yeah. So where's the street, *jefe*?"

"I ain't you fuckin' *jefe*," the boy spat, backing away from the car, gesturing with his hands.

Opening the door of the car, Brodie took a deep breath and stepped out, grabbing the kid by the shirt. She dragged him to the back of the Camaro as Maggie heard long strings of Spanish flying between Brodie and the boy, most of it recognizable in almost any language as profanity. Eventually, she heard laughter and watched the boy stroll away at the same speed he had been going when Brodie stopped him.

"What the hell was all that about?" she demanded as Brodie settled back behind the wheel. "This isn't the kind of neighborhood where you can just grab one of the locals and hassle him. He could have twenty armed friends watching from the windows around here."

"Relax. There wasn't going to be any trouble. Just a lot of macho bullshit posturing. Now he looks good to his homeboys if they were watching because he stood up to the cops and walked away. Val Verde is a couple of streets over."

Less than a minute later they parked in front of a house that looked better than most of the houses surrounding it. The grass was green and the small yard had been edged. Flower baskets hung from hangers along the porch. The stucco-covered building was partially newly painted. Tricycles and other children's toys littered the yard. Brodie followed Maggie up the walkway to the front door. An old window unit hung from one of the front windows. Brodie knocked on the screen door and waited. She was about to knock again when the door opened. A man approximately her age peered at them through the screen. He was holding a crow bar in his right hand and appeared to be slightly out of breath.

She smiled and asked, "Is this the home of Cruz Garcia?"

The man looked at her and then Maggie. "We don't buy nothing," he said.

"I'm not selling," she replied, flashing her badge. "I'm Detective Brodie and this is Detective Weston. We're with the Cedar Springs Police Department. We're looking for Cruz Garcia. Does he live here?"

The man relaxed and nodded, "Si. Yes. Come in."

Opening the screen door, Brodie followed Maggie into the front room of the small house.

"You find my cousin?" the man asked.

"Did you report him missing?" Maggie asked.

"Yes, two, three days ago."

Their conversation was interrupted as a woman in her thirties came quietly into the room accompanied by three young children. One of the children, a girl about two, clung to the woman's leg so tightly that white handprints could be seen on the woman's brown skin. She wore simple clothes, which hid a slim figure. The beginning of tears made her eyes sparkle. Her straight dark hair fell to the middle of her back. She spoke to the man in soft Spanish.

"This is Cruz's wife, Magdalena."

"Does she speak English?" Brodie asked.

"A little, but not so good as me."

"When did your cousin disappear, Mr... I'm sorry. I didn't get your name, sir."

"Alejandro Ruiz."

"When did your cousin disappear, Mr. Ruiz?"

"He go to work Wednesday evening and has not returned. Magdalena is very worried."

"I imagine. Where does Mr. Garcia work?"

"At university in Cedar Springs. He works there as a janitor."

"Does he have a car?"

"No. There is a bus that goes near the university. Cruz walk the rest of the way."

"I see. Does Mrs. Garcia have a recent picture of her husband?"

The detectives waited while Ruiz spoke briefly to the woman. She nodded and left the room, dragging children with her.

"She wouldn't answer the door when she saw you. I had to run over from my house behind here. Have you found Cruz, Detective?"

"We don't know yet, Mr. Ruiz. We have found someone. If it turns out to be Mr. Garcia, someone will have to identify him."

"I understand," the man said weakly. His voice trembled as he spoke. "Cruz wanted to bring his family here for a better life. He is very hard worker. A good husband and father. To come all this way...a sad thing."

"Was Mr. Garcia an illegal?"

"No," Ruiz said, obviously insulted. "I sponsor him myself. He live with me until he save enough to bring Magdalena and the children here. He have a green card."

"So he only has his wife and three children," Maggie asked.

"Five. The older ones are in school. Cruz he go to night school. His English was very good. Will get his American high school paper this year," the man explained with pride.

Mrs. Garcia came back into the room and said something softly as she handed a picture to Ruiz. He looked at it and then passed it to Brodie.

"She said this was taken at Christmas before midnight mass," he said. "This is Cruz," he continued, pointing to a man in a suit.

She held the picture up for Maggie to see. It left little doubt that the head in the aquarium belonged to Cruz Garcia. She led Ruiz onto the porch and explained that they were reasonably certain his cousin was dead and explained the procedures the family would have to follow to identify him and reclaim the body. She explained that considering the circumstances of the death, it would probably be better for Ruiz to make the identification. Giving him her card, she and Maggie left Ruiz, Magdalena Garcia and her children to grieve and try to make sense out of a senseless act.

THE TWO DETECTIVES returned to the squad room shortly after five-thirty and found Nicholls sitting at his desk with his shirt sleeves rolled up, peering at yellow lettering on a green computer screen. When he saw them come in, he stopped and rubbed his eyes. Brodie went to her desk and sat down heavily. While Maggie wandered off down the hallway and entered the restroom, she leaned back and closed her eyes for a minute.

Detective Phillip Romero had seen them come in. A tall, slender, dapper man, he watched Maggie disappeared down the hallway before getting up from his desk and approaching Brodie.

"Hey, Brodie. Who's the new *chica*?" Romero asked, resting against the edge of her desk..

She opened her eyes. "What?"

"The new woman. How come I haven't been properly introduced yet?"

"I guess because you weren't here. Hang around; she'll be back. I tried my damnedest to get her assigned to you, but Donaldson didn't think you could keep your dick in your pants long enough to train her."

"Fuck you."

"Ask him yourself if you don't believe me, Romero."

"Single?"

"I don't give a shit about my trainee's sex life. Ask her yourself. Here comes your big chance now," she said when she saw Maggie coming back down the hallway.

The two of them watched as she stopped at the coffee maker and poured a cup of coffee. She shifted her weight from one foot to the other as she added powdered creamer and sugar to the cup. The fit of her slacks showed off a well rounded butt. Brodie looked up at Romero and smiled.

"Might want to wipe the drool off your chin before you introduce yourself," she chuckled.

"I could be in love," Romero sighed.

"Give me a fuckin' break," Nicholls mumbled into his computer screen.

Romero leaned down next to him and whispered, "Watch and learn from a man with...experience."

"I hope your dick falls off, Romero," Nicholls whispered back.

Brodie watched as Romero went to the coffee maker and refilled his cup while engaging Maggie in conversation. She remembered how it made her feel to know there were others who wanted Maggie and were attracted to her clean-cut good looks. She had never been jealous when other women hit on Maggie. She knew Maggie would be going home with only her each night.

"So what has your little computer told you so far?" she asked Nicholls, dragging her attention away from Maggie.

"The lab sent over a list of part numbers," he answered, turning back to his computer screen. "Apparently we have an '02 Mercedes. The last registered owner is Clifford Jenkins. Checked with DMV and got an Austin address and phone number. There was an answering machine at the other end and I'm waiting for a return call. The car isn't listed as stolen either here or by Austin PD."

"Maybe Mr. Jenkins doesn't know it's missing yet," she offered.

"I contacted Austin PD and they'll send someone by the address, but who knows when that'll be."

"Well, it's about time to call it good for today anyway. Maybe something will come in tomorrow. We got a tentative ID on our other guy."

"That was pretty quick."

"Weston found a missing employee from the university. We checked out the guy's home and got a picture. A family member will be making a positive ID, probably tomorrow. Is the body still at Travis County?"

"Yeah."

She sighed, pulling a piece of paper from her pocket and dialing the number. "I hate this part," she said as she waited for someone to answer.

A few minutes later she replaced the receiver in its cradle and rubbed her face.

"Migraine?" she heard Maggie's voice ask.

"No. Just a garden variety headache," Brodie said, thinking Maggie knew her too well. "Probably just need something to eat," she responded. "I'm about ready to pack it in for the day."

"Me, too," said Nicholls. "I still have a couple more things to check, but I'm about to go blind from staring at this damn screen anyway. Why don't you run what we have past Jacobs? See if she can give us a bead on what this guy's mind looks like."

Brodie got up slowly and fished her keys from the pocket of her slacks. It had been three days since she lost her cool with Camille. She frowned at the thought of trying to explain what had happened Saturday morning. She wasn't sure she knew herself.

Maggie watched as Brodie stopped on the way out and spoke to the officer behind the front desk. She had always been an intense and intriguing woman, but there was something different about her now. Something was lacking from the woman she had once known so intimately. Nicholls typed more information into his computer and sat back to let it digest his newest request. He took a sip of cold coffee from his mug and swished it around in his mouth.

"You going home, too?" he asked.

"Yeah, but I want to go over my notes from today and see if I left anything out. Is it always this busy around here?"

"Nah, you caught us at a really unique time. Two deaths under suspicious circumstances in less than a week is pretty radical stuff for Cedar Springs. Usually it's a bunch of bored, rich juvies breaking and entering for kicks. If a citizen dies around here it's probably from lugging around too much money at one time and they keel over from the strain."

Pausing a moment, Maggie took a deep breath. "Who's Jacobs?"

"What?"

"Jacobs. I heard you mention the name to the lieutenant."

"She's a psychologist friend of RB's. Nice lady." He smiled. "Great legs. I think she works for Austin PD. Or at least consults for them. Since RB was a psych major back in the day, they have a lot to talk about." He looked at his computer monitor for a moment. Turning to look at Maggie, he said, "Look it's none of my business, but I think there's something you should know about RB."

"What's that?" Maggie said as she glanced through another report.

"It won't make any difference in your training or anything, but, well, RB's gay."

"Really?"

"Yeah. I didn't mean to freak you out or anything. As a matter of fact, I think she might be dating Dr. Jacobs."

"Does that bother you?" Maggie asked.

"What? That she's a dyke or that if Jacobs is a dyke too it would be a total waste of a good-looking woman?" he quipped.

"Either one, I guess."

"Well, Brodie's a good cop. Really busted my balls when she was training me. When I found out she was gay, I thought she was taking out her latent hostility against men on me for a while."

"Was she?"

"No, she was just doing her job."

"And it doesn't bother you to be partnered with her?"

"We don't talk about it much. To each their own, I suppose. I heard you did good today, by the way. Identifying Juan Doe."

"Did Lieutenant Brodie say that?"

"Not in so many words."

"That's what I thought."

"Listen, Maggie, RB is okay. Just not very liberal with her praise. Never talks much, so I have to do most of the talking or go nuts in the car listening to some fuckin' country-western station."

Maggie laughed. "Country-western doesn't bother me."

"Then you and Brodie should be real tight."

Somehow I doubt that, Maggie thought, looking back into her notebook, remembering the first time she had encountered the formidable detective.

MAGGIE WESTON WAS a rookie patrol officer partnered with Dale Simmons, a sadistic son-of-a-bitch who made it obvious he didn't want to be saddled with a woman as his partner, even if her father was a commander. When they were called to handle a domestic disturbance, he sent her into the house alone to find out what was going on. What she walked in on was a very large Bubba with a belly full of cheap beer whaling on his girlfriend just because it was Friday night and he thought she needed it. She was forced to draw her service revolver and call for her partner to back her up. When Simmons failed to respond, she called for any available unit for assistance. She was still alone and holding her revolver on the man when a tall, dark-haired female officer and her partner entered the house. The girlfriend was leaning against a hall door and it was obvious she would require a few stitches.

"Problem?" the officer asked calmly in a deep, husky voice as her eyes quickly surveyed the situation.

"This gentleman doesn't seem to be in a very cooperative mood tonight," Maggie answered.

"How about calling the paramedics, Wheeler? And see what's delaying that jackass Simmons," the female officer said to her partner.

Wheeler nodded and jogged out to their patrol car while she kept her eyes trained on the drunk.

"Is she willing to press charges?"

"Doesn't have to. I witnessed the assault," Maggie answered, her revolver still leveled at the man. Adrenaline was pumping through her body, but she felt safer with other officers on the scene. The older officer positioned herself near the young woman and glanced at her nameplate.

"Are you planning to arrest him tonight, Officer Weston?"

"If I could have gotten my son-of-a-bitch partner in here, he'd already be under arrest," she seethed.

"Tell this bitch to get the fuck outta my fuckin' house!" the drunk yelled.

"Shut up, asshole! No one's talkin' to you," the taller officer snapped, pointing at him.

"Fuck you, bitch! I know my rights."

"Then exercise your right to remain silent and put your hands on the wall," the woman ordered. She was an imposing figure, Maggie thought as she quickly glanced at the other officer. Her eyes caught the name on the officer's ID tag. Brodie. She had heard the name during her training, but they had never met.

"Do you want me to take this one?" Brodie asked.

"I got it, but you can keep an eye on him for me," she replied.

Maggie's partner finally found the front door and was resting against the door frame observing the proceedings nonchalantly, chewing on the remains of a toothpick. Wheeler had to push him aside to re-enter the house.

Maggie placed her revolver back in its holster and removed her handcuffs from their case on the back of her belt. "Sir, you're under arrest for assault and battery. Turn around and place your hands on the wall," she ordered in a firm voice as she approached the drunk.

The drunk looked at the two male officers and winked. "You boys need to teach your women to stay in their place," he laughed. Suddenly he jumped toward her and yelled, "Boo!"

As he reached out to grab Maggie's uniform, Brodie and her partner pulled their revolvers and yelled, "Freeze!"

The drunken man looked startled for a second by their reaction. That was all the time Maggie needed to grab him by the arm and slam him face first into the nearest wall. She heard a cracking sound, followed by blood running from the man's nose after his close encounter with the peeling sheetrock. She used the extra time to throw the stunned man to the floor, jamming her right knee into the middle of his back. Grabbing his right arm, she handcuffed it while reciting, "You have the right to remain silent. Anything you say can and will be used against you in a court of law. Do you understand that, sir?"

Before the man could spit out his answer she brought his left arm behind him and completed cuffing him. She finished reading the man his rights and pushed past the female officer and her partner, stopping next to where Simmons was still lounging against the door frame.

"I got him down. Now you can get his fat ass up," she said through clenched teeth.

She walked to their patrol car, straightening her department issue shirt on the way, working hard to control her anger. Leaning her arms against the vehicle, she took several deep breaths and exhaled them slowly.

"Are you all right?" Brodie's voice asked from behind her.

Maggie turned her head around quickly and glanced at her before turning away again. "Yeah, I'm fine. But I'll probably be dead by next week if I don't get transferred away from that motherfucker Simmons."

"Rookie?"

"First week."

"Are you related to Commander Weston?"

"What if I am?" she asked defensively.

Brodie shrugged as she smiled at the rookie. "Make sure you write this up in your report. I'll file a backup report and I'll speak to the Watch Commander about getting you with someone else."

"I don't expect special treatment because of my father," Maggie said as she squared her shoulders and glared at the woman.

"I'm not giving you any," Brodie said. Seeing Wheeler and Simmons leading the man out of his house she called out, "Put that tax-payer in our car, Wheeler."

Wheeler nodded and changed direction with the drunk who was complaining loudly that his nose was broken and he felt sick. Wheeler looked at Brodie and Maggie and smiled before abruptly turning the drunk toward Simmons in time for the man to vomit. Simmons wasn't fast enough to get away out of the way and suddenly looked like he might puke himself. When the suspect was secured in the back of Brodie's patrol car, Brodie looked Simmons over as he walked toward his unit.

"Jesus, Simmons, you look like shit," she said, the scent of regurgitated beer wafting from the officer's uniform.

"Yeah, and he don't smell so good either," Wheeler said with a grin.

"What happened, bud? There's blood on your uniform. Did you get hurt?" she asked with little genuine concern in her voice.

"Naw," said Wheeler. "We had a little trouble getting the moron up and his bloody nose sort of ran into Simmons' uniform. Sorry 'bout that, man."

"Fuck you, Wheeler," Simmons mumbled.

"Well, you better get back to the station house and change. Your shift is about over anyway," Wheeler smiled.

"Y'all be careful now," Brodie said as her soft brown eyes turned to Maggie and winked.

Maggie barely had time to close the door of their patrol car before Simmons peeled away from the scene. Two days later Maggie was transferred to a new training officer, at least in part due to the recommendation of Officers Royce Brodie and Stan Wheeler.

IT WOULD BE three months before Maggie finally saw Royce Brodie again. She hadn't been able to get the tall, confident officer out of her mind. She wasn't much of a socializer, but a friend talked her into going out for a couple of drinks after her shift. DreamWorks was a new women's club a couple of blocks off the interstate in Austin and although she had never been there, she had heard of it. She had been suffering from bouts of insomnia and decided that a few drinks might help her get some sleep.

When she walked in, it took a minute for her eyes to adjust to the low light and high volume level. Colorful neon beer signs decorated the wood paneled walls. She found her friends involved in a serious game of pool and after a round of hugs and handshakes, she excused herself to make her way to the bar which was fifteen feet of polished wood.

"What can I getcha?" the cheerful blonde behind the bar asked.

"Miller Draught, please," Maggie smiled, dropping a five on the bar as she winked at the blonde, placing her in her mental notebook of women to check out more carefully later. Leaning against the bar, sipping her beer, she looked around the bar. About twenty couples with varying degrees of ability moved around the dance floor. Once upon a time she had loved to dance, but it had been a long time since she had taken a spin on a dance floor. Maybe later, she thought.

On her way in she had seen a few interesting faces in the pool room and wandered back toward it. She leaned against a wall and observed the games already underway. Then she noticed a familiar face and a smile made its way across her lips. Fishing quarters from her pocket, she stepped forward and placed them on the side rail of the table, a challenge to take on the winner of the match in progress.

When the match ended, she picked up a cue stick and walked to the table. The winner walked up to Maggie as she shoved the coins into the slots. "Royce Brodie," the winner said. Looking at Maggie closely, Brodie asked as they shook hands, "Have we met before?"

"Sort of," Maggie said.

"Shit! You're the one with the drunk Bubba last month!"

"Is it true what they said around the station? About Simmons," Maggie asked.

Brodie smiled at the mention of the rookie's former partner. "I heard he fell off his roof while adjusting his satellite dish," she said as she shrugged.

"Yeah, I heard that, too." Not long after the incident Wheeler had suggested he and Brodie should give Simmons an off-duty attitude adjustment. When reason hadn't worked they wound up knocking the shit out of him. Maggie laughed as she hoisted her drink. "To the roof."

As the challenger, Maggie racked the balls and watched as her opponent prepared for the break. She guessed Brodie was ten or twelve years older, but still attractive enough for Maggie to consider getting to know her a little better.

"I've got a twenty that says I can take you," the rookie challenged, reaching into the back pocket of her jeans.

"Your money," Brodie said with a shrug.

"I should warn you," Maggie said, her eyes flashing. "I hate to lose."

"Yeah, well, I hate green beans, but that doesn't mean I don't get stuck with them on my plate from time to time."

Maggie lifted the rack from the balls and took a drink of her beer as she stepped back for the break. A solid ball fell into the side pocket and Brodie walked confidently around the table looking for her best shot. Four balls later she missed a difficult shot and had to turn the table over to Maggie. She picked up her beer and leaned against the wall as her opponent surveyed the table. Maggie couldn't suppress a smile as she leaned over the table to line up her first shot and gave her opponent a primo view of her ass.

She studied each shot carefully, considering where the cue ball should stop for her next shot. She never spoke and seemed to be oblivious to the appreciative looks from the older officer. She got down to her last two balls on the table before a ball rattled a corner pocket, but failed to drop.

"Better not miss or your ass and your money will be mine," Maggie said in a low voice as she brushed past Brodie.

"I'll do my best, but suddenly losing doesn't sound like such a bad thing," Brodie responded with a grin.

She sank her remaining balls, but was left with a difficult bank shot the length of the table for the eight ball. Squatting down, she estimated the angle to the corner pocket before tapping it with her cue and leaning over the cue ball. The second her stick hit the cue ball Maggie knew Brodie had hit it perfectly and watched the eight ball drop into the designated pocket. She walked over and extended her hand. As Brodie took it, she smiled broadly. "Keep your money," she said.

"I always pay my debts."

"It wasn't a fair match, you know. I've probably been shooting pool since you were in diapers."

"I never make excuses for losing. You just outplayed me, this time. But you could ask me for a dance to soothe my damaged ego."

Stepping onto the lightly saw-dusted floor, Brodie took Maggie in her arms and glided off into a slow two-step. Maggie followed her every step and spin as they moved effortlessly around the floor.

The way Brodie's body moved against hers made the room seem warmer than it was. Maggie hadn't been with anyone for quite a while and hadn't expected anything more than a dance. The song finally ended and Brodie released her, but Maggie's arms remained around her waist as she looked up at her. Unable to redirect her eyes anyplace except Maggie's lips, Brodie began to lean closer, then pulled away.

Maggie stopped her, wrapping her arms around Brodie's neck, engulfing her senses as she pulled her into a slow, exploratory kiss. As their lips parted, Maggie looked into her eyes. "I like you, Royce," she said, the low timbre of her voice an invitation to more.

"I like you, too, Maggie, but..."

"But what?" she challenged.

"Well, for one thing, no one calls me Royce except my mother," Brodie said.

"It fits you," she said as she teased a finger across the taller woman's mouth. "I like it."

Clearing her throat, Brodie continued, "Your father *is* my watch commander."

"What we do off duty is no one else's business, including his."

"There's a pretty big age difference between us."

"Is that a problem for you?" Maggie laughed.

"Not usually. One of my many faults is that I enjoy the company of attractive women," Brodie admitted. "Of all ages."

"Do you work tomorrow?"

Brodie shook her head slightly. Bringing her mouth closer to Brodie's ear, Maggie said with a smile, "I'm on second shift, but I'll make sure you're up before I leave for work."

For the next two years they were never separated until the night that marked the beginning of the end.

NICHOLLS SLAPPED THE side of the computer monitor, snapping Maggie back to the present. "Come on, you hunka shit, give with the information already!"

Half a minute later the computer finally began doing something constructive. He read the information coming up on the screen and jotted down a few notes.

"Is that about one of the recent cases?" Maggie asked.

"No. We've had a rash of afternoon vandalisms and a witness said she saw some kids hanging around one of the places that got hit. So I tapped into the school computer to check attendance records. Never know, I might get lucky and nail the little shits."

Maggie closed her notebook and got up. "Well, I guess I better get going." She picked up a small stack of papers from her desk and shoved them into a manila envelope before grabbing her purse and heading for the front door. It had been an eventful two days, despite some latent hostility on Brodie's part.

As Maggie walked past the front desk, the desk officer was engrossed in a heated conversation with a tall, patrician-looking older woman. She was dressed like an English housewife in a green wool plaid skirt, white blouse, and tan cardigan sweater. Her gray hair was pulled up into a semi-bun, but it didn't make her face look stark or severe.

Maggie pushed the front door to the police station open, but the desk officer stopped her. "Detective, perhaps you can help this lady."

Maggie glanced at her watch quickly and walked back toward the front desk. "What seems to be the problem?"

"My husband has been missing for five days and the police department doesn't seem to give a damn. That's the problem, young woman."

"Have you filed a missing person's report, Mrs.-"

"Brauner. And I have filed a report and called every day. So far I haven't even had the courtesy of a follow-up phone call. How far up the food chain do I have to go before you people take this seriously?"

The officer behind the desk looked frustrated. "Ma'am, maybe he just wanted to get away for a while."

"Officer, my husband simply would not just get away. He may be sixty-five years old, but despite what you young people seem to believe, people our age do manage to have quite healthy personal relationships."

"When did your husband disappear, Mrs. Brauner?" Maggie asked.

"Thursday evening, but because Elliott hadn't been gone forty-eight hours these fools made me wait until Sunday morning before taking a report."

Maggie was intrigued by the woman's appearance. She was between fifty and sixty years old, but there were few wrinkles on her face or hands. Her manner, even though she was obviously aggravated, was warm and familiar. She was quite tall, about five-ten, and Maggie had to look up to speak to her, which made her feel like a school girl standing repentantly in front of her teacher.

"I'd be happy to talk with you, ma'am. I'm Detective Maggie Weston."

"Helen Brauner," the woman said extending a hand to Maggie. Her grip was surprising strong, not the limp handshake Maggie had expected from the older woman.

Maggie led Helen back to her desk and pulled a chair over for her. Nicholls was pulling his jacket on and preparing to leave.

"Need some help, Maggie?" he asked.

"No, thanks. I've got it, Nicholls."

"When you finish up here why don't you join me at the Super Burger? Cheap food and doesn't taste half bad either."

"Thanks," she said with a smile. "I'll take a rain check."

Nicholls left Maggie and Helen Brauner alone in the squad room.

"I don't have a copy of the missing person reports right now, Mrs. Brauner, so why don't you just start with Thursday night."

"Please, call me Helen. Everyone does," the woman said. "Even my students."

"Okay, Helen. You said your husband disappeared Thursday evening."

"Yes. Elliott came home on time, but later remembered there were some papers in his office at the university that he needed for Friday."

"Your husband is a professor?"

"We both are. I offered to go with him, but he said he'd only be gone a few minutes. We live over on Maple, a few blocks from the university, near fraternity row."

"I'm sorry to interrupt you, Helen, but about what time did he leave?" Maggie asked.

"Between seven and seven-thirty. Right after dinner. It's about a fifteen minute walk so he should have been home by eight or eight-fifteen."

"He walked to the campus?"

"We always do. Elliott doesn't drive. I do, but he likes the company and it gives us a chance to talk on the way to work every morning."

"What does your husband teach at the university?"

"Microbiology."

"And where is his office located?"

"In the Biology Building, third floor."

Maggie felt her heart skip a beat at the mention of the Biology Building. "I see. And is your office in the same building?"

"No. I'm in the building next door. Chemistry. My students told me there was a problem in the Biology Building yesterday. Is that true?"

"Yes, but I'm sure your husband wasn't involved with that."

Helen Brauner looked relieved. "I'm terribly worried about Elliott. This just isn't like him. I called Tony, but he said he hasn't seen Elliott. And neither has Malcolm."

"And who are they?" Maggie inquired.

"Tony is Elliott's graduate assistant. A brilliant student, but a little rough around the edges. Malcolm Roth is another professor in Elliott's department."

"Do you know Tony's last name?" Maggie asked.

"Obregon. Antonio Obregon."

"What did you mean when you said he was rough around the edges?"

"Well, it's just that he doesn't have many social skills. Has a rather nasty temper, according to Elliott, but such promise."

"I see. Do you happen to have a picture of Dr. Brauner?"

"I thought you might want one." Helen smiled as she reached for the worn leather shoulder bag resting against the leg of her chair. "I tried to find a recent picture, but this was all I could find."

She pulled a Polaroid picture from the bag and handed it to Maggie. It showed Helen Brauner standing next to a man who was nearly a head shorter than she. Helen was resting her right elbow on his shoulder and touching his face with her left hand, gazing down at him. Elliott Brauner had his left arm around his wife's waist and appeared somewhat stiff as he posed for the picture. The contrast between the two was striking. Helen wore a floor length evening gown, resplendent with jewelry, her hair a silver halo surrounding a smiling, almost youthful looking face. Elliott, on the other hand, seemed out of place, wearing a rather ill-fitting tuxedo. The red cummerbund made him look shorter than he probably was. Wire-rim glasses sat halfway down his nose at a slight angle. The stockiness of his body betrayed the fact that Helen must have been a good cook.

"It was taken two or three years ago, the same year Dr. Ramsdell was made University President. His inaugural dance. I'm sure you can tell that Elliott wasn't exactly happy to be there. Called it a total waste of time and money." Helen laughed. "Despite his grousing, Elliott actually loves to dance and is quite good at it."

"Um, how tall is Dr. Brauner, Helen?"

"You noticed. Elliott is five feet five inches tall and weighs, oh, about a hundred and seventy-five pounds, I think. We used to make quite a striking couple, Detective Weston. The first time I went out with Elliot, in graduate school, I tried to make myself look shorter. But he told me, no, he ordered me, to stand tall. The difference in our height didn't bother him and if it bothered me, then I should look elsewhere for an escort. Then he said something quite off-color about the advantage of being shorter than me." A slight blush spread over her cheeks as she remembered a private conversation.

"First thing in the morning, I'll get a copy of the report you've already filed and check a few things. The picture will be very helpful. Where can I reach you, in case I need to ask you a few more questions?"

"I'll either be in class or in my office most of the day. I'm worried sick about Elliott, but I can't let my classes go to hell. Elliott would chastise me severely if I neglected my students. My office is 224 in the Chemistry Building and my last class ends around three o'clock. But that class is a lab so it may take me a little while longer to clean everything up. That's in Room 312. Please let me know if you find out anything. Good or bad, I have to know."

Suddenly, Helen Brauner looked older. Maggie placed her hand on Helen's and said, "You'll hear from me tomorrow, Helen, no matter what."

BRODIE TOOK A beer from the refrigerator and headed for the living room. As she stretched out on the couch, Max strolled up next to her and laid his massive head on her lap, looking up at her with soulful eyes. *Might as well get it over with,* she thought as she reached for the telephone receiver and dialed, waiting as the phone on the other end rang.

"Goddammit, Max. Don't you ever stop shedding?" she mumbled as the big dog nuzzled harder against her. She took a long drink of the beer as she continued petting Max's head until she heard a familiar voice on the phone.

"Hi, Camille. How's it going?" she asked more cheerfully than she felt.

"I was hoping you'd call, RB. I've been thinking about you all day," Camille said.

"I'm sorry about last weekend. I don't know what got into me."

"Sometimes things just happen," she said warmly. "How are things at work?"

"You mean how is it having Maggie Weston around, don't you?"

"I don't want to pry into your life. I'm just concerned about you."

"I know that. We've been busy the last couple of days, so I didn't have much time to think about the past," she lied. "Listen, do you have any plans for tomorrow? I need to pick your brains a little."

"I don't think so, but I don't have my appointment calendar here. New case?"

"Yeah, a nasty one and I need to get a handle on this guy as quick as I can."

"How do you know it's a man you're looking for?"

"It's not a female crime, honey. Take my word for that much."

"That sounds a little like stereotyping, RB."

"Well, I'm an equal opportunity cop. After you see the file you can tell me if it could be a woman. It goes without saying, of course, that the department can't pay your usual consulting fee."

"Why don't you drop by my office tomorrow around five?"

"I could pick up a pizza or something and drop by your place later this evening," Brodie offered.

Camille paused before responding. "I don't think that would be a good idea right now, RB. We need to talk anyway."

"That doesn't sound good, babe."

"I'll see you tomorrow."

Brodie stared at the phone for a minute before hanging up. Until three days ago she had been enjoying what she considered to be a satisfying relationship with Camille. She took a long drink of the beer as she looked down at Max. The dog looked like he was asleep and she closed her eyes, too.

THE DAY AFTER Wheeler was killed, Brodie awakened in the hospital, a dull throb in her right thigh. She barely remembered what had happened the night before. Her mouth was dry and her tongue felt like it was sewn to the roof of her mouth. She looked around for water and saw a nurse adjusting an IV line. She opened her mouth to speak, but had to struggle to say anything.

"Water," she finally croaked.

The nurse poured a glass of water and raised the bed far enough for Brodie to drink through a straw.

"You had us scared for a while, Sergeant Brodie," she said. "There's someone waiting outside for you to wake up."

The nurse left the room quietly, returning a few moments later followed by Maggie. She had been in one of the units that responded to her call for help the night before. As soon as the nurse left them alone, Maggie took her hand and kissed her lightly.

"Damn, baby, you look like shit" she said. She looked exhausted.

"It's just a leg wound. I'm not likely to die from it."

"You were in surgery long enough for a transplant. The doc said the damn bullet traveled halfway down your leg. It'll be a while before you can go back to work."

She looked at Maggie and blinked a few times. "Wheeler..."

"He didn't make it, Royce. I'm sorry."

Brodie was suddenly furious as tears pooled in her eyes and escaped down her cheeks. "That bitch! That fuckin' little bitch! It's my fault, Maggie."

"That's not true, Royce. You couldn't have known she had a gun."

"I should have been more careful, but she was just a kid."

"You both should have been more careful. The shooting team thinks she may have been on something."

"When is Stan's funeral?"

"Day after tomorrow."

She grabbed Maggie's arm and pulled her closer. "I have to be there, Maggie."

"You will be, I promise."

Two days later Maggie helped Brodie out of her car. She felt like shit and so far the painkillers weren't doing their job the way they were advertised. She and Maggie were both in their dress uniforms. It took her a while to get used to the crutches, but Maggie stayed at her side until they made it up the front steps of the church. Police officers from cities around the state had turned out to honor the fallen officer and scores of police vehicles from various police departments lined both sides of the street in front of the church. Brodie paused inside the church entryway to remove her hat. As she made her way down the church aisle, other officers looked at her as she passed and she knew they were whispering that she had been with Wheeler the night it happened. It seemed like a million years ago. She and Maggie took seats with other members of the Austin Police Department near the front of the church and she saw Commander Tim Weston turn to glare at them.

Forty minutes later they were standing on the grass in the cemetery. The painkillers either still hadn't kicked in or had and were now wearing off. She tried to think about other things to take her mind off the incessant throbbing in her leg, but she was startled when the honor guard fired its volleys. She wanted desperately for it all to be over, but knew she couldn't leave until she spoke to Stan's wife. When the gravesite service ended she made her way through the line of well wishers to speak to Gloria Wheeler. When she saw Brodie approaching, she went to her and hugged her tightly. Brodie blinked back tears as she told Gloria how sorry she was. She moved on and waited for Maggie to rejoin her.

"Get me out of here, Maggie. My leg is on fire."

"Let me take you back to the hospital, Royce."

"Let's just go home."

They were halfway to Maggie's car when Brodie heard someone call her name and stopped. She saw Tim Weston striding purposefully in their direction followed by Maggie's brothers.

"You shouldn't have come here, Brodie," Weston spat as he stopped inches from her..

"The doctors already told her that," Maggie said.

"I'm not talking about the fuckin' doctors, Officer," Tim snapped as he looked at his daughter. "She doesn't belong here."

"What the hell are you talking about, Dad? She was Stan's partner, for Christ's sake," Maggie said before Brodie could speak.

"And her carelessness cost him his life!"

Maggie started to respond, but Brodie stopped her.

"Is that what you think, Tim? That I'm responsible for Stan's death?"

"You're goddamn right. You know it and I know it, Brodie. You were supposed to be covering his back and you didn't. What the hell were you doing?"

"It happened too quick."

"Everything we do is quick. If you can't handle it, you don't belong on the force."

"That's not fair, Dad," Maggie intervened.

Whipping his head toward his daughter, he spat, "And I suppose you believe that bullshit because she's fuckin' you."

All of Brodie's pent up emotion came to the surface and she forgot about her leg. Dropping her crutches, she grabbed Tim, and shoved him against the nearest tree.

"Don't you *ever* talk to her like that again," she seethed.

"The thought that Stan died because his partner was a fuckin' cowardly dyke turns my stomach," Weston snarled as he shoved her away. "You should have been the one who died and done us all a favor!"

Before she thought about what she was doing, she swung her fist and caught Weston on the jaw, knocking him down. All the adrenalin in her body kicked in and she would have continued pummeling her commander if she hadn't been stopped by Maggie and her brothers.

By the time Maggie got her back to her car, the wound had reopened and was bleeding again. She pressed her hand over the wound as Maggie drove away from the cemetery.

"Dammit, Royce. You need to go back to the hospital," Maggie said as she saw the blood on Brodie's hand.

"It'll be all right. I need to stay off my feet for a while and let it heal a little longer. Just take me back to my place," she insisted.

SHE CLENCHED HER hands into fists to keep them from shaking as the memories overtook her. She downed the remainder of her beer in one long swallow and fought back the tears that found their way to the surface. Rubbing her face with her hands, she couldn't believe the appearance of one woman had opened up every bad memory she had worked so hard to forget. Just a few days earlier she had had her past under control.

Chapter
Four

MAGGIE SWUNG HER forest green Subaru into a visitor's parking space and looked around. There were a few cars parked in an area designated for faculty members and she smiled when she saw them. Some were a little beaten up with a few patches of Bond-O. The university may have been considered a center of higher learning, but many of the vehicles looked as if they belonged in front of a honky-tonk. There was a distinctly Texas appearance to the vehicles. She counted six pick-up trucks with the usual paraphernalia hanging in the back windows. Racks for rifles. Window decals from various country-western radio stations in the area. Advertisements for the owner's favorite alcoholic beverage. Keep Austin Weird bumper stickers. There were two or three small foreign sports cars that seemed to have taken the wrong off-ramp on their way to an Ivy League college huddled among the pick-ups.

It was nearly eight-thirty and classes would be getting underway soon. A few students still straggled across the campus, looking as if they had just rolled out of bed and were still wearing whatever they had slept in.

She knew she should have checked in at the department before driving to the university, but had decided she was capable of conducting a couple of interviews on her own. Brodie might be pissed off and she knew it. To fend off some of her potential anger, she left a message with the dispatcher to notify her training officer of her location and the approximate time she would return. The night before she had gotten a list of professors in Elliott Brauner's department. Even though she didn't have class schedules for them, she decided to prowl the halls of the Biology Building and visit Brauner's office.

She left her purse in her car, locked it, and walked up the steps into the building. A little more than forty-eight hours earlier there had been near panic in the building as students and staff members strained to see what all the excitement had been about. Now it seemed as if nothing remarkable had happened. Inside the front door was a directory listing the office assignments for professors in the building. She didn't remember seeing it the day Garcia's head had been found and reprimanded herself for missing a detail like that.

Looking at the list of names, she checked the directory. Dr. Malcolm Roth's office was listed as 316. Dr. Elliott Brauner was 330.

As she climbed the stairs to the third floor, the smell of formaldehyde grew increasingly stronger. With most of the labs located on the second floor, it was understandable, but the smell seemed to rise and permeate into the third floor and grow stronger. Maggie could hear the sound of keyboards clicking rapidly when she reached the top of the stairwell. Occasionally a phone rang behind one of the doors. Fluorescent lighting lit the walls and floor making them seem slightly yellowed. The hallway was T-shaped and Maggie looked to see which direction the room numbers ran before moving farther down the hall. Near the end of the T, she found 316. The name Malcolm Roth, Ph.D. was neatly stenciled in black on the opaque glass door. Below it, in slightly smaller lettering, "Microbiology".

Maggie decided to skip Dr. Roth for the moment and locate Brauner's office. Halfway down the T was Room 330. There were no lights on inside and the same stenciling she had seen on Roth's door was also on this door. Elliott Brauner, Ph.D., Microbiology. She tried the doorknob, but the room was locked. Returning to Roth's office, she knocked on the door. A moment later the door was opened by a handsome young man in his late twenties, a cell phone pressed between his shoulder and ear.

"May I help you?" he asked.

Maggie smiled and showed him her badge. "I hope so. Detective Weston with the Cedar Springs Police Department."

"Is this about what happened Monday?"

"No. I'm investigating a missing person. Dr. Brauner's wife filed a report that he hasn't been home for a few days."

The man smiled at her and opened the door wider, ending his conversation and clipping the cell onto his belt. He was medium height and weight and his light brown hair was neatly styled. He wore tan Dockers over a polished pair of loafers. Maggie hadn't seen a man wearing loafers in a while.

"I'm sorry, Detective. Please come in. I'm Daryll Chambers, Dr. Roth's assistant. He doesn't like students dropping by without an appointment and I thought you might be some eager coed looking for free answers to the next exam."

Maggie stepped into the office and glanced around. Anti-everything posters hung on the walls of the outer office. A wooden desk was pushed against one wall. A computer cursor blinked where Chambers had apparently stopped when he answered the door. Next to the desk was a row of four-drawer file cabinets. The room was in moderate disarray, but no more than one would expect in any college office. "Is Dr. Roth in class now?"

"Until ten," Chambers nodded looking at his wristwatch. "Then he has a break until after lunch. If you need to talk to him you might try back then."

"I noticed that Dr. Brauner's office is locked. I don't suppose you have a key."

"Only Dr. Brauner and his assistant have a key to his office as far as I know."

"I gather you know his assistant, Mr. Obregon, since you're both in the same department."

"Everyone knows Tony. We were all a little surprised when Brauner made him his assistant. But then Brauner is a little unusual himself."

"How so?"

"Distant. Never associates with anyone else in the department unless his wife is with him and forces him to. Tony's pretty much the same way, so I suppose that's why they're able to stand one another."

"Are Mr. Obregon and Dr. Brauner friendly?"

Chambers laughed lightly. "About as friendly as a cobra and a mongoose. They fight all the time. Just last week I was on my way here and came up the back stairs. When I passed Brauner's office they were practically screaming at each other."

"Really? Could you tell what they were arguing about?"

"No, and I didn't want to know. Although I did hear Brauner use his favorite phrase when he deals with students."

"Which is?"

"This establishes a new standard for incompetence and carelessness," Chambers said raising his voice and smiling.

"Was he addressing Mr. Obregon or another person?" Maggie inquired.

Chambers seemed to think a second and then shrugged. "I assumed he was talking to Tony because before I got to my office I heard a door slam. The next thing I heard was Tony calling Dr. Brauner a stupid old fucker." Chambers smiled sheepishly and said, "Excuse my language."

"Do you remember which day last week you overheard the argument?"

"I'm sorry, I don't. But it must have been near the end of the week. Definitely after Wednesday."

"I'd like to get into Dr. Brauner's office and take a look around. Do you know anyone who might have a key to the other offices?" Maggie asked, glancing to a key ring lying on Chambers' desk.

"I only have a key to this office," Chambers said as he picked up his key ring. "I can call maintenance or security. One of them might have a master key for all the rooms."

"I'd appreciate that, Mr. Chambers," Maggie smiled as he picked up the desk phone and started to pocket his keys while punching in a few numbers. The keys missed his pocket and fell to the floor.

Maggie picked them up and handed them back to him as he explained the situation to whoever answered the phone, said thank you, and hung up.

"Thank you, Detective. The security supervisor said he'll send someone over in a few minutes. You can wait here if you want," Chamber said casually.

"Thanks, but I'll go back to Dr. Brauner's office. Thanks for your help," she said. As she reached the door, she looked back at Chambers who had already sat back down at his desk.

"I'll be back around ten. Please tell Dr. Roth I'd like to speak with him," she said.

"Will do," Chambers said without looking up.

Maggie waited outside Brauner's office for about ten minutes before she heard footsteps trudging up a back stairway to the third floor. Finally she saw a gray head appear over the top step. A man in his fifties, wearing dark brown work pants and a short-sleeve tan work shirt, displaying a patch with the university seal on the right sleeve, appeared to be winded by the time he reached the top step. As he took a deep breath and approached her she could read the name "Ralph" embroidered over his left shirt pocket. He was carrying a large metal ring with dozens of keys hanging on it.

"You the one who wants in 330?" he asked as he reached her.

"Yes," she replied.

"You got permission from somebody?"

Pointing to the badge hanging over the waistband of her slacks, she said, "Yes, again."

"Sorry, but, as I'm sure you know, we've had a little trouble here recently," Ralph said as he fumbled through the keys looking for the right one. "And I sure don't want no trouble from Dr. Brauner on account of me letting someone in here."

"Who else would have keys to this office?"

"Besides this one, probably only three or four. Dr. Brauner's a little paranoid about who has access to his office. He has us change the lock every time he gets a new assistant. Must have somethin' top secret in there. Ah, here is it," he said absently. He turned the key and opened the door.

"Thanks. I'll make sure it's secure before I leave," Maggie said as she reached in and flipped on the light switch. She looked around the room as Ralph searched for the key to Brauner's inner office. When he finally opened the door, he turned to leave. "Tell you what I'm gonna do, Officer. I'll set the doors to lock automatically when you close it. It'll save me another trip."

Maggie stepped back out into the hallway as half the man's body disappeared down the steps.

"Ralph!" she called out.

"Yeah," he answered, stopping to turn halfway around.

"Would the janitorial staff have a master key, too?"

He scratched his head a second before answering. "Yeah, I think they might, now that you mention it."

"Do you know a janitor named Cruz Garcia?"

"Heard the name. I believe he works evenings and I only work days."

She nodded and walked back into Brauner's office. The office was set up in the same configuration as Roth's with a small outer office and a slightly larger room which served as Brauner's office. The difference between Roth's office and Brauner's was striking. No posters decorated the walls and there were no stacks of papers. The outer office looked unoccupied. There was a wooden desk, which she assumed was for his assistant. An older model computer sat on one side of the desk. There were no file cabinets in the front office. Sitting at the desk, she opened the drawers and looked through a few small stacks of papers. Apparently the papers were student assignments waiting to be graded. Other than the papers, everything else in the drawers was what she would have expected to find; typing paper, a bottle of correction fluid, pens, pencils, paper clips. Maggie turned on the overhead light in Brauner's office. The room was certainly not overly decorated, but had a homier look than the outer office. A bank of file cabinets lined the wall just inside the door. A striped Roman shade covered the window and three potted plants sat on the windowsill. Maggie poked a finger into each pot. The soil was dry and the plants probably hadn't been watered in several days.

Turning away from the window, she surveyed the contents of the room. There were pictures and documents on the walls and she read each one. Three college degrees hung directly behind Brauner's desk and she speculated they would seem intimidating to anyone sitting in front of the desk. An undergraduate diploma from Columbia and graduate diplomas from the University of Chicago and Harvard. Remembering the picture his wife had shown her, Elliott Brauner had not exactly fit the mental image anyone would have of an Ivy Leaguer. Hanging alongside the diplomas were commendations from the National Institutes of Health, the Center for Disease Control, and a few other governmental agencies she had never heard of. On a side wall between two large bookcases were a series of pictures Maggie assumed to be family pictures. Several pictures were of Helen, but there were none that included Brauner himself. Either the professor had been camera shy or was extremely modest. One of the bookshelves held a small compact disc player.

Next to it was a collection of CDs, mostly classical with a smattering of jazz recordings.

Brauner's desk was cleared except for an ink blotter/calendar combination and a picture of Helen leaning against a huge tree, smiling broadly. Maggie sat down at the desk and pulled a drawer open. A stack of official looking papers embossed with the university seal were paper clipped together and lying on top. Maggie took them out and was glancing through them when she was interrupted by a loud voice.

"How the fuck did you get in here?"

She looked up quickly and saw a menacing looking Hispanic man standing in the doorway of Brauner's office. He was clenching and unclenching his hands and she reflexively touched the service revolver under her left arm. The man appeared to be in his mid to late twenties and reminded her of more than a few of the Hispanic gang members she had encountered on patrol. He had curly black hair and dark brooding eyes that seemed to drill through her. He was dressed in khaki work pants and a white t-shirt. A gold chain hung around his neck and although she couldn't see what was hanging at the end of it, she would have made book it was a crucifix. There was an old, but still noticeable, scar on the right side of his forehead.

"You deaf? I asked how you got in here?" the man asked loudly, taking a step forward.

"That's close enough, sir. There's no need to get worked up," she said as she stood. The man's eyes dropped to her waistband.

"You a cop?"

"Detective Weston, Cedar Springs Police. Who are you?" she asked.

"Brauner's assistant."

"Tony Obregon, right?" Maggie said with a slight smile. "I was hoping I'd have a chance to speak to you."

"About what?"

"Dr. Brauner's wife has reported him missing. I'm checking to see if anything here would tell me where he might be."

"Well, he ain't here, that's for damn sure. You got a warrant?"

"I don't need one when the family requests assistance. When was the last time you saw Dr. Brauner?"

Obregon shrugged. "Thursday, I guess."

"So you didn't see him Friday."

"I just told you when I saw him. I came in Friday and the office was locked. I figured Brauner must have gotten sick or something."

"What did you do then?"

"What do you think? I went home and went back to bed with my old lady."

Obregon turned and stalked back into the front office. Maggie followed him. He sat down and opened a drawer in his desk.

"I suppose you've already been through this," he sneered.

"How long have you been Dr. Brauner's assistant?" she asked, ignoring his comment.

"Eighteen months, three weeks, four days, and counting."

"That's pretty precise."

He looked at her and smiled wryly. "Working for Brauner makes you that way. Almost like counting the days on a prison sentence."

"You didn't get along with him?"

"No one gets along with Brauner. They tolerate him."

"And vice versa?"

Obregon stood up and placed his hands on top of his desk.

"Meaning what?" As he glared at her she noticed the distinct markings of homemade tattoos on his forearms and the backs of his hands.

"Are you still a member of the Latin Lords?"

He took his hands off the desk and shoved them into his pockets.

"You bet. This is an equal opportunity university just crawling with Black Panthers, Latin Lords, and a dozen other gangs."

"It's not easy to break away from a gang like that. Has it caused you any problems?"

"Only with the white academic establishment," he answered. He looked her in the eyes and lowered his voice as he spoke. "The homeboys won't bother me as long as they think I'm still the meanest motherfucker in the neighborhood."

"Tell me about Dr. Brauner," Maggie said, taking her notebook from her pocket.

"Ain't that much to tell. He's a son of a bitch."

"Maybe you could be a little more specific. Is he a tough employer?"

"The little Jew is a tough everything, lady. Most hated professor on this campus. The students tried to get him fired a couple of years ago, but of course, the bigwigs didn't want to hear any shit about that."

"Isn't he a good teacher?"

"For the five percent who can pass his class, he's a fuckin' genius. To the other ninety-five percent he's a fuckin' son of a bitch," Obregon said with a grin.

"Which group are you in?"

Obregon stopped grinning. "I'm one of the select five percent, but still think he's a son of a bitch. The guy's sadistic toward students. Nothin's ever good enough. Perfection's all he gives a damn about. Musta been one of those Jews who turned their own kind in. Loves to humiliate students in front of everyone."

"Is that what you argued with him about last week?"

"Who told you that?"

"I just heard it. Did he call you incompetent and careless?"

"Every fuckin' day."

"Did it make you mad?"

"No, I love bein' called a moron. What do you think?"

"Mad enough to do something about it?"

"Oh, I get it! Brauner takes off for parts unknown and you think I helped him pack for the trip."

"I don't think anything, Mr. Obregon. I'm just asking questions."

"Am I a suspect or something? Cause if I am, I know my rights and you better Mirandize me. Otherwise, I got nothin' else to say to you."

"No, you're not a suspect right now, but I wouldn't leave the area for a few days in case I have more questions for you later."

"Oooh, I'm shakin' all over, officer," he sneered. "That it?"

"Do you know what Dr. Brauner's schedule for Friday was supposed to be? Did he have anything unusual planned?"

"Brauner is a very predictable man. The only thing he had planned for Friday was another exam which was guaranteed to fail the usual ninety-five percent."

"Are you in Dr. Brauner's class?"

"I'm his assistant. I can't very well be in his class and be expected to grade the damn tests, now can I."

"Did you administer his tests?"

"Sometimes, but I never see them until he hands them to me in the classroom. You'd think they contain the secret to how the universe was formed the way he guards them. Didn't even trust me to type them. Just hand them out and grade them."

"Did he ever accuse you of creative grading?"

"Nope. I can't stand most of the elitist little pricks in his classes and he knows it."

"Okay. If you think of anything else that might be useful, give me a call at the police department," she said as she handed him a business card.

Obregon nodded as she walked toward the office door. "It was that asshole Chambers who told you about me and Brauner, wasn't it?"

"I'm afraid I couldn't say," she answered with a smile. Turning back toward him as he grabbed the door to close it, she asked, "By the way, do you know a man named Cruz Garcia?"

"The janitor?"

"Yes."

"Met him once when I was working late in the lab. Jackass thought because I'm Hispanic I broke in to steal something. Why?"

"No reason. I wanted to ask him a few questions."

"Come back later. Pretty sure he works the night shift."

Obregon slammed the office door as she began walking down the hallway toward Malcolm Roth's office. The hallway seemed amazingly quiet and she could hear her own footsteps as she walked. When she turned the corner into the main hallway, she heard music coming from the direction of Roth's office and it took her a moment to remember where she had heard the same music before. Brodie had played it for her once. The Grateful Dead. Somehow the image of The Grateful Dead and Royce Ann Brodie never seemed to go together. She smiled and shook her head as she knocked on Roth's office door and waited. No one answered. Turning the doorknob, she looked in the front office. Seeing no one, she went to the door of Roth's private office and knocked. A minute later the door opened and Malcolm Roth smiled down at her. She smiled back, but more from amusement than friendliness. Roth was wearing a bright tie-dyed t-shirt over faded jeans and sandals. His graying hair was long and pulled back into a ponytail. Round wire-rimmed John Lennon glasses made his long thin face appear even longer and thinner. His eyes were wide and it was obvious that he hadn't taken time to shave that morning.

"Can I help you, miss?" Roth asked.

"Dr. Roth?" Maggie inquired.

"Yes."

"I'm Detective Weston with the Cedar Springs—"

"Ah, yes. Daryll told me you had been by," he interrupted. "Please come in, Detective."

She followed him into the office. He plopped down in a chair behind his desk and reached behind him to turn his stereo off. As she sat down across from him, she noticed the distinct odor of marijuana in the room, thinly hidden by the pungent scent of burning incense. Glancing around the room she saw a couple of Grateful Dead posters and a number of photographs of Roth apparently taken during another time in his life. Except for his graying hair, he hadn't change appreciably over the years.

"Are you old enough to remember the sixties, Detective Weston?" Roth asked.

"Not really," she answered, "but I've heard about them."

"The last great era of personal and academic freedom," he said with a touch of sadness in his voice.

"There certainly aren't any groups like the Dead around anymore."

"You know the Dead?" he asked with a smile.

"I had a friend who listened to them."

"Well, I'm sure you didn't come here to discuss the sixties, as fascinating as they may have been. How can I help you?"

"I'm checking on a missing person report on Dr. Elliott Brauner. His wife hasn't seen him for several days."

Roth leaned forward. "Now that you mention it, I haven't seen him around lately either. But no one keeps tabs on Elliott. He's a very private person."

"When was the last time you saw him?"

"God, I don't know," Roth said scratching his beard. "Must have been at least last Wednesday or Thursday."

"Are you close to Dr. Brauner?"

Roth laughed softly. "Elliott Brauner doesn't have friends, Detective. Merely acquaintances. A shame really. I confess that I did force myself on him a few times, but mostly about academic matters. He has an exceptional mind, you know. And was educated at the finest institutions. It was a genuine coup when the university convinced him and his wife to teach here."

"It's my understanding he isn't very popular with students."

"That's a polite way of putting it. An extraordinary number of students fail his courses. But please notice I didn't say he failed an extraordinary number of students. If a student works hard for Elliott, they pass. A 'C' in his course is considered an academic achievement."

"Do you think anyone dislikes him enough to harm him?"

"I doubt it, but with students today you never know. They're a fairly mediocre bunch. I doubt many of them ever had to work for a grade before they graced us with their presence. They're not terribly motivated, so even if they thought about doing something to Elliott I doubt any of them would have the initiative to do it. And unless you're a believer in the paranormal, thoughts usually won't hurt anyone."

"What do you know about Dr. Brauner's assistant, Mr. Obregon?"

"All I know is what Elliott told me once in a rare burst of enthusiasm. According to him, Tony has the most potential of any student he's taught in years."

"I got the impression that Mr. Obregon doesn't care much for Dr. Brauner."

"That's Elliott's way. He's not generous with his praise. He believes it will cause students to slack off if they know he's impressed with their work. He is hard on Tony, but I get the impression he likes him. At least academically."

"Your assistant said he overheard Brauner and Obregon arguing."

"I wouldn't doubt it, but I wouldn't take what Daryll says too seriously. Personally, I think he's a little jealous of Tony."

"Why is that, Doctor?"

Roth rubbed absently at his day-old beard growth. "How can I put this politely. Daryll is no genius, Detective Weston. He's one of Elliott's students this term and it's a coin toss whether he will pass or not. I'm not too happy with the work he does for me, but there simply weren't any other assistants available to choose from. If I could have stolen Tony away from Elliott, I would have. And believe me, there is no way in hell Elliott would consider Daryll as his assistant. Elliott called him something quite appropriate once," he said looking at the ceiling. "What was it? Oh, yeah. A wealthy sniveling sycophant."

"Why do you keep him as your assistant then?"

"Needed someone to answer the phone," he shrugged. "And he is an adequate typist. This is his last year with us anyway. If he can pass Elliott's course, that is."

IT WAS NEARLY noon before Maggie finished interviewing Malcolm Roth. The only impression she came away with was that Roth seemed to genuinely like Elliott Brauner. Including his wife, that brought the grand total of his fans to two. As she drove to the police department she tried to piece together what she knew and concluded it wasn't much. She pulled her car into a parking space in front of the station. The early spring air was warm and felt good against her face. She was glad she had moved to Cedar Springs.

Brodie and Nicholls, their shirtsleeves rolled up, were going through a stack of folders when she entered the squad room. She noticed with a smile that Brodie hadn't lost her habit of running her hand absently through her hair when she was preoccupied.

"Sorry I'm late," she said as she sat down at her desk and pulled out her notebook.

Nicholls looked at her and nodded without smiling. Brodie closed the folder she was reading and tossed it on her desk as she stood up.

"With me, Weston," she said tightly as she walked away.

Maggie glanced at Nicholls, but his eyes remained riveted on the papers in front of him. She pushed herself out of her chair and followed the lieutenant, who was already halfway across the squad room. Walking down a narrow hallway, Brodie looked into rooms as she went, finally stopping and opening the door to a vacant interrogation room, holding the door open as she waited for Maggie to catch up to her. Motioning her trainee into the room, she entered and closed the door behind her.

"Do you know the meaning of the word 'trainee', Detective Weston?"

"Of course," she answered, unsure what Brodie meant.

"A trainee is a person, male or female, who doesn't know their ass from their elbow. Which is the reason that person is placed under the supervision of someone more experienced. So they can learn to at least find their ass," Brodie intoned, her voice rising slightly.

"I'm sorry, Lieutenant Brodie, but I...," Maggie began.

"What the hell do you think you were doing this morning?"

"I was checking on a missing person at the university. His wife..."

Brodie took a step closer, her eyes penetrating Maggie's as she spoke through clenched teeth, her voice low and lethal. "Your job, for the time being, Detective Weston, is to report here every goddamn morning. Successfully achieving that assignment, your second job is to do what the fuck I tell you to do, when I tell you to do it."

"I understand that, but..."

"There are no buts here, Detective Weston. There are no Lone Rangers here. If you hope to succeed as my trainee, you *will* do things my way. Do you understand me?"

Maggie's eyes never wavered from Brodie's and she could see the woman was working hard to control her anger.

"Yes, Lieutenant. I understand."

"If anything like this ever happens again, I'll recommend to Captain Donaldson that you be relieved of your duties here. I will write this incident on your performance evaluation. Am I making myself clear?"

"Perfectly."

Brodie turned and left the room, slamming the door behind her, leaving Maggie alone and slightly shaken. She had known there could be problems working with her former lover, but hadn't expected to have them quite so soon. By the time she composed herself and returned to her desk, Brodie was engrossed in a conversation with another officer. Nicholls looked at her and handed her a couple of folders. "Go through these. We have a John Doe from Thursday night."

She took the folders and began reading through the reports on the burned vehicle and victim. Her reading was interrupted by the phone ringing.

"Cedar Springs Police Department. Detective Weston speaking," she said as she continued to look through the folder. She handed the receiver to Nicholls.

"Austin PD," she said.

Nicholls took the phone from her. "Nicholls," he said.

He grabbed a pad and scribbled as he wrote. Finally he said, "Appreciate it." He handed the phone back to Maggie and looked around until he spotted Brodie.

"Hey, Brodie. That was Austin PD. They located Clifford Jenkins."

She walked to his desk. "What's his story?"

"The vehicle was his. He reported it stolen this morning. Out of town on business for about a week and left it parked in long-term executive parking. He called it in as soon as he couldn't locate it. Austin PD is going to fax us his statement."

"Well, at least we know the victim wasn't the owner of the car."

"Austin's interviewing the parking lot attendants to see if anyone remembers the car, but that's a real long shot. You know how many cars go in and out of there every day?"

"Several hundred, I'd guess." She seemed to be deep in thought, trying to re-organize the information they had on John Doe. "This is giving me a headache, Nicholls. Up for some lunch?" she asked.

"Can't. I got a line on a new couch and it's today or never."

"Okay," she said as she looked at her watch. "I'll be back in about an hour. Page me if anything comes up," she said as she grabbed her jacket and left the squad room.

Before Maggie could get back to the folders on her desk, the phone rang again. She rested the receiver on her shoulder as she answered it and repeated her introduction. For a moment there was silence on the other end.

"This is Detective Weston," she repeated. "Can I help you?"

"I'm sorry," a woman's voice finally said. "Is Lieutenant Brodie there, please?"

"She's just left for lunch, ma'am. Can I take a message?"

"This is Dr. Jacobs. Is Detective Nicholls there by chance?"

"Just a moment," she said and pointed the receiver in his direction.

"Shit. How can I get any work done if the friggin' phone keeps ringing?" he said to himself as he took the phone. "This is Nicholls," he said.

"Nicholls, this is Camille Jacobs."

"How are you, Doc?" Nicholls said smiling. "What can I do for you?"

"I'm fine, thanks. When Lieutenant Brodie gets back from lunch, would you tell her I had a cancellation in my schedule and she can come by my office at four instead of five. She wanted to discuss a case you're working on."

"Which one?"

"I didn't know you had more than one. She only said a woman couldn't have done it."

"I've warned her about that sexist bullshit, but she never listens to me. I'll give her the message."

He handed the phone back to Maggie and floated a note over to Brodie's desk. "What's your plan for the afternoon, Maggie?"

"I'm going to finish this report and then I'm going to sit right here on my ass until Lieutenant Brodie tells me what to do next."

Glancing at the clock on the back wall of the room, he said, "Guess I'd better get a move on about that damn couch. Want me to bring something back for you?"

"No. I'm good, but thanks."

Alone in the squad room, Maggie ran her hands through her hair and took a deep breath. She had known Brodie might be mad, but hadn't anticipated the level of her anger. She remembered the last time she had seen that much anger in her former lover's eyes and absently touched the scar on her forehead.

IT WAS SUPPOSED to be a relaxing evening out with friends. Brodie was coming off another double shift and Maggie was relieved her lover would finally have a two-day break. Since Wheeler's death, her father had made Brodie's life hell, but she insisted she could handle it.

As soon as Brodie walked into the apartment they shared, Maggie sensed something was wrong. Without stopping to acknowledge Maggie, Brodie walked directly into the kitchen and took a beer from the refrigerator, leaning against the counter to take a long drink.

"Are you all right, Royce?" Maggie said as she rested against the door frame.

"Great," Brodie said dully, filling her mouth with the amber liquid.

Crossing the room, Maggie touched her on the cheek. Brodie jerked her head away. "Not now, Mag." Draining the bottle, Brodie walked past her and tossed it in garbage before taking a second from the fridge. "My two days were cancelled," she said as she opened her beer and took a long drink.

"What? You haven't had a day off in over two weeks! You should call your union rep," Maggie said.

Whirling around, Brodie said, "And do what? Admit that I can't take it? Let your father tell everyone I can't handle my job? Fuck that!"

"I'm sorry, Royce. I'll call Carrie and tell her we can't make it tonight."

Finally looking at Maggie, Brodie's face softened. "No, don't cancel. Just give me a few minutes to catch my breath and take a shower. It'll be all right, baby." Brodie set her beer down and took Maggie in her arms, holding her tightly for a few minutes. "I'm sorry, honey. I didn't mean to take it out on you."

Brodie had seemed more relaxed during dinner, but Maggie noticed she was consuming more alcohol than usual. By the time they arrived at a local club, Brodie had become sullen and distant. It was nearly midnight when a group of women entered the club and made their way toward a table. Brodie stood up quickly and staggered slightly. "Fuckin' son of a bitch!" she seethed.

Following Brodie's glare, Maggie said, "What's wrong, Royce?"

Ignoring her question, Brodie left their table and walked toward the new group, Maggie following close behind. One of the women was standing, taking drink orders from the rest of her group. Suddenly she was grabbed roughly and spun around to see the florid face of Sergeant Royce Brodie. Pushing her away, the woman said, "Brodie! What the hell are you doing?"

"What the fuck are you doin' here, Santos? I was told you had the flu and wouldn't be at work for a couple of days. I got stuck with your for shit shift!" Brodie accused.

"I was ordered to take the next couple of days off," Santos said.

"By who?"

"The watch commander."

"What?" Maggie exclaimed.

Santos grinned at Maggie. "Looks like your daddy ain't as hot for your girlfriend as you are, Weston." Shifting her eyes to Brodie she said, "They changed me to first shift beginning tomorrow. Hope you can sleep off whatever you been drinkin'."

Brodie grabbed Santos and would have hit her if Maggie hadn't stopped her. "Let's go, Royce. It's not worth it."

As Brodie made her way out of the club, Maggie made their apologies to their friends. She had to run to catch up to Brodie, insisting that she drive. Brodie sat silently in the car all the way home and remained silent as they entered their apartment. Brodie walked into the kitchen and took a bottle of Jack Daniels and a glass from the cabinet.

"What are you doing, Royce? You've already had enough to drink tonight."

"Don't tell me what to do," Brodie said as she threw back the drink. Before the liquor finished burning its way down her throat she poured another.

"Don't do this," Maggie said as she came to stand next to Brodie. "Please. Let me call in and tell them you're sick."

"No!" Brodie said loudly. "I guess now you think I can't do my job either!"

"That's not it and you know it. You're not going to be in any shape to work tomorrow. You've had too much to drink." Reaching in front of Brodie, she took the bottle from her.

"Fuck you, Maggie!" Brodie screamed. "Go to bed and leave me the fuck alone!"

"Not while you're like this," Maggie said. "You've been drinking more and more since Stan was killed. You need to talk to the department psychologist."

Great!" Brodie laughed. "Then your daddy can get my ass run off the force for being a nut case! That's good, Maggie. That's really good."

Running her hand across Brodie's back, Maggie said, "Come to bed, Royce."

Turning to look at Maggie, Brodie grinned. Bringing her face close to Maggie's she said, "Sure, baby. Let's go to bed."

"Not when you're drunk, Royce."

Maggie had never been able to describe what she saw pass through Brodie's eyes the second before she felt the slap. She couldn't believe her lover would strike her. The force of the slap and the shock of it stunned her. Brodie grabbed her and began pulling at her clothes, breathing heavily. Maggie shoved her away. "Stop it, Royce!" Turning, she walked into the living room.

"You belong to me!" Brodie shouted as she followed her.

"Not when you're like this."

"Well, maybe I'll have to find someone more willing."

"Fuck you!" Maggie turned to walk away from her.

Brodie reached out and shoved her toward the couch. In an instant the arguing stopped as Maggie's foot caught on a small rug and she fell face first onto the coffee table, shattering the heavy glass top. Maggie's fall seemed to happen in slow motion as Brodie tried to stop it, but couldn't. As blood seeped into the carpet under Maggie's head, Brodie fell on her knees, calling out her name and dialing 9-1-1.

MAGGIE WAS STILL running her fingers over the scar on her forehead when Brodie's voice broke into her thought. "You asleep?"

"I was just thinking, Lieutenant," Maggie said, dropping her hand away from the scar that reminded her of that night every time she looked in the mirror. She looked at Brodie. How had it all gone so wrong? Over the last few years small things had reminded her of what she had had with Brodie. The tenderness, the gentleness of her touch, the way her heartbeat increased every time Brodie looked at her. Just as it was now. Would there ever be a time when the sight of Royce Brodie wouldn't cause the same physical reaction?

"Could I run an idea past you?" Maggie finally asked.

Leaning back in her chair, Brodie said, "Shoot." When Maggie brought her eyes up to speak, Brodie barely heard what she was saying as she met her gaze. It was more than politely looking into the eyes of a person speaking. It was a reflection of the past. A time when everything had been right.

Maggie faltered for a moment as she and Brodie looked at one another. "I've...um...been going over the Garcia file and the one on your John Doe. See what you think."

Brodie leaned onto her elbows. "Okay."

"Okay." Maggie smiled as she took a deep breath. "We know Garcia left home around four Thursday and disappeared until he was found the following Monday morning. The missing person case I was checking this morning is Dr. Elliot Brauner, a professor at the university."

"So what's the deal? He run off with one of his sexy young coeds?"

"No. Or if he did it was the best kept secret in the universe. There are a few things about his disappearance you might be interested in though."

"Such as," Brodie said, still looking at the file folder.

"Dr. Brauner went to the university about seven-thirty Thursday evening and didn't return."

"So."

"His office is in the Biology Building."

Brodie looked up at her without raising her head. "You think there's a connection with Garcia?"

Maggie shrugged. "I don't know, but it seems too coincidental to be ignored and I don't believe in coincidences any more than you do. Isn't it possible that whoever killed Garcia did it to steal his keys? Maybe they wanted to get into one of the offices and Brauner caught them."

Brodie pushed her glasses to the top of her head and rubbed her eyes. "It's possible, but do we have any hard evidence any of the keys were used after Garcia's death? They could have been thrown away and we just haven't found them yet."

"Can I have permission to at least contact Brauner's wife and ask her to check her husband's office?"

"It can't hurt, but it might be a dead end. Let me know if anything comes of it."

IT WAS A little after four that afternoon when Camille's receptionist showed Brodie into the psychologist's office. She was bent over a chart, jotting down notes from her last patient's visit.

"Have a seat, RB. I'll be through with this in just a second," she said without looking up. Brodie had been to Camille's office many times since her departure from the Austin Police Department. One year for private counseling sessions designed to help her deal with her guilt over Wheeler's death and seven of a more personal nature after they began seeing one another. She hadn't heard Camille sound so detached in a long time. She glanced around the familiar office while she waited.

A few minutes later, the psychologist removed her reading glasses and placed them on her desk. Sitting back in her chair, she said, "I assume those are the files you wanted me to look at."

"Yeah," Brodie said as she leaned forward and slid the folders across the desk. Something was wrong. Camille had never been so distant toward her before. Now she would have to wait while she looked through the files.

"Pour yourself a cup of coffee, RB. You know where everything is," Camille said as she became engrossed in the first folder. Brodie poured two small cups and set one in front of the doctor. It took nearly ten minutes for Camille to go through the file, stopping once or twice to flip to a previous page to re-read a section of the report. Finally she closed the folder and removed her glasses. "You're right. A woman didn't do this one," she said.

"Well, that eliminates over half the population as suspects. What can you tell me about the guy who did do it?"

She re-opened the folder and sipped her coffee half-heartedly.

"Probably young and white. Methodical. Patient. Precise. He is either fairly strong physically or he knew the victim. He might have cultivated a recent friendship with the victim which would have allowed him to overpower him easily. Do you have a scenario yet?"

"Just guesses. We think Garcia may have been lured someplace and rendered unconscious. Then the killer took the body into the old tunnel system under the university where he could work undisturbed, decapitated him, dumped the body and then returned to the campus to put the head in the lab."

"Decapitation is a pretty messy business and certainly not a spur of the moment act. He had to have planned it. Probably over several weeks or even months."

"According to the family, the victim was last seen Thursday afternoon when he left for work. The head was found early Monday morning. The body was located Tuesday after what we think could have been an anonymous tip from the killer."

"Were there classes in that particular lab Friday?"

"Yes, and they used specimens from the tank. So the head was placed there sometime between late Friday and early Monday."

"The coroner said the time of death, based on the body, was between two and four days before it was discovered," Camille read.

"Unless the killer kept the body on ice for a while and then disposed of it after he finished whatever the hell he was doing with it. Why do you think he put the head in the aquarium?"

"Considering that it could have been the killer who led you to the body, it looks like a taunt of some kind. Look what I did. That sort of thing. He's proud of his work, but you weren't moving fast enough for him and he had to give you a clue about the location. He may believe he's smarter than the average person. Possibly a superiority complex and just as likely undeserved."

"Yeah, that's what Weston said. You think he could've done this before?" Brodie asked.

"A serial?"

"Maybe not a serial. We would have heard about other police departments finding human heads lying around. But the sort of no-muss-no-fuss way he did it makes me think he isn't a beginner."

"It's possible he's done it before, but maybe not on a person. Any reports about mutilated animals?"

"I don't know. I haven't checked with animal control lately, but I will. Could it be a doctor?"

"If it was, he wasn't a surgeon," Camille answered, reopening the folder and looking through the enclosed photographs of the body. "The cuts appear to be pretty good from what I could see in the pictures, but are not professional quality. Looks like he might have felt hurried for some reason."

"You mean he took all that time to plan and set everything up and then got in a hurry."

"It's possible he was becoming bored. He might not have derived the thrill he thought he would from the act."

"Great. A killer with attention deficit disorder," Brodie said, finishing her coffee.

"Why do you think he chose this particular victim?" Camille asked as she sipped her coffee.

"I don't know. Weston has a theory, but we can't confirm any of it yet. Maybe he thought no one would miss the guy. Maybe he cruised the whole town looking for someone to hack up. Maybe he's in Alaska fileting Eskimos by now."

"I doubt he's left the area," Camille said, removing her glasses. "He'd want to stick around to see how close you can get to him. Then he might leave. Of course, if it is a superiority thing, he might stay even then, believing he's smart enough to evade capture."

"Well, everyone slips up sooner or later no matter how smart they think they are. As soon as I can come up with a motive, I'll be on his ass."

"What if there wasn't a motive?"

"There's always a motive, honey. It might be a lame one, but there'll be one. I just have to find it." Brodie rubbed her temples, the nagging headache she'd had the last four days still lingering.

"This case is only a few days old and it's getting to you already.

When did your headaches start?"

"Over the weekend. We've got a John Doe that's probably a homicide, too. Weston thinks it could be related to Garcia's case, but we haven't found any positive evidence of that."

"Rough week."

"Yeah, and it's not even half over."

"How is everything else at work, RB?"

"Fine," she lied tersely.

Camille didn't say anything. She picked up the folders and handed them to Brodie. "Tell me about Maggie," she said.

"Not much to tell," Brodie shrugged, trying to avoid the subject of her ex-lover.

"How hostile have you been toward her?"

The question seemed to surprise the detective. "Probably more than I need to be. I'm not sure I can evaluate her objectively," she said.

"How does she treat you?"

"What do you mean? I'm her training officer."

"So she's forced to at least put on a facade of respect due to your position?"

"Pretty much."

"She's bound to have changed over the last seven or eight years. Tell me about her."

Looking uncomfortable, Brodie had to think a few minutes to carefully choose the right words. "She hasn't changed much. A little more mature, I guess."

"Attractive?"

"Yeah, I suppose. Why all the questions, Camille? I can handle it. It was a surprise when I found out she'd be here. That's all. I'll adjust like I always have."

Camille took a long breath and looked at Brodie a moment before speaking again.

"Maybe your feelings for Maggie haven't changed as much as you thought they had."

"Look, I'm sorry for the shitty way I acted last weekend. How about you let me take you out next weekend to make it up to you?"

"I don't think that would be a good idea right now, RB," Camille said softly.

Brodie looked at her and frowned. "I made a mistake and overreacted, but Maggie Weston is nothing more than a trainee."

Camille chuckled slightly. "I haven't been doing my job very well," Camille finally said. "I advise my patients every day to face the reality of their lives and move on. I should have taken my own advice. I like you, RB."

"I like you, too. Is that a problem?"

"It's becoming one. You obviously haven't gotten past your feelings for Maggie. It was always there before, in the shadows like the bastard child at a reunion, but now... Well, it won't get any better."

"Are you jealous of what I had with Maggie?" Brodie asked, beginning to feel somewhat defensive.

"I'm not jealous of what you had with Maggie, but what you still want from her. Most women dream of a relationship like that. You and I have been seeing each other a long time, but realistically I know you don't love me the way I might expect you to after all these years. I've never demanded anything from you and I'm not now."

"Are you insinuating I've been using you in some way?" Brodie's voice had begun to rise.

"Last weekend..." she started, looking down at her hands, "last weekend told me a great deal. I'm not prepared to let myself be used as a surrogate for the woman you really want, RB." Twisting her lips into a half smile she added, "It's bad for my self-esteem. I want more from our relationship and I'm not sure you're willing to, or even capable of giving me that. I need someone who wants me and loves me as much as I think you still want and love Maggie Weston."

She knew Camille was right. She hadn't gotten over Maggie and wasn't sure it was something she could ever erase from her memory. She had never entrusted her emotions, her happiness, her very soul, to another woman until she met Maggie. She had never admitted to anyone, not even herself really, how much losing Maggie had shattered her life. Periodically, unexpectedly, the smallest thing would trigger the random memories lying dormant in her mind.

"I...I don't know what to say, Camille," Brodie finally said, her voice shaky.

Camille got up and handed Brodie the file folders as she took her hand and walked toward the office door. "Call me in a few days," she said as she leaned over and kissed Brodie on the cheek, wishing there were more she could do for the troubled woman who had been her lover for nearly six years. "We can talk about it some more...if you want to."

MAGGIE TOOK A deep breath as she stepped out of her car in front of her parents' home. She had been dreading dinner with her family since she accepted her mother's invitation. She hadn't been home for a dinner with her parents, her brothers and their families since Christmas. That one had ended badly and she hoped tonight wouldn't be round two.

Walking to the passenger side of the Subaru, she lifted a covered casserole dish from the floorboard and closed the door with her hip.

Peg Weston was waiting on the porch, drying her hands on her ever-present apron as Maggie made her way up the front steps. Balancing the dish in one hand, she hugged her mother quickly before stepping inside. She took in the smell of food cooking. She couldn't remember a time when the interior of the Weston home hadn't been filled with the smell of her mother's cooking. The sound of raucous laughter floated down the hallway from the family room.

"I'll take that, dear," Peg said. "Go say hello to your father and brothers."

"Where are the wives and kiddies?" Maggie asked. "Shuttled off to watch television quietly so they won't disturb the menfolk?" She saw the look of disappointment on her mother's face and almost regretted making the remark.

"Don't start anything with your father tonight, Maggie. Let's enjoy a meal together like the family we have always been."

Maggie carried her dish toward the kitchen. "I'll see them in a minute, Mom. How are you doing?"

"Why I'm fine, as always. Why do you ask?" Peg asked as she flipped on the inside oven light to check a pan of home baked rolls.

"I thought maybe Dad was driving you crazy being around all the time now that he's retired," Maggie shrugged.

"Oh, no. Your father still visits his friends from the department and we have them over for poker night. He'll never really retire," Peg said with a smile.

Maggie never understood how her mother could remain so calm. Nothing seemed to faze her. Her husband and all five of her children were police officers. Usually one was enough to make most wives babbling neurotics after a short period of time. But Peg Weston considered it as nothing more than a family tradition. Three of her sons were with the Austin Police Department. Sean and Liam were both detectives and Sean was up for a promotion to watch commander. Daniel was a sergeant in the patrol division. Until Maggie resigned from Austin PD to take her new position in Cedar Springs a month earlier, the only black sheep in the family had been her youngest brother, Carl, who had jumped ship and joined the Department of Public Safety as a state trooper.

As she looked in the refrigerator for something to drink, strong arms wrapped around her body and lifted her in the air. "That beer better be for me, girl," Liam said as he carried her away from the fridge.

"Put me down, you big ox," Maggie said through her laughter.

Setting her back on the floor and grabbing the bottle from her hand, he said, "Why're you hidin' out in here?"

"I thought I'd talk to Mom before I had to listen to the rest of you grunt and groan about your jobs the rest of the night. Where's Ruth?"

"Washing the kids up for dinner. Dad wants to know how much longer, Mom?"

"Tell your father five minutes," Peg said as she pulled the rolls from the oven. "Maggie, find out what everyone wants to drink."

She took a deep breath and sauntered into the family room. It was a familiar sight. Her brothers surrounded their father as if he was the king of an empire, hanging on his every word. Tim half-smiled when he saw Maggie. "Good to see you again, Margaret," he said.

"Mom wants to know what everyone wants to drink with dinner," she said as she crossed the space between them to lean down and place the expected kiss on her father's cheek.

"Milk for the kids," Tim said. "Everyone else will probably have tea or coffee."

Dinner was on the table by the time she finished filling everyone's drink request and she took her usual seat to her mother's right at the table. After a quick prayer, everyone erupted into conversation. For the first time she was glad to be seated next to her mother and surrounded by her sisters-in-law. The children were all seated at a separate smaller table in the nearby kitchen.

Just when she thought she might escape talk about her new job, Tim asked, "So how are things out there in the boonies, Margaret? Catch any jay-walkers yet?" Full mouths chuckled as they waited for her reply.

"No. No, I haven't, Dad," she said tersely. "But we have a couple of interesting homicides right now."

"Homicides? Tell me about them." It was obvious that his interest was piqued, but Maggie glanced quickly at her mother before speaking.

"Maybe later. You know Mom doesn't like shop talk at the table with the kids here."

"Okay," Tim nodded. "Fair enough, in deference to your mother. How's your training going? Fred Donaldson is a good man. He'll see you're trained right."

"My training's fine so far, but I've only been on the job a couple of days. I've still got a lot to learn. Everyone has been extremely helpful in teaching me the paperwork. They do things a little differently than you do in Austin."

She hoped that would be the end of the questions about her new position and turned to compliment her mother on the meal. "So who's your training officer out there?" her father asked as he sliced into the meat on his plate. "If he does a good job we can transfer you back in a few months."

She hesitated before looking down the table at her father. "I'm not planning to transfer back to Austin. I like living in Cedar

Springs. It's not as...political...as Austin."

"You'll get bored there soon enough," Tim smirked. "You can earn twice the money here if you're properly trained."

"I'm being properly trained."

"So who did you say your TO was? Maybe I know him."

Maggie looked around the table. Her father and brothers were staring at her, waiting while they chewed. She had hoped to enjoy the evening with her family, but obviously that idea was soon going to be shot to shit. "Lieutenant Royce Brodie," she finally stated in a clear voice.

Tim stopped cutting through the meat and his eyes narrowed as he brought them up to meet Maggie's. He glanced at the smaller table behind him where his six grandchildren were sitting. Keeping his voice low, he asked, "Did you know who your training officer was going to be before you started work?"

Raising her chin defiantly, she said, "Yes."

"And how long will it be before you let that bitch back in your fuckin' pants?"

"Calm down, Dad," Sean said, casting a glance at the children.

Peg looked nervously toward the smaller table. "Are you children ready for some dessert?" she asked, trying to keep her voice cheerful. Eager faces looked up, not believing their luck at getting an early treat. Pushing her chair back, she stood and smiled. "Go on into the den and I'll bring it to you."

Maggie looked down at her plate of half eaten food and shoved it away. She rested her elbows on the table and rubbed her forehead with the tips of her fingers until her nieces and nephews had disappeared from the kitchen. She knew there was nothing she could say that wouldn't lead to a monumental argument. Turning her head to the side she glared at her father. "I already know what you think about me because I'm a lesbian, but that's insulting."

"It's been eight goddamn years and I know you haven't been a nun, sleeping with one woman after another, doing God knows what..."

"That's enough!" Maggie said as she stood up quickly. "I don't need a fuckin' morality lesson from you. Royce barely tolerates me as a trainee."

"You can't expect me to sit back and watch her teach you how to get killed! Is she still a drunk?"

"She has never been a drunk!"

"Give it up, Mag!" Tim stood and stepped away from the table. Striding toward his only daughter he continued. "She was a drunk! And when you confronted her about it, she lost it and beat the shit out of you! You spent three days in the fuckin' hospital!"

"She didn't beat me!"

Tim reached out quickly and grabbed her roughly, pushing hair away from her face. "This scar on your forehead tells me different."

"If you hadn't had a fuckin' hard on about getting her fired because of Stan nothing would have happened!"

"She let my best friend get murdered because she didn't back him up. She admitted it to the review board!"

"That's a lie!"

Pulling her closer to him, he said, "She told the board she was distracted by thinking about fuckin' you on her day off."

"I read the transcript of the review board. You were the one making that accusation. You didn't know a damn thing about my relationship with Royce," Maggie said as she jerked her arm away. "You assigned her to a duty you knew would make her stand all day on her injured leg. You assigned her to the worst patrol sectors alone hoping she'd be injured or killed. You ordered other officers to call in sick so you could double-shift her when you knew she was already exhausted. You did everything you could to break her, but you couldn't!"

Stopping in front of Maggie, he sneered, "I made her miserable enough to resign. I didn't plan on her smacking you around, but at least you saw the light and kicked her ass out."

"You were the reason she drank too much that night. If you had done that to any other officer under your command you would have been fired and you know it. I had to force her to leave before you got her killed! What happened was an accident you created. Face it, Dad. You can't stand the idea that your daughter is a dyke and you took it out on Royce. Well, you know what? Even though Royce isn't a part of my life anymore, I'm still fuckin' women every chance I get. I was before I met her and I always will. Get used to it!"

Her head snapped to the side as Tim slapped her. Tears burned her eyes, but she refused to let them fall as she glared at her father. He was shaking with rage when Sean and Dan pulled him away from Maggie. "Get out of my home, Margaret."

She threw her napkin on the table and glanced at the faces of her brothers and sisters-in-law. One side of her mouth curved into a half smile. "Well, it's been a fun evening. Tell Mom it was a great meal." Turning away, she walked out of the dining room and toward the front door.

"Mag!"

She was halfway into her car when she saw Carl running toward her. "What?" she shot testily.

"I'm sorry, Maggie," he said.

"No. I'm sorry you and the others had to see that little scene." Looking at her brother she asked, "You feel the same way, Carl?"

"I only met Royce once..."

"Not about Royce. Are you ashamed because your sister is a lesbian?"

Carl looked uncomfortable and paused before answering.

"Guess that says it all," Maggie said. "Tell Mom I'm sorry, okay."

"Wait, Mag. I'm not ashamed of you. I just don't understand it, that's all."

"Yeah, well, neither do it. I know who I am, Carl. And this is who I'll always be. I can't change that and I can't change what you and the rest of them think about me." Smiling slightly, she said, "But if it makes you feel better, I don't think it's catching."

"This will blow over, Mag. You know how he is," Carl shrugged.

"Yeah, I'm afraid I do," Maggie said as she started her car.

WHEN BRODIE STRODE into the squad room before daylight the next morning, she was surprised to find Maggie already at her desk. "You had breakfast already, Weston?" she asked her trainee.

"Uh...no, Lieutenant. I sort of got involved in going over notes and reading reports."

Pulling her jacket off, Brodie said, "Go grab something to eat while I brief Donaldson."

Maggie watched Brodie stack a few file folders together. She had been the recipient of her training officer's harsh penetrating eyes, but also remembered the liquid softness in them when they had been alone. It was a look she had never found with another woman. The memory brought the beginning of a smile to her lips. Brodie frowned when she caught Maggie looking at her.

"Something on your mind, Weston?"

"Sorry...no...just trying to put a few things together in my mind."

Brodie glanced at her wristwatch and then back at Maggie. As Maggie pushed hair behind her ear, Brodie noticed a bruise on Maggie's cheek. Frowning, she asked, "What happened to your face?"

"Oh, I wasn't paying attention to what I was doing. Ran into a door when I took some clothes to the Laundromat," Maggie said.

"Yeah, well, my briefing won't take long so you only have about half an hour before we have to start earning our pay again."

She watched her trainee maneuver through the desks in the squad room, appreciating the fluid way she moved. Mentally snapping out of it, she quickly picked up the folders and went to Donaldson's office, knocking lightly on the door before entering the Captain's inner sanctum.

"What's up, Brodie?" Donaldson said as she stuck her head in the door.

"Thought I would give you a briefing on the cases we're working, Fred. I was hoping you might have a few insights."

"Sure. Come on in and pull up a chair. It's bound to be more interesting than the departmental budget."

It took Brodie about ten minutes to bring him up to speed on the two new cases. Glancing through the files she handed him, he leaned back in his squeaky chair and puffed his cheeks out as he sighed slightly.

"Any ideas about the perp?" he finally asked.

"I ran it past Dr. Jacobs yesterday. Based on her evaluation, it's possible he might have done something similar before. We're running an inquiry for similar crimes," she explained.

He frowned as he leaned forward on his desk. "How is Weston doing?" he asked, changing the subject to something more tangible.

"Has an independent streak that could get her in trouble, but she'll be all right. Plays well with others."

"I was rudely awakened a couple of hours ago by Tim Weston demanding I remove you as her TO."

Brodie frowned, recalling the bruise on Maggie's cheek and wondered if Tim had caused it. "I guess that's up to you and Detective Weston," she said.

"Well, I told him to go fuck himself and let me sleep," Donaldson said. "And Weston hasn't earned the right to make demands around here yet. So just go out there and do your job. Catch me a couple of murderers before there's mass hysteria in the suburbs. I like my town nice and uncomplicated."

"I'm sorry if my past has complicated things for you, Fred."

"Yeah, well, that's why I get the big bucks. So everybody and their dog can take a dump on me if you fuck up. Anything else we should discuss?"

MAGGIE CARRIED A cup of coffee into the living room that evening, picked up the phone and dialed. It was answered on the second ring.

"Dr. Brauner? This is Detective Weston. I'm sorry to call so late, but I promised...," she began.

"Have you found, Elliot?" Helen said quickly.

"No, we haven't Mrs. Brauner, but I assure you we're working on it. I've talked to a few people on the campus, but no one seemed to know anything. Mr. Obregon and Dr. Roth thought he was sick. I didn't see anything out of place in his office either, but, of course, I wouldn't notice if something was missing. It was very neat."

"Elliott is a very neat man, Detective."

"Perhaps if you were to check his office, you might notice something out of place. Do you have a key?"

"Yes. I'll look tomorrow and if I notice anything I'll call you."

"That would be very helpful, Dr. Brauner."

"You said you talked to Tony and Malcolm."

"Yes."

"I hope Malcolm won't get in any trouble."

"Why would he?"

"I'm sure you couldn't have missed the peculiar odor in his office, Detective."

"I noticed it," Maggie laughed softly, "but I didn't see him doing anything illegal."

"Malcolm is such a sweet man, but I'm afraid he's stuck in a time warp."

"He did seem to be sort of a throwback to the sixties."

"Well, you know what they say about things coming back. It's a little ironic that his wife is making a small fortune with tie-dyed shirts now. Students are so ignorant of the past that most of them think it's a new fad. Marj is as bad as Malcolm. When you see them together, it's like reliving Woodstock. Of course, I'm sure other people have some interesting things to say about Elliott and me. They're both really lovely people who'd do anything for a friend."

"Dr. Roth seemed very fond of your husband."

"Yes, he is, and Elliott likes Malcolm as well. He just doesn't express his feelings very well."

"Did your husband know Mr. Obregon is or was a member of a gang, Dr. Brauner?"

"Yes, we both know, but he's overcome his past."

"I was told that he and your husband had an argument last week. Do you know anything about that?"

"No, Elliott didn't say anything to me about an argument, but it's certainly possible. They frequently have disagreements. Elliott is a perfectionist about his field. He detests sloppy work. I think occasionally Tony may not be as meticulous as Elliott believes he should be."

"So far I'm afraid I don't have much more to tell you, Dr. Brauner, but we'll continue looking into it."

"I appreciate that."

Maggie leaned back on the couch and closed her eyes. She rubbed her jaw absently and winced. Where was Elliott Brauner? Everyone she had talked to so far had described him as meticulous, predictable, not given to sudden changes in his routine. You could practically set your clock by his actions. The only deviation in his schedule she had detected was his last-minute trip to the university the previous Thursday evening to retrieve something he had forgotten. His disappearance that night had obviously not been planned.

Chapter
Five

HELEN BRAUNER CLIMBED the stairs to the third floor of the Biology Building slowly as she fumbled through her purse searching for a large key ring which held a dozen keys of various sizes and shapes. Some of them she had never used before, and it would only be guesswork on her part as to which ones would fit Elliott's office and file cabinets. By the time she reached the third floor landing she found what she was looking for. The building was quiet and the clicking sound made by the heels of her shoes echoed down the hallway. Glancing at her wristwatch, she realized it would be at least an hour before anyone else except the most dedicated students and professors would begin making their way into the labs and offices.

It took her a few minutes to find the key that opened Elliott's office and she made a mental note to label her keys when she got home. To her relief the inner office door was unlocked and when Helen saw her husband's desk, tears suddenly filled her eyes. In the back of her mind Helen had the nagging feeling she would never see his face again. Setting her purse down, she sat behind his desk and ran her hands over the leather bound blotter covering the desk top. She tried the desk drawers and found them locked. She tried several keys on the key ring before finding one that opened the lock on the desk. She hadn't really been sure there was a spare key, so she had collected every key she could find at home and hoped for the best.

The first drawer revealed nothing that seemed out of place or out of character for Elliott Brauner. Mostly office supplies and a few file folders containing reminders for faculty meetings. The other drawers contained nothing of importance either and Helen wondered why Elliott bothered to lock the desk. She picked up the key ring and crossed the office to three file cabinets inside the office door. She was trying the fifth key that looked like a file cabinet key when Tony walked into the office. She smiled when she saw him.

"Good morning, Tony. You're in early this morning."

"I have a couple of things to check on in the lab, Dr. Brauner. What are you looking for?"

"The police asked me to look around and see if I noticed anything out of place."

"You still haven't heard from him?"

"No. But at least the police are finally looking into it. I don't suppose you have a key to these file cabinets."

Tony chuckled slightly. "Mrs. Brauner, you know damn well your husband wouldn't trust me with the keys."

"He trusts you, Tony. He's just overly cautious."

"If you ask me, ma'am, he's just paranoid."

She smiled at him. "He wasn't always like that."

"I've been meaning to call you. The doc was supposed to give an exam to his grad class last Friday. When he didn't show up, I wasn't sure what to do so I told them to keep studying and it would probably be sometime this week."

"Is it in one of these cabinets?"

"I suppose. I never saw it."

A key finally turned in the cabinet lock. Helen opened the top drawer and looked through the file folders.

"What are these, Tony?"

He looked over her shoulder for a moment. "Student records. He kept a record on the progress of all his students. Sorta like efficiency reports or something."

"Have you read them?"

"A few. Not very complimentary."

"Elliott is really only interested in the best students, especially at the graduate level. He spoke very highly of your work."

"You coulda fooled me."

"Well, he believes too much praise can ruin a scientist. Sometimes he doesn't consider the person inside the scientist," she said absently as she opened the second file drawer.

A small stack of papers sat in the back of the drawer behind a section of file folders. Helen picked them up and showed them to Tony. "Is this the exam for last week?"

"Must be. It was supposed to cover a lab on the properties of carcinogens."

"I'll let you take these, Tony. Have the students prepare to take it day after tomorrow," she said as she handed him the exams. She thumbed through the files in the drawer, which appeared to contain master copies of other exams. She pushed the drawer shut and was preparing to open the last drawer when she stopped and glanced at the exams in Tony's hand. "Let me see those again for a minute."

She took the papers and sat down at her husband's desk. She looked at each set of exams and counted them. "How many students are in Elliott's graduate class?"

"Twenty-four. Why? Is an exam missing?"

"No, but there is something wrong."

"But they're all there."

"They are, but not in the right order."

Tony looked at her and she smiled. "You're right about Elliott being paranoid," she said. "He has a system of stacking his exams so he can tell immediately if they've been tampered with."

"How?"

"See this class and section number?" she said pointing at the top of the exam.

"It's got a typo in it. It should be Micro 2201, not 0424."

"Look at the next one."

"6006. I don't get it."

"Normally, students simply come in and take the exam," she explained, leaning back in the desk chair. "They never look at ordinary things such as the course number. Elliott uses a method that rotates six numbers throughout the exams and he always uses the same six numbers. First, our anniversary and then my birth date. The exams should always be 04-24-60-06-12-43. These are in the wrong order. This exam should be 1243. Someone has rearranged the stack."

"Maybe the doc dropped them or something."

Helen looked at Tony and smiled. He smiled back at her and shook his head. "He'd rearrange them if he had, wouldn't he?"

Helen nodded and went back to the stack. "Most of them seem to be in the right sequence. It's just a few on top that are wrong. I think I should keep these for the police, Tony."

"What about the exam?"

"Write a new one. I know Elliott would trust you to do that, but don't tell the students it's a different exam. Just be sure to cover the same material. Would you do that?"

"Sure. Do you want to see it before I give it?"

"No. I'm afraid that even after all the years I've lived with Elliott I'm still not that great in microbiology."

WHEN BRODIE ARRIVED at work Friday, Maggie was at her desk looking through a file folder. She stopped reading when she saw Brodie and closed the folder. "This report from Travis County came in this morning. I hope you don't mind if I looked over it."

"Which report is it?"

"The traffic accident. Doesn't seem to have been an accident after all."

"That's what they said last week. At least now it's official," Brodie said as she sat down and opened the folder. "How's the face? You know, it almost looks like a bruise you might have gotten in a fight."

"It's fine, Lieutenant," Maggie said, ignoring the speculation. "Coffee?"

She glanced around the office. "Who made it?"

"I did, but it may be weaker than you're used to."

"Mud would be weaker than we're used to," the lieutenant grunted.

She continued reading the report from the medical examiner until Maggie returned and set a cup in front of her. Reading over her shoulder as she turned the pages of the report, Maggie rested her hand lightly on Brodie's shoulder. Although she felt the warmth of Maggie's hand through her shirt, she chose not to say anything about the uninvited contact between them. It had once been an instinctive, natural touch. She had missed it more than she realized.

"Anything you didn't know before?" Maggie asked between sips of coffee.

"Seems our guy had a leg injury at some point. Screws in the right ankle."

"No dental?"

"Nope. Teeth were conveniently removed."

"Except for the ankle screws there doesn't seem to be much to work with. Could be anybody."

"Well, Detective, that's why they pay us the big bucks. To make something out of nothing."

Maggie continued to sip her coffee as she returned to her desk.

"Lieutenant Brodie," she said.

"Yeah."

"I want to apologize if my being here has complicated things for you."

"Why would it?"

"I just thought that..."

"Thought what?"

"Nothing. Forget it."

"Look, Weston, your job is to do what I tell you and my job is to teach you the way we do things here," she said calmly. "Okay?"

Brodie was saved from further conversation when the phone rang. She sat up and grabbed the receiver. "Cedar Springs Police Department. Lieutenant Brodie." She listened for a few seconds and then handed the phone to Maggie who took it with a questioning look on her face.

Brodie shrugged and said, "Your fan club, I guess."

"This is Detective Weston."

"Detective, Helen Brauner."

"Good morning, Dr. Brauner. How can I help you?"

"You asked me to call after I checked Elliott's office."

"Did you find something?"

Maggie listened for a few minutes before speaking again.

"When can I meet you, Dr. Brauner?"

"I'll be in my office a little before noon. Can we meet then?"

"Of course. I'll be looking forward to it."

Maggie hung up and looked at Brodie, who was still going over the file from the Medical Examiner.

"That was Helen Brauner from the university. She reported her husband as a missing person last Sunday."

"That the one you were playing Lone Ranger on Tuesday?"

"Yes."

"Are you meeting with the wife again?"

"Around noon if it's all right with you."

"She didn't say what she wanted on the phone?"

"I asked her to check her husband's office to see if she noticed anything out of the ordinary. Something I wouldn't have noticed. I assume she found something and preferred not to discuss it on the phone."

"Okay. Follow it up," Brodie said, returning to her file folder. "Maybe I'll tag along to evaluate how you conduct yourself during an interview."

"What about Nicholls?"

"He's spending the morning going over our burned-out Mercedes from Thursday night and interviewing the owner. Probably won't be back until after lunch some time."

BY ELEVEN FORTY-FIVE, the two women were climbing the stairs leading to the second floor of the Chemistry Building in the university Science Quadrangle.

"Jesus, it stinks in here," Brodie said.

"Didn't you take chemistry in high school? There are always strange smells coming from the chemistry labs."

"You'd think with all the brain power around here they could at least come up with chemicals that had a pleasant smell."

"I think those are called perfumes and deodorants."

"Which office is hers?" Brodie asked as they reached the second floor.

"224," Maggie said looking around. "Must be down this way."

Brodie followed her down the hallway until they found a door that looked identical to the ones Maggie had seen in the Biology Building. The same block lettering identified the occupant, Helen K. Brauner, Ph.D., Chemistry. Maggie knocked on the office door and someone called out, "Come in."

Maggie opened the door and looked around the outer office. The office was homey looking with curtains hanging from the windows. Helen Brauner appeared in the doorway of the inner office. She smiled when she saw the rookie detective.

"Sorry to yell like that Detective Weston, but I let my assistant go to lunch early and I was heating my own. Please come in."

"Dr. Brauner, this is Lieutenant Brodie," Maggie said. "My training officer."

Helen smiled warmly at Brodie and extended her hand. "Please, come in. Can I offer you some lunch? I always have too much. Elliott usually shares it with me."

"No, we're fine, Dr. Brauner, but thank you," Brodie smiled.

They sat on a couch in Helen Brauner's office. Brodie looked around the office as Helen removed her lunch from a small microwave. She picked up two coffee cups and filled them, handing one to Brodie and the other to Maggie.

"If you'd like cream and sugar, there's sugar on the table and cream in the refrigerator," she said as she sat down with her lunch.

"This is fine," Maggie said. "You said you found something in your husband's office."

"Yes. I don't know how important it is, but it was something out of place." Helen stood and handed a stack of papers to Maggie.

"What are these, Dr. Brauner?" Maggie asked.

"Exams. I got them from my husband's office this morning. Elliott was supposed to give the exam last Friday, but since he disappeared Thursday it was never given."

"And you think there's something unusual about them?"

"Absolutely. They're out of order."

Helen Brauner explained her husband's system of stacking exams to the detectives.

"You'll excuse me, ma'am," Brodie said, "but that seems like an awful lot of trouble for an exam. Did your husband suspect one of his students of cheating?"

"Tony, that's Elliott's assistant, called him paranoid and perhaps he was. Personally, I prefer to think of his system as a means of showing his affection for me in some small way. It may seem silly or sophomoric, but Elliott was never one to show affection in a grandiose manner."

"So you believe someone tampered with the exams prior to them being given?" Maggie asked.

"It looks that way even though none of the exams are missing. I presume someone either read it or made a copy of it."

"Who would be in a position to do that, Dr. Brauner?" Brodie asked.

"Certainly the people who would benefit most would be his students, but I have no idea how any of them would gain access to them," Helen answered.

"What about Obregon?" Maggie asked.

Helen laughed lightly. "As far as I know, Tony didn't have a reason to copy the exam. He isn't a student in that particular class and he doesn't have a key to the file cabinet where I found them."

"Maybe he has a key you don't know about," Maggie said.

"I asked him and he said he didn't. I don't believe Tony would lie to me, Detective."

"Would he take a copy for another student in class? I'm sure there are students who would have been glad to pay for a copy."

"Tony doesn't like any of the students well enough to steal for them and I can't believe he'd be involved in selling an exam."

"Money can be a powerful motivator, Dr. Brauner," Brodie said.

"Lieutenant Brodie, Tony Obregon has too much to lose at this point in his academic career to risk being caught in such a scheme. He has literally dragged himself up from nothing to attain his current level of education. He is a doctoral candidate in Microbiology and any monetary gain he might make now is certainly surpassed by what lies ahead for him in research with any number of major research facilities. I know for a fact that my husband has personally recommended him for possible positions once he graduates."

"Does Mr. Obregon know that? From what I gathered he and your husband are not the best of friends," Maggie said.

"Elliott recognizes Tony's enormous potential, but it isn't his desire to be Tony's friend. As a matter of fact, and I probably shouldn't even tell you this, Elliott is responsible for Tony's remaining at the university and finishing his degree. He couldn't stand the idea of him wasting his intellect. Last year, when his partial scholarship ran out, Elliott personally arranged to finance Tony's final year. Anonymously, of course."

"That was very generous of your husband," Maggie said.

"Generosity had nothing to do with it, Detective. Elliott knows talent when he sees it and he would do anything to prevent losing it. He believed if Tony left school until he had enough money to complete his education, he might never return."

"Well, I think we have a few leads to work with now, Dr. Brauner. I appreciate your help," Maggie said, closing her notebook. "We'll take these exams with us, if you don't mind."

"Of course."

As Helen escorted them to her office door, Brodie stopped and looked back at the pictures she had hanging on the wall behind her desk.

"Are those pictures of you and your husband, ma'am?" she asked.

"Yes. A family album of sorts," Helen said, smiling.

"I notice your husband is on crutches in one of them. Did he have an accident?"

Helen laughed. "Yes, and I'm afraid it was my fault. When I was younger I had a passion for ice skating. After I met Elliott I harangued the poor man into joining me. He tried for my sake, but it was the first and last time."

Brodie smiled. "I can understand that. Trying to impress the woman he loved, huh?"

"Yes. He did pretty well for a while, but then his ankle gave way and ended a promising skating career."

"He broke his ankle?" Maggie asked, following Brodie's lead.

"Shattered it. The doctors had to use screws to hold everything in place. But it never bothered him, especially after we moved to the warmer climate here."

Brodie touched Maggie on the arm and said, "We appreciate your help, Dr. Brauner. We'll let you know if we find out anything."

"Lieutenant," Helen said, with a slight tremor in her voice. "You believe my husband is dead, don't you?"

Brodie had difficulty looking at Helen Brauner as she spoke, "I'm afraid it's a possibility, Dr. Brauner. I'm sorry."

Even though tears filled her eyes, Helen Brauner stood up straight. "Thank you for your honesty, Lieutenant. When will you know for sure?"

Brodie reached out and placed her hand on the woman's shoulder. "We'll let you know as soon as possible, ma'am."

Brodie was quiet as she and Maggie walked back to their car. She started the engine, rolled her window down and lit a cigarette.

"Damn fuckin' shame," Brodie said as she exhaled. "Get the name of Brauner's doctor and see if he has any x-rays showing the screw placement. We'll send them over to Travis County for a comparison. Then at least she'll know what happened to her husband."

Brodie backed the car out and drove toward the police department. She and Maggie didn't speak for several blocks.

"Do you think Brauner and Garcia's deaths are related now?" Maggie finally asked.

"It's sure beginning to look that way. And that should make our job a little easier, I suppose. Have you thought about a timetable of events yet?"

"Not really, but my guess would be that both crimes occurred Thursday night, probably early evening. Mrs. Brauner told me her husband went to the university a little after seven. We haven't found Garcia's keys, but he must have had them in order to clean the offices. If Mrs. Brauner is right about the exams being tampered with, Garcia's killer might have murdered him for his keys and used them to get into Brauner's office."

"Where he was probably interrupted by Brauner returning at seven or so," Brodie continued.

"In the meantime, he had Garcia's body stashed in the tunnel."

"Look it up when we get back. I wonder why no one missed Garcia that evening. The Biology Building is pretty big. Surely there was more than one janitor assigned to the building."

"According to the supervisor there are three, one for each floor. It's possible they wouldn't see one another."

"He probably couldn't get rid of Garcia's body right away and then his problem was compounded by Brauner's unexpected appearance. He would have been forced to kill him to prevent Brauner from turning him in. Do we have any suspects?"

"At least twenty-four if you think it might have been a student," Maggie said holding up the exams. "And that doesn't include Obregon, the assistant. He and Brauner had a fight on Wednesday about something. When I talked to him, he said it wasn't any big deal, but he could have been lying. He is, or was, a member of the Latin Lords. Has the tats to prove it."

"According to the professor's wife, he done seen the light though," Brodie quipped.

"We'll need to talk to him again."

"Who else have you talked to about Brauner?"

"Dr. Roth in the same department and his assistant, a graduate student named Daryll Chambers."

"What did they have to offer?"

"Not much, but I didn't know much when I talked to them except Brauner was missing. Roth's sort of a strange bird. Smokes pot in his office and looks like his karma got stuck in the late sixties."

"Sounds like my kinda guy," Brodie said with a smirk.

"You'd love his Grateful Dead collection," Maggie said as she grinned across the seat at Brodie.

"Who else you got?"

"The assistant, Chambers, looks straight arrow. One of those Ivy League types. Very clean cut. He told me about an argument he overheard between Obregon and Brauner."

"When we get back to the office we'll fill Nicholls in and start dividing up what we've got so far. Better set up a schedule for interviewing the students, but you can eliminate the women in the group."

"Why? You think a woman couldn't carry off a crime like this?"

"Not without help and this doesn't look like it was a group project."

NICHOLLS WAS AT his desk with the telephone receiver resting on his shoulder when the two women returned to the squad room. He waved quickly when he saw them and returned to his phone conversation. Maggie poured coffee for herself and one for Brodie and carried them back to their desks. She got Nicholls's attention and pointed at his cup. He smiled and shook his head.

"I'll get a roster of students in Brauner's class this afternoon. How do you want to handle the interviews? Here or at their places?" Maggie asked.

"I kinda prefer the element of surprise by just dropping in on them personally," Brodie answered. "Sometimes they don't show up when you call them in and, if our boy is among them, I wouldn't want him to skip town."

"I can get their addresses from the registrar, but spring break at the university will be starting at the end of next week. We might not be able to get to all of them before then."

"We'll do what we can and catch the rest after."

Nicholls hung up the phone and leaned back in his chair.

"So, where have you two been?" he asked.

"We got a possible I.D. on Charcoal Bill," Brodie said.

"Great, I guess. Who is he?"

"Dr. Elliott Brauner, a professor in the Biology Department. What did you find out about the vehicle?" she asked.

"Pretty much what we already knew. Jenkins was definitely the owner. In fact, I just talked to him on the phone again. He's given a statement to Austin PD, but won't be much help. Wants his insurance company to take a look at what's left. Worried he won't get a new car out of it."

"When did he leave it at the airport?"

"The Sunday before we found it. Out of town all week for a business conference or something. Has absolutely no idea who might have stolen his car. Surprise, surprise. But it seems that Mr. Jenkins has this, uh, how can I delicately put this? Snob complex? Anyway, he always parks his car in Executive Long Term Parking. The airport has a special area for big business types who travel frequently."

"Is he a frequent flyer?"

"Apparently."

"Well, the car wasn't your regular freeway trolley. Maybe we'll get lucky and the guy at the ticket booth will remember it," Maggie interjected.

"How do you think our guy got to the airport?" Nicholls asked.

"Your guess is as good as mine," Brodie said.

"Think he had the bodies with him?" Maggie asked.

"That'd take a pretty ballsy guy. Lug along two dead bodies. Hot wire a car and then transfer the bodies to it," Brodie said.

"Since Brauner's was the only body found in the car, maybe he didn't have both bodies with him. Wouldn't even have to worry about hiding it. Just pass it off as a sleeping passenger," Nicholls said.

"Shit. This Jenkins guy left the car at the airport on Sunday, we found it after it became a barbecue grill on wheels Thursday, and Jenkins didn't report it missing until the following Monday. Whoever took it could have done it anytime between Sunday and Thursday. Wouldn't have had to have either body with him." Brodie said, rubbing her face.

"But that's assuming he planned the two murders in advance," Maggie jumped in. "I think Brauner was an accident. Just stumbled into his own murder. He shouldn't have even been on the campus Thursday evening."

"Think he might have witnessed Garcia's murder?" Nicholls asked.

"I don't know, but suppose our guy hadn't figured on murdering Brauner. Suddenly he's stuck with two dead bodies. Burning the body in a fake accident seems like a hastily put together plan," Maggie offered.

"Why go to the airport to steal a fuckin' car? He coulda stolen one closer to home," Nicholls said.

"Probably figured a car stolen from the airport in Austin wouldn't be reported for at least a day or two. Especially one in long term parking," Brodie said, looking at Maggie. She could sense Maggie was beginning to get excited by the idea of pieces falling into place. It was becoming harder for her to find much wrong with the trainee's work.

"Right," Maggie said. "It would give him time to distance the two crimes from one another. Or at least he thought so at the time."

"So how do you think it went down, RB?" Nicholls asked.

"Well, Weston thinks Garcia was killed to get his office keys, in particular the keys to Brauner's office. An exam was scheduled for Friday and the wife confirmed the exams had been tampered with. He was interrupted by Brauner and forced to kill him, too," she answered. "Probably took Brauner's key to the file cabinet after he killed him. Worked out for him in the end since there was no reason for a janitor to have keys to anything other than the office itself."

"Sounds logical to me, but isn't he practically pointing the finger at himself then? I mean, how many people would have wanted into Brauner's office bad enough to kill two people."

"That's the illogical part," Maggie said. "There are twenty-four people in his graduate class and if you eliminate the women that leaves nineteen."

"Maybe it isn't one of Brauner's students," Nicholls said. You said the assistant, what's his name, argued with the professor. Maybe he's sending us off on a wild goose chase after he got his rocks off getting even with the old man."

"Then why kill the janitor?" Maggie asked. "Obregon had a key to the office himself. I don't like him for this."

Brodie ruffled her hands through her short hair. "Well, now that we've completed that circle and seem to be right back where we started, I think it's time to call it a day. Let's sleep on it over the weekend and we'll start interviewing people Monday. See if we can eliminate anyone and make the circle smaller."

BRODIE CARRIED HER coffee cup to the restroom and washed it out before leaving for the weekend. They had made some progress on the two cases and it was more than she had initially hoped for. As she left the restroom on her way back to the squad room, she heard loud voices and quickened her pace. It seemed a little early for their usual contingent of Friday night drunks. As she rounded the corner into the squad room she stopped dead in her tracks. What she saw wasn't anything she would have anticipated and felt the urge to turn and walk in the opposite direction. The eyes of Tim Weston glaring at her prevented that option. She glanced quickly around the room at her fellow officers and walked toward her desk.

Maggie was seated behind her desk, obviously embarrassed by the scene her father was creating. The look Brodie saw in her eyes broke her heart. But Maggie Weston wasn't hers to protect any longer. Nicholls was attempting to determine what the problem was, using as reasonable a tone as possible.

"Sir, I suggest we move to an interrogation room. This is a personal matter between you and your daughter and shouldn't be aired in front of these other officers."

"Why? My daughter has made it perfectly clear she isn't in the least ashamed or embarrassed about being a lesbian," Weston said derisively.

Nicholls appeared dumbfounded by the accusation and stared at Brodie.

"That's enough, Tim," Brodie said as she approached the scene, trying to keep her voice as calm as possible. "Take Detective Nicholls' suggestion. Let's go someplace more private. If you insist on continuing your tirade out here I'll have you arrested for creating a disturbance."

"You don't have the guts to do that, Brodie," Tim sneered.

She stepped closer to him and kept her voice low. "Don't test me, Tim." Turning away, she was stopped by Nicholls' hand on her arm. "Romero! Take Detective Weston and her father to interrogation two. I'll be there in a minute." She jerked her arm away from Nicholls and walked back down the hallway and into interrogation room one with Nicholls following her.

"Is it true, Brodie?" he asked as soon as the door closed.

"Which part?"

"Is Weston a dyke?"

Brodie glared at him. "Her sexual orientation is none of my business or yours. You'll have to ask her."

"Are you sleeping with her?"

"I'm not ready to throw away my career by fuckin' a trainee, Nicholls! I knew Maggie when I was with the Austin PD and that's it, so drop it. If you have a problem, see Captain Donaldson."

Brodie left the interrogation room and leaned against the wall to calm down and take a deep breath before moving to her next problem. When she entered the second interrogation room Maggie was seated at the table and Tim was pacing like a caged animal.

"You want me to stay, Brodie?" Romero asked.

"No. Where is Donaldson?"

"He ran out to grab something to eat. Should be back soon."

"Ask him to join us when he gets back, please."

She closed the door as Romero left and turned her attention Maggie and her father. She could see the apology in Maggie's eyes, but ignored it. "Sit down, Mr. Weston, and tell me what your problem seems to be, considering you're not a resident of our fair city."

Although he refused to sit, Tim placed the palms of his hands on the table and leaned toward Brodie. "You're my fucking problem, Brodie, and you damn well know why."

"I only know what your problem was eight years ago."

"I know you'll try to work your way back into my daughter's bed, if you haven't already," he spat, staring at Maggie. "Your fellow officers should be made aware of who they're having to work with every damn day."

"They are aware for the most part. All you've succeeded in doing today is humiliating your daughter. I don't give a shit what my fellow officers think about me, but I do care what they think about my trainee. I didn't ask for this assignment and I tried to get out of it because I knew you'd pull a stunt like this eventually. I guess I didn't think you'd be this vindictive against your own daughter. She's going to be a damn good detective. She's thorough and has good instincts. I'm guessing she got those traits from her mother because she sure as shit couldn't have gotten them from you. Your problem is you can't accept Maggie for who she is. While it is a problem, it's a personal one between the two of you. I won't have your personal problems dragged in here interfering with our jobs. Believe me when I tell you I won't hesitate to have you arrested if you *ever* create a scene like this again. I've had a hard week and am going home. Alone. I am not sleeping with your daughter and I don't ever want to have to discuss this with you again." Brodie turned on her heel and yanked the door to the room open. She almost ran into Donaldson on her way out of the room.

"What's the problem, Brodie?" he asked.

"We have a citizen with a complaint," she said tersely. "Let me know the outcome. I'm going home."

She didn't pause to acknowledge the stares of others in the squad room as she left for the weekend. Her hands were shaking as she sat in her Camaro and tried to light a desperately needed cigarette.

Chapter
Six

MAMA JEAN'S WAS a well-known women's bar and dance club a block off the main drag in Austin. Brodie parked her Camaro in a pay parking lot and strolled slowly to the club three blocks away. She stopped and looked at items displayed in the store windows along the way to take her mind off the scene earlier. Finally taking a deep breath, she pushed open the front door of the club and immediately felt her body relax. She hadn't been out in months and, after her confrontation with Tim Weston, decided she owed herself a night away from work and stress and unwanted trainees. She had been to more than a few women's bars that would have only looked good if she had been drunk. Mostly pick-up bars where almost anyone could score a one-night stand as long as they weren't too picky. She knew her fellow officers wondered about her, but they never asked any questions. Nicholls knew about her preferences, as did Donaldson. As long as she performed her duties successfully and kept her private life private, he didn't seem to care. What she did off duty wasn't anyone's business. She hadn't considered settling down permanently, not even with Camille. And now Camille had made it clear that their status-quo relationship was no longer enough for her. Even though she missed waking up every morning next to the warmth of a woman's body snuggled closely against her, she wasn't willing to take an emotional risk like that again.

She whiled away nearly two hours watching women and listening to the mostly country-western music. Periodically, a woman approached her for a dance and she had been glad to accept. She enjoyed dancing and, for the most part, the conversation had been pleasant as well. She began to relax and felt her body fall into a comfortable rhythm. The more she danced and the more women she met, the more she ventured to ask others to dance. Even sober she was having a surprisingly good time.

HE SHIFTED HIS car into park and sat patiently, waiting for Maggie Weston to enter her duplex. He'd give her a little time to get comfortable or perhaps wait until the lights were turned off for the night. He pulled the tab on a soft drink can and settled in, waiting for the right time. She could tie him to the murder of Cruz Garcia. He mentally slapped himself for being so stupid. The dumb bitch probably didn't realize why she had to die.

He blinked when headlights from an on-coming vehicle hit him. He ducked his head, not taking any chances. The car, a flashy red Mustang, slowed in front of the duplex and turned into the driveway. "Shit," he muttered. He watched as a woman dressed in jeans and a short-sleeve pullover readjusted her clothing and ran a hand through her medium length dark hair as she approached the front door to Maggie Weston's home. *Now what*, he thought. He wanted to finish his business and get back to his life.

MAGGIE WAS EXHAUSTED after the scene with her father and had only arrived home from work a few minutes before her doorbell rang. She groaned and contemplated not answering until the doorbell rang the second time.

"Carrie!"

"Hey baby," the woman said with a smile. "You don't look ready for a night out. Just get home?" she asked as she stepped into the room and pulled Maggie into a warm embrace.

"I've just had the worst day of my entire adult life," Maggie answered, returning the hug.

"Well, sit down and tell me all about it." Carrie Landers said. She smiled as Maggie ended the embrace. "You may be tired, but you still look good enough to eat." She kissed Maggie softly. "We can stay home if you want to."

"No. It's just that with everything that happened today, I forgot about our date. Maybe a night out will take my mind off the problem."

"So what's the problem?" Carrie asked.

"My father showed up at work today and outed me," Maggie answered, her voice quiet.

"Why would he do a dumb thing like that?"

"Because he thinks I'm sleeping with my training officer."

"What?! Why would he think something as stupid as that?"

"Because it's Royce Brodie," Maggie admitted.

"Oh, I see. You didn't tell me that."

"I didn't need to tell you," Maggie said angrily. "That was eight years ago, for Chrissakes! There's nothing going on between me and Royce. She barely tolerates having me in the squad room."

"Take it easy, sweetie. I wasn't accusing you of anything. I'm not the enemy here," Carrie said.

"I know you never liked Royce, Carrie, but I can handle my own problems."

"I didn't like the way she treated you is all." Carrie took Maggie in her arms again and held her. "I'll never treat you like that, Mag."

"I know. Let me grab a quick shower and change clothes, okay? Then you can take me someplace fabulous for dinner. I'm starving!" Maggie laughed.

HE FOLLOWED THE Mustang into Austin and found a parking slot nearby where he could observe Maggie and her companion walk hand-in-hand into Suzi's China Bar and Grill on Anderson Lane, just off Loop One. *Why you little dyke*, he thought with a smile. He'd eaten there a couple of times and it was good enough to impress his dates. It also meant he'd be waiting for at least an hour and probably longer, judging from the number of vehicles in the parking lot.

He opened his car door and got out, walked across a side road to a convenience store where he purchased another soft drink and a bag of popcorn. If he'd known killing Maggie Weston was going to take all night, he would've brought a book.

Nearly ninety minutes later he sat up straighter in his car seat when he spotted Maggie leaving the restaurant. She was laughing at something the other woman had said. The Mustang backed out and turned onto the side road to get back on Loop One. He followed at a discreet distance and turned behind them at the Fifth-Sixth Street exit. They were driving into the downtown area where traffic would be more congested. The Mustang finally turned onto Sixth Street and entered a public parking garage. Across the street he saw the flashing neon sign for Mama Jean's, a local gay and lesbian bar. He drove around the block and pulled into the parking lot of a post office sub-station. Paying the attendant five dollars, he walked across the busy street and turned the corner in time to see Maggie and her companion jog across the road and walk into the bar.

MAGGIE FOLLOWED CARRIE into Mama Jean's. Carrie Landers had been her best friend since their training days at the Austin Police Academy, and they began dating not long after Maggie passed her detective's exam. Before she and Carrie started going out she had been to Mama's alone many times, but there hadn't been many nights she had been forced to go home alone. She almost always managed to find a passing fancy to take her mind off her loneliness. To celebrate Maggie's new job Carrie had planned a special evening beginning with dinner, a little dancing and something much more intimate later. While Carrie went to the bar to buy the first round, Maggie went in search of an out-of-the-way table. When Carrie re-joined her, they tipped their drinks back. As she set her glass down on the table, a familiar figure on the dance floor caught Carrie's eye. "Well, there's a face I hoped I'd never see again," she said.

"What?" Maggie asked, following Carrie's gaze.

"It's your ex."

Brodie directed a dazzling smile at the woman she was dancing with. *A beautiful smile,* Maggie thought. *It used to take my breath away when she smiled at me like that.* She watched as the dance ended and Brodie escorted her dance partner from the floor, her fingertips barely touching the small of the woman's back. They took long, thirsty drinks from the bottles they had left along the dance floor railing. As Brodie brought her bottle to her lips, Maggie felt her stomach clench and she longed to be that damn bottle, just to feel Royce's lips touch hers again. Jesus Christ! She shook her head to clear her mind. She was losing it. Brodie ran her hand slowly to the back of the woman's neck and pulled her closer as she said something to the woman that brought a smile to her face.

"How about a dance?" Carrie asked as she ran her hand down Maggie's back.

Smiling, Maggie took her hand and followed her to the dance floor. The song was a slow tune, and Carrie drew Maggie close to her. As they made their way around the floor, Maggie caught a glimpse of Brodie. The woman she had been talking with was gone and she was watching the couples dance. As they made their second turn around the small floor, Maggie turned her head to look for Brodie. A moment later their eyes met and stayed on one another. Maggie wanted to reach out to her. She had made a mistake by going to Cedar Springs. After the fiasco with her father that afternoon, Maggie wasn't certain she could still hold her head up at work. She had been completely blindsided when he appeared.

She turned toward Carrie and said, "I need to speak to Brodie for a moment."

Resting a hand on top of Maggie's, Carrie said, "You're better off without her."

"I know, but we're working on a case and I forgot to tell her something before I left this afternoon," Maggie lied.

Brodie's white long-sleeve shirt seemed to glow under the black lights scattered around the club as she chatted amiably with the woman she had been dancing with earlier. Taking a deep breath for courage, Maggie tapped her on the shoulder. As soon as she saw her former lover, Brodie's smile evaporated

"Weston," she said, her eyes turning cold. "Enjoying your evening?"

"Could I speak to you privately for a moment?" Maggie asked, casting a glance at the woman with Brodie.

Turning back toward the other woman, Brodie said, "Don't go away. It's a work thing."

Maggie followed Brodie to a corner of the bar and waited for her to turn around.

"I wanted to apologize for my father. We had a fight earlier in the week and I didn't know he'd show up where I worked. I...I'll turn in my resignation if you want."

"What's done is done. You can do what you want, but don't let him force you into doing something you don't want to do. He's pissed because he doesn't control you any more and he can't stand that. Never could."

Maggie looked around the club nervously and spotted Carrie talking to a group of women. On an impulse she asked, "Would you like to dance?"

"Aren't you with someone?" Brodie asked. She had seen Maggie dancing with Carrie and privately confessed a twinge of jealousy to herself. She wasn't particularly happy with the way she was feeling about Maggie, but the memory of dancing with her was too strong to ignore.

"Yeah, you probably remember my friend, Carrie."

"I remember her calling me a good-for-nothing drunk after you were hurt."

"A lot of people said a lot of things they shouldn't have back then, including me. One dance can't possibly hurt anything. It's just a dance."

For a moment, the corners of Brodie's mouth looked as if they might actually curl into a smile. "Why not?"

As the driving beat of Melissa Etheridge's *I'm the Only One* began, the disc jockey announced in a husky, sultry voice over the microphone, "Shadow dance, ladies. Show your partner what you've got to offer her tonight."

As Brodie started toward the floor, Maggie stopped. Maybe asking for a dance hadn't been such a great idea after all.

"Do you want to dance or not?" Brodie asked.

Glancing at the dancers already on the floor, Maggie looked back at her and took her hand. As soon as they were on the floor, Brodie spun Maggie in front of her and slid an arm around her waist, pressing her hand firmly against Maggie's abdomen, pulling her closely against her own body. "Just relax," she breathed softly into Maggie's ear, sending a chill down her body. Shadow dancing was as amazingly sensuous as Maggie remembered as their bodies began moving together as one. There was something erotic about feeling but not seeing her partner's body move against hers as she trailed one hand slowly down Maggie's arm and side. It could have been her imagination or the sensations her body was feeling, but it seemed as if Brodie's hand had slipped slowly down her abdomen, her fingers spread. Maggie felt her body reacting to the movement of Brodie's body against hers.

Almost without Maggie realizing it, the tempo of the music changed and slipped smoothly into another song. Taking her cue from the beat of the music, Brodie stepped around her gracefully, facing her as the dance continued. Maggie felt her hand slip to the small of her back, drawing her closer once again.

"How long have you been dating Carrie?" Brodie asked.

"A few months," Maggie answered.

"I hope you have better luck this time."

As she opened her eyes, the coldness she had seen in Brodie's eyes was replaced by something softer, something that took her breath away. Hurt? Disappointment? She ran her hand along Brodie's neckline and rested her head in the hollow of the taller woman's shoulder, feeling contented ... secure for the first time in years. Brodie shifted her body, allowing her lead leg to slip slightly between Maggie's thighs. She felt her breath quicken at the movement and hoped Brodie couldn't feel her heart beating faster against her chest. She had wondered how she would feel if Royce ever touched her again and now she knew. Every cell of her body remembered. When the music began to fade away, she didn't want to release her grip on the taciturn detective.

"Thanks, Weston," Brodie said as they finally left the dance floor.

Maggie laughed. "Even off duty you can't bring yourself to call me by my first name again."

"It was just a dance," Brodie shot back. "Don't make more out of it than it was."

"Perhaps," Maggie said to herself as Brodie walked away.

HE ORDERED A beer and found a nice secluded spot partially in the shadows next to the bar. He stood there a while, leaning against the wall. He watched Maggie and the brunette glide around the dance floor and felt nauseated. He would be doing the world a favor by killing her. *One less dyke in a world that was sick enough already.* When the two women returned to their table, Maggie looked around the club and sipped her drink. A moment later she said something to the woman with her and left their table. She walked directly toward a tall, older woman and spoke to her. He nearly panicked as the two women moved toward the corner of the bar where he was watching. Had Maggie seen him and gotten reinforcements to confront him? He shook the idea away in his mind and shrank back father into the shadows. *You tramp*, he thought when he heard Maggie ask the other woman to dance.

He thought he saw Maggie hesitate when the dance was announced. Apparently a shadow dance was something special. Once the dancers began to move, he licked his lips. The way Maggie embraced this woman was different, more intimate. There was a sense of familiarity in the way they touched one another that he found extremely arousing. Maggie Weston was turning out to be a much more interesting person by the minute. His eyes followed the older woman as she wove through the crowd.

BRODIE MADE HER way to the ladies room and splashed cold water on her face. Damn, Maggie felt good in her arms. She had danced with a dozen women that evening, but none had caused her body to react the way it had with her. It was stupid and senseless. She couldn't allow it to go any further. It wouldn't be fair to Maggie. She was with someone else now and Brodie knew she wouldn't be able to handle the rejection that would come from anything more serious. She was drying her hands and face when the bathroom door opened and Carrie stepped into the small room. She leaned against the wall, gazing down at the floor until they were alone.

Brodie turned and leaned against the sink as she tossed the damp paper towel into the nearby garbage can. "Something I can do for you, Landers?" she asked.

"You can leave Maggie the hell alone."

Brodie smiled. "What's your interest?"

"Maggie has finally gotten over you, Brodie. We're together now."

"Congratulations. Isn't that what you always wanted?"

"I knew you'd self-destruct eventually. I'm a very patient woman."

"Well, I've heard that's supposed to be a virtue. It sounds like you don't trust her much though."

"It's you I don't trust."

"That's a group that seems to be growing by leaps and bounds lately," Brodie said as she walked toward the door.

Carrie grabbed her arm. "Stay away from her, Brodie," she threatened in a low voice.

"Or what?" Brodie asked as she jerked her arm away and opened the door. "You'll ruin my career?"

Brodie skirted her way around the edges of the crowd, stopping to speak to one or two women. When she turned to leave the club, she caught a glimpse of Carrie drawing Maggie closely against her on the dance floor and paid no attention to the man exiting the club in front of her.

ON AN IMPULSE, Brodie turned the Camaro east onto Congress Avenue toward the Omni. It had been a long time since she'd been to the Renaissance Tavern inside the hotel. She considered it a special place. The Renaissance appeared to have its usual contingent of late-evening diners as she pulled into a parking space.

The rich dark paneling in the dimly lit bar exuded a sense of calm as soon as she entered the room. Taking a seat at the bar, she decided what the hell, she hadn't reached the limit on her credit card and might as well get what she wanted for a change. Ordering a double Chivas on the rocks, she tried to relax and looked around the room. Her thoughts were interrupted by a woman sliding onto the bar stool next to her.

"Excuse me," the woman said, "would you mind sharing your ashtray with me?"

Brodie slid the heavy leaded-glass ashtray toward her.

"Thank you," the woman said with a smile as she pulled a silver cigarette case from her black beaded clutch purse and flipped it open.

Brodie picked up a matchbook from the bar and opened it. When the match ignited she held it toward the woman, who played with the cigarette between her lips for a moment while looking at her before lowering her cigarette into the flame.

"Thank you again," she said softly.

"No problem," Brodie said, picking up her drink. Glancing at the woman, she asked, "Would you like a drink?"

"I'd love one. Are you alone?" she asked.

"Seems like," Brodie answered, signaling to the bartender.

The woman ordered a glass of white wine and tapped ashes from her cigarette into the ashtray. "Do you come here often?" she asked.

"No. You?" Brodie said as she turned slightly toward her.

"Not as often as I'd like," the woman smiled as she exhaled a thin stream of smoke.

Brodie's eyes took in the whole package seated next to her as she inhaled the light scent of an expensive perfume. The woman had shimmering auburn hair braided into an elegant French twist. Her hair was set off by a simple black cocktail dress with a neckline that plunged far enough down her chest to make Brodie wonder what kept her breasts from slipping out. The skin of her cleavage was evenly tanned and inviting.

"You look a little stressed," the woman said nonchalantly. "Rough day?"

"You could say that," Brodie said, as she remembered the way she had held Maggie in her arms earlier.

"Are you from out of town?"

"Sort of," Brodie answered as she tossed down the rest of her drink and motioned for a refill.

"Actually, I was supposed to have a date tonight, but got stood up," the dark-haired woman said.

"Someone's loss," the detective smiled. "You're very attractive."

"Thank you. I'm Kara," she said, extending a slender hand toward Brodie.

"Brodie," she said as she took the woman's warm hand in hers. The soft lighting around the bar shimmered in Kara's green eyes.

They chatted until they finished their drinks. As Brodie got up the leave, Kara stopped her. "I don't want to sound forward or anything, Brodie, but I have some Chivas in my suite if you'd like a nightcap," Kara offered.

"Sure. I don't have any other plans." She couldn't help but smile at Kara. She hadn't been fooled for an instant, but she wasn't about to tell that to the woman.

HE WASN'T SURE what it was, but there had been something about the interaction between Maggie and the tall, older woman that made him decide to follow someone new. The body language between Maggie and this woman practically broadcast an interest in one another simmering just below the surface. Whatever it was, it had driven the older woman to seek out companionship. He shuddered to think what she would have to pay for an evening with the beauty who accompanied her on the elevator. It was late and not many people milled around the elevators waiting to return to their rooms. He watched as the elevator the two women entered rose and finally stopped on the sixth floor. He would remember that. The auburn-haired woman reminded him a little of Maggie. Maybe that was what the woman from the bar wanted. Someone she could substitute for what she couldn't have that night. *Ah, Maggie, such a fucking tease. You were going to be mine tonight, but I can wait a while longer. I know where you live.*

AS THEY STEPPED from the elevator on the sixth floor, Kara opened her purse and found the key card to her room, handing it to Brodie with a smile. She unlocked the door and followed Kara inside as the woman switched on the overhead light. She moved across the room toward a small wet-bar, taking two glasses from a cabinet over the bar, and pouring Chivas into them. When she turned around, Brodie was standing at the sliding glass doors leading onto a small balcony. Walking up next to her, Kara handed her a glass.

"Nice view." Brodie said.

"The city looks different at night and from this height," Kara commented. "Almost clean-looking, isn't it?"

"Yeah," she answered, taking a deep drink from her glass.

She looked at Kara as she sipped her drink. Her unexpected meeting with Maggie earlier had filled her with a need she hadn't wanted to acknowledge. Setting her glass down, she stepped closer to Kara and held her eyes with her own as she slipped her hand into the open neckline of her dress, pleased to discover nothing underneath. She heard the quick intake of breath as she slowly fondled Kara's breast, smiling as she felt the nipple harden beneath her touch. Running her hand under the skirt of Kara's dress, she pulled her closer. She could taste the Chivas that lingered on the inviting mouth as she kissed her hungrily, hoping to erase her memory of Maggie's lips on hers. It was an expensive drink and Kara was an expensive call girl. Both were outside her budget.

Kara took her hand and pulled her toward the bedroom. As she backed into the room, she pulled a few pins from her hair and long auburn tresses cascaded over her shoulders. Brodie slid the dress off Kara's shoulders and let it fall to the floor while Kara slowly began unbuttoning her shirt as Brodie kissed her and explored her slender body. Neither was in a hurry. She needed to drive the feel of Maggie's body out of her mind, if only for a few hours. It had been an emotionally difficult week and she owed her body everything it was about to give and receive.

BRODIE WAS AWAKENED by lips on hers and for a split second didn't remember where she was. Instinctively, she grabbed whoever it was and deepened the kiss. The early morning fog lifted from her brain as Kara's body moved on top of hers.

"Good morning," Kara said, tossing hair back from her face.

She reached up, stroked Kara's velvet breasts and smiled, "Morning."

"Are you feeling better?" Kara asked.

"Absolutely."

Kara had a light laugh. She didn't know how much Kara usually got for her services, but she was worth every damn dime. The truth was she did feel better, despite a general lack of sleep. Kara had awakened her every two hours, resuming their lovemaking, and had seemed pleased with Brodie's response. For the first time she could remember in a long time, she had made love to another woman without seeing the face of someone else. Kara was alive and warm and tender and reminded her she was alive as well. She almost felt guilty that the call girl had worked so hard for nothing more than her gratitude.

"I ordered breakfast from room service," Kara said softly. "Are you hungry?"

"Starving," Brodie said, grabbing her and pulling her down toward her. She was losing herself in the woman's body again when she heard knocking on the door of the room.

"Why don't you take a quick shower while I get breakfast?" Kara suggested.

She watched Kara's naked body slide out of bed and into a short, silk kimono-style robe. As she stood, Brodie felt light-headed and didn't know whether it was from hunger or exhaustion.

When she came out of the shower a few minutes later she felt much better. The last of the cobwebs had evaporated in the steam from the shower. She quickly slipped back into her clothes before leaving the bedroom. A rolling cart from room service was parked near the coffee table. She looked around and found Kara standing at the sliding glass window, looking down at the early morning traffic that had begun to clog Congress Avenue. She walked up behind her and slid her arms around Kara's waist, kissing the nape of her neck.

"Why didn't you tell me you were a cop?" Kara asked bluntly, but without anger.

"How'd you find out?" Brodie asked, releasing her.

"I took some money for a tip from your wallet and the gold from your badge sort of jumped out at me. Are you going to arrest me?"

"For what? You didn't bring up the subject of money last night and it'd be a pretty safe bet you're not going to now. Last time I checked it wasn't against the law for two consenting adults to make love."

"As long as it's free," Kara said.

"When it's free and consensual, it's called making love, Kara. When you pay for it, it's just fucking."

"When did you know?" Kara asked with a smile.

"As soon as you said you had been stood up. I figured you might be looking for a way to recoup your loss."

"Guess that didn't quite work out the way I thought it would," Kara laughed.

"I don't usually have other women try to pick me up in a straight bar, even an expensive one."

"Actually, some of my best lovers have been women," Kara smiled.

"How will you explain it to your employer?"

Running her hand down Brodie's chest, she said, "I'm my own employer. But even a working girl needs a little vacation. Let's eat before our breakfast gets cold."

HE WAITED IN his car outside the hotel all night. He mentally shifted between anger and fantasy. He would have enjoyed watching the women getting it on, as perverted as that might have seemed. Then he could have shown them both what they had been missing all along. He smiled and rubbed his face. He was exhausted. At least the women upstairs had been horizontal and not stuck sitting halfway up in a cramped car. He needed a cup of coffee and something to eat, followed immediately by a hot shower and eight hours sleep.

A little after ten-thirty in the morning, he watched as the woman from the bar pushed open the glass front doors of the hotel and stepped out, squinting into the sun with a self-satisfied look on her face.

THE LATE MORNING sun was shining brightly as Brodie left the Omni. She was surprised that she actually felt relaxed and refreshed. As she started her car and prepared to return to Cedar Springs, she looked up and smiled. She knew she would remember the night Kara had given her exactly what she had needed, but she also knew she would never see the woman again. Kara had accepted her as she was and hadn't asked any questions. Regret over leaving her mixed oddly with a twinge of guilt. She felt strangely unfaithful to Maggie, a woman with whom she no longer had any kind of relationship, and to Camille, a woman with whom she had until a few days earlier.

Chapter
Seven

WHEN BRODIE ENTERED the squad room Monday morning, she didn't bother to sit down at her desk. Maggie and Nicholls were engaged in early morning chit-chat in an attempt to get their juices going when Brodie walked in.

"Grab your stuff, kiddies, and let's go."

"Where to?" Nicholls asked.

"The university. Did we get anything from Brauner's doctor yet?"

"Came in early this morning," Maggie said. "The position of the screws looks like a match."

"First, we'll tell Mrs. Brauner we've identified her husband's body. Then we'll divide up the list of graduate students and start talking to them. I want to speak to this Obregon guy myself."

"Are we keeping the Garcia and Brauner cases separate or lumping them together?" Nicholls asked.

"I think Weston's right and one case led to the other, so I'm sure we're looking for the same killer for both crimes. Two cases of real bad luck."

"What do you mean?" Maggie asked.

"It was bad luck that Garcia was a janitor in the Biology Building and bad luck that Brauner left something he needed in his office the same night."

"Anything else?" Nicholls asked.

"Yeah. I want an inquiry sent out to see if there have been any other crimes similar to this at any other universities. This guy was too cool about what he did to be a first timer. Keep a list, Weston, of the things we need to do."

"I think we should check out the other cars in long term parking at the airport," she said.

"Good idea," Brodie said. "Any other thoughts you'd like to share with us?"

"Not right now, but I'll let you know if I think of something, Lieutenant."

"When we get to the university drop me off at the Chemistry Building. Then you and Nicholls swing by the registrar's office and get class schedules and addresses on the graduate students. We can jerk their asses out of class if we have to. Be sure to watch their reactions to being questioned. See if anyone is too cool."

"I'd like to go with you to see Mrs. Brauner," Maggie said. "I spoke to her originally and I like her."

"That's okay with me, RB," Nicholls said. "I can get the info from the registrar pretty quick. I'm sure they're computerized."

"Okay. Let's go before the trail gets any colder," Brodie said.

As Maggie started toward the entrance of the police station, Brodie stopped Nicholls. "About what happened Friday. There's nothing going on between me and Weston."

"But there was in the past, right?"

"Yeah, there was. I know you're not comfortable with my lifestyle and I didn't see any reason to reveal our past relationship to you. It ended years ago."

"At least that explains why you were so hostile when she first got here."

"Any time you think I'm stepping over the line, just say so and I'll back off."

"Shit! Why should she have it any easier than I did?"

NICHOLLS DROPPED THE women in front of the Chemistry Building and pulled away from the curb. Brodie readjusted her sunglasses before starting toward the entrance to the building.

"You ever broke the bad news before?" she asked.

"No," Maggie frowned.

"Want this one? Gotta do it some time."

Maggie took a deep breath and exhaled audibly. "Yeah, I'll do it."

"Just be sympathetic and don't give any details. She doesn't need to know any specifics right now."

"What if she asks how we identified him?"

"Tell her we matched his medical records to the body and leave it at that. She'll find out the condition of the body soon enough from the funeral home. It's a safe bet there won't be an open casket funeral."

Maggie nodded and entered the building as Brodie held the door open. She knew notification of next-of-kin was never going to be her favorite part of the job. She tried to think what she would want someone to say to her if their roles were reversed. Before she could think about it any further, she heard Brodie speaking to her again.

"Be direct. There aren't any good ways to tell a woman her husband has been murdered by some sorry s.o.b. She probably already suspects she's a widow. Just tell her and then tell her you're sorry. Try to keep eye contact with her while you're talking. Ask if there is anyone we can call for her."

Instant death notification lessons between floors of a building.

Helen Brauner was in her office preparing a cup of tea when Maggie knocked on the open door. She knew the moment she and Helen looked at one other that the woman knew why they were there. There was a slight catch in her voice as she invited the two detectives into her office.

"Dr. Brauner," Maggie began. "I'm sorry, but I have to notify you we've found your husband."

"He's dead, isn't he?"

"Yes, I'm afraid so."

"How?"

Maggie glanced at Brodie and then back at Helen. "He was murdered, Dr. Brauner. I can't tell you more than that right now."

Helen placed a hand on the corner of her desk and sat down. Tears formed in her eyes and the overflow ran slowly down her cheeks. She leaned back in her chair and closed her eyes, forcing more tears down her face. She sniffed quietly, but there was no hysteria. Maggie pulled a tissue from a box on Helen's desk and walked behind the desk to give it to her. Helen opened her eyes and looked at Maggie before taking it and dabbing at her eyes and nose.

"Is there anyone I can call for you, Dr. Brauner?" Maggie asked gently.

Helen shook her head slightly. "I wouldn't know who to call. I haven't needed anyone except Elliott for the last thirty years."

"Can we take you home?"

Helen blew her nose softly as she shook her head. "I can't say I wasn't expecting this, you know. But even then, there was a glimmer of hope. Just denial, I suppose. I'll be fine. My assistant can take my last class today. What should I do now?"

Maggie looked at Brodie.

"Whichever funeral home you choose can contact the Travis County Medical Examiner, Dr. Brauner. They're holding your husband's remains for now, but they can be released at any time," Brodie said quietly.

"Thank you, Detective," Helen said.

"Ma'am, there isn't any easy way to say this, but Dr. Brauner's body was burned in an attempt to hide his identity. There's no need for you to view the remains. It might be some consolation for you to know the medical examiner believes Dr. Brauner was already deceased and didn't suffer. I'm sorry," Maggie added.

Tears dropped from Helen's eyes as she squeezed them tightly shut and drew a deep breath, as if she were trying to block out the image in her mind.

"I know this is a very difficult time for you, Dr. Brauner. But is there anything else you've thought of in the last couple of days we should know about? Something your husband may have said or something you overheard, that might help us find the person responsible," Brodie asked.

"I honestly cannot think of anything, Lieutenant Brodie. But I haven't spent much time thinking about it either."

"Please call us if you think of something later or if you need our help," Maggie said. "You have my card."

"Yes, I'll try to think over everything we did last week. I'll call if I remember anything."

Brodie followed Maggie out of Helen Brauner's office and into the hallway.

"I wish there was more we could do," Maggie said.

"The only thing we can do now is try to find whoever killed him," Brodie responded. "Nothing else will help put this behind her."

They weren't in a hurry as they went down the stairs to the first floor.

"By the way, you handled that fine, Weston," Brodie said.

"I hope I never have to do it again."

"Then you better find other work. But it's not as bad here as in Austin. Murder is a pretty rare occurrence in Cedar Springs."

As they left the building. Nicholls was parked at the curb in a No Parking zone waiting for them.

"Can't you read signs, boy?" Brodie asked as she and Maggie reached the car.

"Who's gonna give me a ticket? The campus cops?"

"Did you get the schedules and addresses?" she asked as she slid into the car.

"Yep. All computerized, just like I thought. Took about fifteen minutes."

"Let's see it," she said.

He handed her a small stack of computer printout sheets and started the car.

"Where to?" he asked.

"Let's go over this list to see where everyone is this morning. Then we can divide it up."

He pulled away from the curb just as a campus security car was slowing down next to him. The campus security officer squinted hard at Nicholls as he smiled and waved at the officer.

"Did you see that moron? Trying to stare me down. Jesus, what an idiot. How did the widow take the news?"

"About as well as could be expected," Brodie said. "And either she doesn't know anything useful or she does and isn't telling."

Nicholls parked their car in the parking area reserved for

professors in the Science Quadrangle.

"We'll meet back here in about an hour unless one of us happens to trip over something promising. Remember we only have this week before everyone rabbits out of here for spring break. Work as fast as you can, but be thorough," Brodie instructed.

"Some of the kiddies may be leaving mid-week," Nicholls said. "It's pretty common for students to ditch classes the last two or three days before break begins."

"Well, maybe graduate students are a more dedicated bunch," she said as she looked around the parking area.

Nicholls and Maggie had lists with five names each on them. Except for Brauner's class, most of his graduate students didn't have many classes in common. Brodie decided to interview Tony Obregon first. The graduate assistant's background still bothered her even if Helen Brauner thought he was a born-again intellectual.

When she approached Brauner's office, the door was half open and the lights inside were on. She pushed the door open farther and saw a Hispanic male in his late twenties sitting at a desk in the front office looking over a stack of papers. Obregon looked up as the door opened. He was wearing cheap, black frame glasses and apparently hadn't bothered to shave in a day or two.

"Can I help you?" Obregon asked, looking over the top of his glasses.

"Are you Antonio Obregon?"

"Who wants to know?"

"Detective Lieutenant Brodie," she said flatly as she pulled her badge out.

"If you're here about Brauner I already told some chick from the police that I didn't know nothin'. Haven't seen the old man since last Wednesday or Thursday."

"Which was it? Wednesday or Thursday?" she asked as she entered the room and looked around.

"Brauner taught a class on Wednesday. I saw him then. I was in Thursday afternoon, but he wasn't here."

"So Wednesday was the last time you saw him?"

"Didn't I just say that?"

"Timing is very important in this case, so I'd appreciate it if you can be specific where times are concerned. Considering the experience you've had with the police in the past, I'm sure you can understand that, Tony."

Obregon pushed his chair back and got up to face her.

"You want somethin' specific from me, ask. Otherwise, get the fuck outta here. I got papers to grade and a lecture to prepare."

"You teaching Brauner's classes now?"

"Until you geniuses at the police department find him, yeah."

"We already found him, Tony. And he won't be back. He's dead."

For an instance she saw a flash of disbelief cross his face, but it disappeared as quickly as it appeared. In the years he had spent in and around gangs, he'd probably seen his share of people who died before they should have through no fault of their own.

"When?" he asked.

"I can't say much about the case right now, but we're questioning everyone associated with Brauner."

"There isn't nothin' I know that can help you, okay. I saw Brauner after his last class on Wednesday. I was back up here Thursday in the lab, but I didn't see him."

"What were you doing in the lab?"

"Brauner had been bustin' my chops about my research project. Thought I wasn't spendin' enough time watchin' germs grow."

"Was that what you argued with him about on Wednesday?"

Obregon laughed humorlessly. "That other lady cop tell you that?"

"Did you argue with Brauner about the project?" she asked again, ignoring his question.

"Yeah, we discussed it."

"The way I hear it, it was a little more than a discussion."

"Okay, I got steamed at him and we had a few words. The old bastard thought he was Jesus Christ on a stick and everyone around him was expected to be a dedicated disciple. Unfortunately, I ain't perfect. I'm smart, but he thought I wasn't being dedicated enough, so I told him to get off my back about it. We might have gotten a little loud, but it wasn't no big deal, okay."

"Guess he must have been hard to work for."

"But I only got this year to go and then I'll be away from him."

"Looks like you got your wish a little sooner than you expected."

"Yeah, but I didn't have nothin' to do with his death. I hated his guts, okay, but I didn't kill him."

"I didn't say he was killed, Tony. I just said he was dead. Why do you think he was killed?"

"You ain't here checking out no traffic accident."

"You'd be surprised. Know anyone who'd want to see him dead?"

"Everyone who ever took his class. Check all them out and you'll be workin' this case until you retire."

"Ever hear anyone threaten him?"

"Not to his face, but there was plenty of mumblin' goin' on behind his back."

"Just sour grapes or the real deal?"

"Who the fuck knows?"

"Where were you Thursday evening, Tony?"

"Here until about six and after that I was fuckin' my old lady."

"And I suppose she'll back you up on that."

"What do you think?" he asked with a grin.

"Guess that depends on whether you're any good or not," she smiled back. "What's her name?"

"Rosa Delgado. She lives on McKinney in South Austin."

"You know her from your gang days?"

"She ain't connected with a gang. Works here at the university. In payroll."

"She know about your past?"

"Yeah, I told her."

"You grade all of Dr. Brauner's papers?"

"Most of them."

"Ever have anyone try to bribe you to change a grade?"

"All the fuckin' time."

"Ever do it behind Brauner's back?"

"Nope. Most of these little pricks ain't got enough money to make me change a grade. Buncha snotty, spoiled bastards who never worked for nothin' in their lives."

"I gather you don't care much for them."

"Must be why they made you a detective, huh? Those highly developed powers of deduction."

Brodie chuckled. "Is that Brauner's last exam?" she asked as she looked at the papers in front of Obregon.

"Yeah. Just gave it. Pathetic."

"Is it the one Brauner had made up?"

"No," he said with a grin. "I wrote this one. Brauner's wife asked me to."

"How'd they do?"

"Shitty so far. There's one or two who always do okay. The rest don't know shit."

"Sounds like you're as hard as Dr. Brauner."

"I know what he expects them to know, that's all."

"Did anyone seem upset about the exam? Complain that it wasn't what they expected. Anything like that."

"I didn't hear anything, but I pretty much ignore it when they bitch about the exams."

"Anything else you can think of I might need to know?" she said, closing her notepad.

"No," he answered. "That it?"

"For now, but I assume you'll be around if I need to talk to you again."

"I'm going out of town for a few days during spring break, but

I'll be around. Have to keep an eye on my bacteria," Obregon smirked.

She turned to leave as he sat back down at his desk. "By the way, Lieutenant, you might want to talk to Dr. Roth."

"Why's that?"

"I don't know exactly. But him and Brauner had some serious discussions the last couple of weeks."

"They argue?"

"Not that I heard, but the old man always closed the door when Roth showed up and I thought Roth looked a little shook up the last time he was here. Came out of the office all kinda sweaty and nervous. Brauner never said anything to me, but Roth looked like a kid that just got caught whackin' off by his mama."

She left Obregon grading papers and walked down the hall until she found Roth's office. She didn't knock on the door, but turned the doorknob and walked in. Daryll Chambers looked up from his computer keyboard and frowned. *The woman from the bar. This couldn't get any better.*

"Need something?" he asked.

"I'm looking for Dr. Roth. He in?"

"Not unless you have an appointment. Dr. Roth doesn't do walk-ins."

She pulled her badge out again and showed it to the young man. "Maybe he'll make an exception this time."

He got up from his desk. "I'll check, officer." He knocked lightly on the door to Roth's inner sanctum and then entered. A minute later he came out and held the door open for her. As she entered the office, she turned to Chambers. "You're one of Dr. Brauner's students, aren't you?"

"Well, yes, I am. Why?"

"I'll need to talk to you when I'm finished here. Don't disappear."

She closed the door to Roth's office behind her and turned to face the professor.

"Dr. Roth, Lieutenant Brodie, Cedar Springs Police Department. I'd like to ask you a few questions."

Roth was standing behind his desk and motioned a thin white arm toward a chair facing his desk. She sat down and pulled her notebook from her jacket pocket.

"What can I do for you, Lieutenant Brodie?" he asked with a smile as he sat down.

"I'm investigating the death of Dr. Elliott Brauner. I understand the two of you were friends as well as colleagues."

"My, God! Elliott's dead?" he asked. He looked stunned as he tried to digest the news. He leaned back in his chair and closed his eyes for a moment. "When?"

"I'm afraid I can't give any details right now, Professor. Would you mind answering a few questions?"

"Of course not. Poor Helen. How did she take the news?"

"As well as can be expected. When was the last time you saw Dr. Brauner?"

Roth rubbed his forehead before answering. "Must have been Wednesday afternoon sometime, but I don't remember the exact time. After my last class so probably around four-thirty."

"Did you discuss anything in particular or was it just a visit?"

"He sent me a note saying he needed to talk to me and asked me to meet him in his office after my class."

"What did he want to talk about, Dr. Roth?"

"It was sort of a personal matter."

"His or yours?"

"Actually, it's a little embarrassing."

"Considering the circumstances, I'm afraid you'll have to be more specific."

Roth took a deep breath and exhaled loudly. "Are you familiar with publish or perish, Lieutenant?"

"Vaguely."

"Well, it means that every faculty member is expected to produce something, an article, a book, a research project, in their field every couple of years. Without publishing, even a tenured professor can lose their job. I hadn't published anything for a while and am facing a deadline to get something written."

When she didn't say anything, he continued. "It's a stupid policy and if you look at some of the crap that gets published, you'd have to laugh. Pure shit. Just anything to get in print and preserve their tenure. And nobody reads it. Not even others in the same field. They know it's shit just to cover your ass."

"And were you getting ready to publish?"

"Yeah, I was working on something. Somehow Elliott read a copy of it and that's what he wanted to talk to me about."

"Did he have a problem with it?"

Roth coughed nervously. "Look, Lieutenant, I'm a good teacher, but I don't have time for some bullshit writing that no one but the higher-ups care about. I told Brauner that."

"How about if you just cut to the chase and tell me what the problem was Dr. Roth?"

"Some of the material wasn't mine. I sort of plagiarized from some old tract I found buried in the library archives. Brauner was probably the only person on the planet who had read the original except the moron who wrote it. He called me on it in his office."

"Was he planning to report it?"

"He said he wasn't, but he wanted me to take out the parts I'd lifted."

"And did you agree to do that?"

"Well, I didn't have much of a choice, now did I?"

"What would happen if Brauner had reported the plagiarism?"

"Adios amigo," Roth said with a shrug.

"Would it be fair to say your academic career would be over?"

"That sums it up pretty well," he said as he looked at her. "Sounds rather like a motive, doesn't it?"

"Sure does, sir."

"Lieutenant Brodie," Roth said leaning forward on his desk. "I've done a lot of things in my life I'm not particularly proud of, mostly in my youth. But I have *never* harmed another person. An original card carrying member of the peace and love generation. Even if Elliott had waited until my piece was published and then exposed me as a plagiarist, I would have understood. Elliott Brauner is...was a pure scientist, a dedicated researcher and I admired him for those qualities. He wasn't an outgoing man, but the fact that he offered me the chance to rectify my plagiarism showed he wasn't the heartless ogre most people believed him to be. It was as close to a demonstration of friendship as he ever got."

"Did you eliminate the plagiarized parts of your paper?"

"No," Roth said as he brushed a string of hair out of his face. "I've abandoned that article and started a new one. This one is also shit, but it's all my own shit."

She smiled slightly, remembering how she had skirted the edges of plagiarism herself as a college student. She always figured the professors knew, but hadn't gotten too worked up over beginner undergraduate papers. In a way she sympathized with Roth's situation. She wondered who would check his paper for plagiarism now that Brauner was dead. She closed her notebook and stood as she stuffed it back in her jacket pocket.

"I trust you'll be around if I have any further questions, Dr. Roth."

"Of course, Lieutenant. If I'm not here in my office, I'm in the book."

"Not planning to get away for spring break?"

"I'd love to, but unfortunately the kiddies at home are still in school. And I do have that paper to write."

"What's your assistant's name? Chambers?"

"Daryll Chambers. You need to talk to him, too?"

"We're talking to all the graduate students in Dr. Brauner's classes. See if any of them noticed anything unusual before his disappearance."

"Frankly, Lieutenant, most of these students don't notice much of anything except the clock and the opposite gender sitting next to them in class."

"How long has Chambers been your assistant?"

"Oh, not too long, but it seems like an eternity. Personnel sent him to me right before the Christmas break. He seemed all right at the time."

"Not working out for you?"

"Not working period. He's a coaster. He'll probably slide by and get hired by a mediocre little company to do mediocre work until he dies or finds some mediocre rich young thing willing to marry him."

"What do you know about his social life?"

"As little as possible. I don't mean to sound like a snob, but the sexual exploits and conquests of younger men tend to remind me of what I've lost with age, so I try to avoid finding out what I'm missing."

"I understand completely, Professor," she chuckled. "I appreciate your cooperation."

Roth walked around his desk and escorted her to the door of the office. "Please let me know if there's anything I can do, Lieutenant."

As she left Roth's office, Daryll Chambers was on the phone and, from what she could overhear, she speculated he was arranging a date for the weekend. When he saw her, he made a quick apology to whoever was at the other end of the line and promised to call back. As he hung up the phone, he swiveled his chair around to face her.

"Do you have a few minutes, Mr. Chambers?" she asked.

"Sure. Please. Have a seat, ma'am."

There was something in the way Chambers said "ma'am" that suddenly made her feel old.

"You'll be finding out soon anyway, so I'm going to tell you up front that Dr. Brauner is dead. Would you mind answering a few questions, Mr. Chambers?"

"Jesus, what happened?" he asked, surprise in his voice. "We've all been wondering where he was. The last exam we took didn't seem quite right somehow."

"In what way?" she asked, her interest suddenly piqued by the mention of the exam.

"Don't get me wrong, it was still a difficult exam, but it didn't seem like something he had written. You get used to the way a professor phrases his questions after a while. Know what I mean? Do you think it was foul play?"

She smiled at the question. It sounded as if he had watched too many bad police movies. Not murdered or killed. Foul play.

"That's what we're trying to determine. How well did you know Dr. Brauner?"

"I don't know if anyone really knew him. Except his wife, of course. He is...was very highly regarded in his field. It's an accomplishment for a student to say they studied under Elliott Brauner."

"I've heard not many students manage to pass his courses."

Chambers laughed lightly, "I said it was an accomplishment, Detective. Dr. Brauner had very high expectations for his students."

"You're a student in his graduate class, aren't you?"

"Yes."

"And how're you doing?"

"I'm managing to keep my head above water so far. It's tough though."

"Separates the men from the boys, huh?" she asked with a smile.

"Yes, ma'am. It sure does."

"What about the other students in the class? How're they doing?"

"I don't know for sure, but I'd guess the majority are failing. Dr. Brauner has a very high failure rate."

"Anyone particularly upset about that failure rate?"

"At this point anyone would be upset if they were failing the class. It's required for the degree and there's only two or three months left before the end of the semester. If this was one of their last classes and they failed it, they'd have to stick around next fall and take it again. After all the money most of us have invested in our educations, further delay just means more money and possibly the loss of a job offer at the end of the semester."

"You got anything lined up yet?

"I've got a few feelers out and a couple look promising. In fact, I have an interview during spring break with a pharmaceutical company back East."

"Well, good luck, if that's what you want."

"Yeah, I'd be happy if I could get something close to home."

"You're not from around here?"

"No, ma'am. My family lives in upstate New York."

"And you came all the way to Cedar Springs for a graduate degree? I heard the universities back East were pretty good."

He laughed again. "Yes, they are, but I did my undergraduate work and some graduate work back there. Got a little tired of the scenery. Plus, even if I have to pay out-of-state fees, it's still cheaper to go to school down here."

"Don't tell the state legislature that or they'll raise their fees."

Chambers smiled and nodded at her. "Uh, can I get you a cup of coffee or something?"

"No, thanks. Have you ever had any disagreements with Dr. Brauner as a result of his class?"

"No. I try to keep as low a profile as possible. If Brauner told me to get on my hands and knees and bark like a dog, I'd do it, just to get out of the class unscathed. It's a game, but sooner or later, everyone has to learn to play it."

"What game is that?"

"The academic survival game. Do whatever you have to do to survive and then move on to the next challenge."

"Sounds like a plan. You told Detective Weston a couple of days ago that you overheard an argument between Dr. Brauner and his assistant. Is that correct?"

"I overheard what *sounded* like an argument to me. But they could have just been talking loudly."

"Did Dr. Brauner have a hearing problem?"

"Not that I'm aware of."

"Could you hear what they were saying?"

"No. Just the sounds of their voices from inside Brauner's office. I wasn't eavesdropping. I just happened to be passing by when I heard them."

"Why are you so sure it was Brauner and Obregon? Couldn't it have been Brauner and another person? Like Dr. Roth, for instance."

"It couldn't have been Dr. Roth, Lieutenant. He was in class at the time. And before I could even get to our office here, I heard a door slam and saw Tony come around the corner. He looked upset and was saying something about Dr. Brauner being a stupid old fucker. I guess I just drew the assumption that he was the one in Dr. Brauner's office."

"Sounds logical enough. What do you know about Obregon?"

"Not much there either. I'm afraid I'm not being very helpful."

"That's okay. Just tell me what you do know."

"Actually, Tony's a good graduate assistant for Dr. Brauner. Neither of them is very social. And Tony's lucky to have an assistantship. He doesn't have any money and probably wouldn't be here without financial help."

"He'd have to leave school if he didn't have his job?"

"Probably, but I don't know anything about his personal finances. He could have saved up enough to finish the semester, I suppose. But from the way he dresses and that hunk of junk van he drives, I seriously doubt it."

"So you don't socialize with the other graduate assistants?"

"I didn't say that. I just don't socialize with Tony. Most of the graduate assistants get along and try to help each other out. But Tony never wants anything to do with the rest of us. Never even attended any of the parties we throw periodically. A real loner. Might be some of that Hispanic macho bullshit I've heard about. He always acts like a tough guy. Kind of a bully." Chambers leaned forward conspiratorially. "I've heard he has a police record, but it's only a rumor. If it's true, he'll have a hard time finding a good position once he graduates."

"Maybe his academic record will help him overcome that."

Chambers shrugged, "Maybe, but he still needs to learn how to play the game, Lieutenant."

BRODIE WAS LEANING against the car when she saw Nicholls and Maggie coming toward her. The temperature had risen and she knew it wouldn't be long before the heat and humidity reached a level where she wouldn't want to wear her jacket any more. As she looked around the campus, students strolled between buildings or cruised by on bicycles. She always loved being on the campus and wondered if the students she saw realized they were in the best time of their lives. There was so much to be learned and she regretted not having realized it sooner in her own life. Now she had to satisfy herself with an occasional course in night school just to keep her hand in.

Nicholls was laughing as he and Maggie reached her. "What's so funny?" she asked.

"Nothing. We were just comparing notes on how some of the folks on our lists took being dragged out of class and questioned by the police," he answered with a smile.

"Find out anything interesting?"

"Only if you're interested in who's doin' marijuana or who's bangin' who," he said. "Scared the hell out of most of mine. Probably never even had a parking ticket before, let alone been questioned about a homicide."

"One of mine wanted to know how Brauner's death was going to affect his grade," Maggie added. "Finally decided it couldn't make his grade any worse than it already was."

"Sounds real choked up about losing his professor," Brodie said as she slid into the front passenger seat.

"Didn't question anyone who got depressed when they heard about it," Nicholls said as he turned the key in the ignition.

"So how many do we have left to interview?" Brodie asked.

"We've got a couple left on each list. If they're not at their addresses, then they're probably about ready to hit the beaches at Padre by now. We can check the addresses after lunch and if they're not in, we'll have to catch them when the session resumes," Nicholls said.

"I think most of them are going to be a dead end anyway," Maggie said as she settled in the back seat.

"Why's that?" Brodie asked as she turned to look at her.

"From the reactions I got. None of them denied hating Brauner, but they all seemed genuine in their disbelief that he was dead."

"Probably genuine disbelief at their good fortune. Anyone have anything to say about the last exam?" Brodie asked.

Nicholls and Maggie both said they hadn't heard any complaints.

NICHOLLS PULLED THE car into the parking lot of Swanson's on Central Boulevard. The small family-owned diner was almost full by the time they arrived, but they assured Maggie the food would be worth the wait. Most of the lunch customers had already been seated by the hostess and they only had to wait a few minutes before a large woman dressed in a denim skirt and western blouse approached them. She grabbed three menus from a rack and smiled.

"Usual place, Lieutenant?"

"Or as close as you can get to it, Ruthie," the detective answered with a warm smile.

They followed the woman as she made her way through the tables with an ease that showed she'd had plenty of practice at running the obstacle course of tables and customers. She climbed the four steps into another room and set three menus at a booth table near the back of the smoky room.

"Take your time, folks. I'll be back with your water in a minute."

The booth had well-worn red vinyl seats and a plastic red and white checkered tablecloth over the table. A small jukebox hung on the wall next to the table. Maggie looked around and noticed a similar jukebox at each table. She glanced at the selections available on the jukebox and saw that there was nothing newer than the seventies on the machine. Even if the food was horrible, she knew Royce would be a regular customer due to the restaurant's smoking section, as well as the music. The dining room was decorated with old license plates representing every state. One wall was completely covered by a sign for motor oil. It was a brand she had never heard of, but she guessed it had once been a popular brand. In the middle of the room was a salad bar with a large assortment of raw vegetables, cheeses and other ingredients for making a salad. Two large metal containers of steaming soup sat on one end of the salad bar.

Brodie had already closed her menu by the time Ruthie returned with their water.

"Are you ready to order or do you need a few more minutes to decide?" the waitress asked with a smile.

"I'll take the chicken fried steak, Ruthie," Brodie said.

"You want the usual with it?"

"Yeah, that's good."

Ruthie scribbled on her order pad and looked at Nicholls and Maggie.

"Go ahead, Nicholls," Maggie said.

"I think I'll give the catfish a whirl. And I'll have the coleslaw and hush puppies with it. Tea, and can I get a couple of extra pieces of lemon on the side?"

"Sure thing," she said writing. "And how about you, dear?"

"Ruthie, this is Detective Weston. She's new and this is her first time at Swanson's," Brodie said, as she lit a cigarette. She saw the look of disapproval in Maggie's eyes. She had convinced Brodie to stop smoking when they first met, but it had been an easy habit to fall back into without Maggie there to support her.

"Well, welcome to Cedar Springs, Detective. I hope you can stand working with these two clowns. Don't let 'em run you ragged. What can I get you today?"

"The chicken fried steak sounds good. With mashed potatoes and a small salad."

"Tea?"

"Yes, please."

Ruthie picked up the menus. "These'll be ready in just a few minutes. Enjoy."

They smiled at Ruthie and leaned back in the booth.

"Did anyone you talked to know Garcia?" Brodie asked as she exhaled a cloud of cigarette smoke.

"I got the idea not many of them associated with the janitorial staff," Nicholls said. "They might know his face if they saw it, but no one seemed to be on a first name basis with the guy."

"Same here," Maggie said. "If he worked evenings, it's unlikely they would see him unless they happened to be working in a lab where he was cleaning up. Even then janitors seem to be a part of that invisible group people know are around, but generally ignore. They see them without actually seeing them."

"Who did you interview?" Nicholls asked, glancing at his partner.

"Saw Obregon first, then Roth and his assistant. No love lost between Obregon and the other graduate assistants apparently. But I did find out that Roth could have had a motive."

"Really?" Maggie said.

"Yeah, seems Brauner caught him plagiarizing in an article he was writing and called him on it. He claims to have written another article and dropped the plagiarized one."

"Publish or perish?" Nicholls asked.

"Yeah."

"Think it's enough to make Roth a good suspect?"

"It's as good a reason as any. Roth could have lost everything if

Brauner turned him in."

"What about the exams that were tampered with?" Maggie inquired.

"Obregon claims he wouldn't lift a finger to help out the other graduate students. And I believed him."

"Still money can be a pretty powerful motivator," Nicholls said.

"How much you think a copy of the exam could go for? A hundred bucks? You'd have to be desperate for money to sell something worth as little as that," Brodie said.

"It could be worth a lot more than that if you had a graduate degree riding on passing the class," Maggie said. "He could have asked for more and probably gotten it."

"But if the graduate students dislike Obregon as much as he dislikes them, they might think it was a better idea to pay him some money and then turn him in and get rid of him," Brodie said.

"So you think someone decided to save a few bucks, became a do-it-yourselfer and it got screwed up," Nicholls said.

"Possibly. But if it was one of Brauner's students they had to have been fairly desperate to pass to risk getting caught like that."

Ruthie returned with a large tray containing their food and placed the plates in front of each of them.

"Anything else I can get you?" she asked.

"Looks fine, Ruthie," Brodie said. "Thanks."

"Wave if you need something," she said, picking up the tray to leave.

They ate in silence for a while, all beginning quickly and gradually slowing down to a more leisurely pace. Maggie took a long drink of her tea and paused between bites.

"This is really good chicken fried steak," she said as she cut another bite.

"Best in town," Brodie said. "Specialty of the house."

Nicholls popped the last bite of catfish into his mouth and leaned back in the booth. "Well, what's the plan for this afternoon, boss?"

"Finish interviewing the kids we can find and then go over our notes and see if anything jumps up and bites us on the butt, I guess. Are we waiting for anything else to come in from the lab?"

"We're still working on the preliminary reports on Garcia, but I don't think there'll be anything new or exciting in the final report," Maggie said.

"Have we found anyone who saw Garcia after he left his home Thursday?"

"When I talked to his supervisor, he said he saw Garcia clock in and didn't see him again after his shift." Maggie said.

"What time was that?" Brodie asked.

"A little before five Thursday afternoon."

"Do we have an approximate time for Brauner's death?"

"Mrs. Brauner said he left home between seven and seven-thirty Thursday evening to pick up something at his office."

"If Brauner was killed the same evening, then our guy must have been a busy boy. There's only three and a half hours between the last time anyone saw Garcia and the time Mrs. Brauner last saw her husband," Nicholls said.

"This is ridiculous," Brodie said. "It's barely dark at seven-thirty or eight o'clock. It was a weeknight. There had to have been people around. Someone must have seen something, even if they didn't realize it at the time."

Chapter
Eight

BRODIE WATCHED NICHOLLS and Maggie leave the squad room the next afternoon and pulled her notebook from her jacket pocket to review the notes she had taken over the last few days. Halfway through her notes on Obregon, Maggie walked back into the squad room and threw her purse down on her desk.

Brushing her hair back with both hands, she asked, "Know any good mechanics?"

"Try Frankie over at Cedar Springs Automotive. I've used him once or twice."

Maggie pulled a phone directory from her desk drawer and started dialing. She glanced at her watch as she waited for someone to pick up the phone.

"Yeah, is Frankie there? This is Detective Weston at Cedar Springs Police Department. Thanks."

She tapped her fingers on the desk and waited a few more minutes.

"Come on," she said. Finally, Frankie answered the phone.

"How can I help you, Detective?"

"My car seems to have died and Detective Brodie recommended you. Would it be possible for you to take a look at it?"

"It's getting late, but I can probably swing by there on my way home. Say about a half hour or forty-five minutes."

"Fine."

"I can't promise to get her runnin', but I'll look at her."

Maggie placed the receiver in its cradle and rested her elbows on the desk.

"I gather your car bit the dust," Brodie said as she read her notes.

"It was on its last legs, but I hoped it would hang in there until I got a few dollars ahead."

"Well, if it can be resuscitated, Frankie will do it. Fairly reasonable price usually."

She picked up a folder and tossed it on Maggie's desk. "Look through that again to kill time."

An hour later Frankie reported that Maggie's car would need intensive care and wouldn't be going anywhere except his repair shop that evening. He would tow it to the garage and try to work it in the next day, but he couldn't make any promises about when it would be ready. As soon as Maggie's car was attached to Frankie's tow truck, Brodie offered to drive her home.

MAGGIE LIVED IN a one-story duplex in a relatively quiet neighborhood not far from the university. Not exactly upscale living, but it looked like a safe enough place. It was a red brick building with a flat roof. Flowers had been planted along the walk leading to the front door and the lawn was mowed and neatly trimmed. A homemade slat privacy fence separated her half of the building from the other occupant who she said was a priest at the local Catholic church.

"How are you getting to work tomorrow?" Brodie asked.

"I'll call one of my brothers if they're still talking to me. One of the four is bound to have an extra car he can loan me until I get mine back. I can make some coffee if you'd like to come in," Maggie offered.

"I should be getting home, but thanks anyway."

"I thought it might give us a chance to talk a little," Maggie said.

"Except for work, there isn't much we need to talk about," Brodie said with a shrug.

Maggie was beginning to feel uncomfortable and she cleared her throat. Looking at Brodie from the corner of her eye, she said, "I'd like to clear the air between us."

"I let go of the past a long time ago."

"I haven't," Maggie said softly. She waited until Brodie looked at her. "What happened between us after Stan was killed wasn't your fault, Royce."

When Maggie saw Brodie's face darken, she continued. "My father said and did some horrible things to you, but not everyone believed what he said."

Brodie swallowed hard. "Enough did."

Suddenly, the car seemed warmer to Brodie and she was desperate to separate from Maggie. "I have to go," she said abruptly in a hoarse voice that threatened to betray her thoughts.

"I'm sorry I hurt you," Maggie said.

Brodie looked at Maggie, the hurt showing in her eyes. "I did exactly what you told me to do. I sobered up and got on with my life," she said, her tone biting. "So just drop it, okay."

"Please, Royce," she said.

Too much bitterness still lived deep with Brodie.

"What happened eight years ago was my fault. No one else's. No one forced me to drink to drown my problems. No one made me hi...hit you. I hurt you. I was the only one responsible for that. You did the right thing when you kicked me out."

"I'm sorry," Maggie said, leaning back against the car seat.

Chapter
Nine

THEY COULD HEAR the roar of planes taking off and landing as they stepped out of their vehicle at the Austin airport and stretched. The pungent smell of airplane fuel and exhaust hung over the parking lot. Hundreds of people were going in and out of the automatic doors leading to the terminals of over a dozen airlines. Skycaps whistled for taxis and loaded and unloaded baggage from rows of cars temporarily stopped in front of each terminal entrance.

"What are we looking for?" Nicholls asked.

"I'm not really sure," Brodie said as she looked around.

There were nearly a hundred cars parked in the executive long-term parking area. Most of them looked as if they belonged to people who earned a lot more money than the two detectives combined.

She hadn't been to the new Austin airport since it was moved to the old Bergstrom Air Force Base. Ruling out writing down the license plate numbers of all the cars in long-term and executive long-term parking as an exercise in futility, she decided to speak to whoever was in charge of parking in general and was directed to the office for airport security.

They were greeted by a military-looking older man whose desk plate identified him as George Jackson, Chief of Security. As soon as they were seated across from Jackson's desk, he smiled, "What can I do for you, detectives?"

"A car was stolen from your executive parking area about a week ago," Brodie explained. "The same vehicle was later involved in a homicide in Cedar Springs. The owner didn't report it missing until he returned from an out-of-town business trip. We need a few facts about your procedures for vehicles entering and leaving your parking areas."

"You'll have our full cooperation, Detective Brodie. What do you need to know?"

"When a vehicle enters your parking area what kind of security is there?"

"The driver takes a ticket from an automated system and parks. When the vehicle is reclaimed the driver stops at a toll booth and pays whatever the fee is for the length of time the vehicle was here."

"But the booth tellers assume that the driver is the owner of the vehicle, correct?"

"Pretty much. We don't cross check vehicle registration and driver's licenses."

"Would someone be able to walk into the parking area and steal a car?" Nicholls asked. "Do you have roving security in the parking areas?"

"Yes, but we rely primarily on video cameras which sweep the areas."

"We'll need to see all your tapes for the last week," Brodie said.

Jackson punched a button on his desk phone. "Just for executive parking?" he asked.

"Unfortunately, we'll need the videos for all the parking areas," Brodie frowned.

"Y'all are gonna need a super-sized bottle of No-Doze," Jackson chuckled.

After he completed his phone call, Brodie asked, "Is there any chance a vehicle might be abandoned in airport parking?"

"Rarely," he shrugged. "If a vehicle has been parked two weeks, we request a DMV check for the owner and attempt to contact them. Usually, if travelers are going to be gone longer than that, they take a cab to the airport to avoid the parking fees which can get pretty steep after about a week."

More than an hour passed before Brodie and Nicholls returned to their car. They had been handed a box containing more than fifty security videos.

"Well, this should kill the rest of the month," Nicholls said.

"You're always telling me how great technology is."

"Okay, okay. I knew my words would come back to bite me in the ass one of these days."

"Guess I'm frustrated because we don't have much to go on in this case," she said as she pulled a pack of cigarettes from her jacket pocket and shook one out.

"Maybe we'll get lucky with these videos," Nicholls said as he put the car into reverse. "Maybe Maggie'll turn up something in the files."

Brodie laughed. "We're supposed to be professional investigators, dealing in facts. But lately 'maybe' seems to be our favorite word."

"If we get really desperate, I have an old Ouija board someplace."

NICHOLLS LEANED BACK in his chair and rubbed his eyes. "Jesus, RB, this is less exciting than watching paint peel."

They had been watching cars come and go for nearly three

hours. Brodie looked at her watch. "Well, I think I've had enough for today, kiddies. Probably a wild goose chase anyway."

"Free at last, free at last!" Nicholls said as he stood up. "Thank you, massah."

"I can watch some at home where I can kick back and relax," Maggie offered.

"Go for it," Brodie said as she stretched.

"Jenkins left his car in executive parking Sunday afternoon and it became rubble Thursday night. If I had to take a guess, I'd bet it wasn't stolen until sometime late Thursday. Our doer probably wasn't expecting to have to dispose of multiple bodies. That's less than twenty-four hours of video tape" Maggie shrugged. "It's as good a place to start as any. Besides, department insurance pays for work related injuries, right?"

"What work-related injury?" Nicholls asked.

"Going blind from staring at these tapes comes to mind." Maggie said as she picked out tapes covering the times in question.

Brodie and Nicholls laughed in spite of themselves.

MAGGIE POURED A cup of coffee and sat down heavily at her desk early the following morning, pushing her hair back with her hand.

"Long night?" Nicholls asked with a smile.

Turning her head slightly toward him, she said, "Yeah, I spent an exciting evening watching America's Most Boring Security Tapes. Remind me not to volunteer for shit like that again."

"It was a long shot at best," Brodie said.

Reaching into her purse, Maggie held up a single video. "But not a total waste of time and sleep," she announced with a grin.

"What's that?" Nicholls asked.

"Excerpts showing Jenkins' car and a van that could have been used to transport a body to the airport," she answered as she sipped her coffee.

"You have got to be kidding!" Brodie said as she sat up in her chair.

"Do the bags under my eyes look like I'm kidding?" Maggie retorted.

"Show us," Brodie said.

The three detectives took the tape to an interrogation room with a video player and switched on the television. Maggie took the remote control and stood next to the television as the tape began.

"I copied the pertinent parts of the security tapes to save time." Less than a minute into the tape she paused the video.

"This shows the Jenkins car when it was parked at 1545 the

Sunday before the murders," she explained as Jenkins removed a suitcase from the trunk and rolled it toward the terminal.

"Well, it was a nice looking car at one time," Nicholls commented.

"The next clip shows the vehicle being removed," Maggie continued as she pressed the play button. Obviously a night shot, the picture became grainier as they observed a figure approach the car and, after looking briefly around the parking area, slide something alongside the driver's side window. "Looks like he used a slim jim to open the door. This particular tape was made Thursday evening at approximately 2015. Fortunately for the perp and unfortunately for Mr. Jenkins, the vehicle was surrounded by rather large trucks or SUVs which obscured ground security from noticing anything unusual," Maggie went on.

"And obviously no one was watching the television screens in security," Brodie observed.

"I checked the security tapes for vehicles leaving executive parking and put together the remainder of the tape." Although the tape was a little jumpy from the starts and stops of the dubbing, they watched as the Jenkins car exited the parking area and stopped at a tollbooth.

"Long-term parking is to the left of executive parking," Maggie explained. "So I guess this last part is worth one sleepless night."

The Jenkins vehicle was picked up by another security camera as it moved into long-term parking and came to a stop behind a light-colored van. As they leaned closer to the television screen, the driver exited the car and opened the rear of the van. In less than two minutes the van door closed and the Mercedes pulled away. Maggie stopped the tape while Brodie and Nicholls looked at each other.

"Guess Maggie'll be getting an okay evaluation, huh?" Nicholls said.

"Looks like," Brodie said. "It also looks like we'd better get back to the airport and find that van. Too bad we can't tell anything about the person who took Mr. Jenkins' car, but we can't have everything."

"I can send the tape over to the lab and see if they can enlarge and enhance those parts of the tape," Nicholls offered.

"Can't hurt, but this guy covered himself pretty well," Brodie shrugged as she stood up. "We'll meet you at the car, Nicholls."

An hour later, accompanied by airport security, they approached an older, rusting tan Dodge van with a cracked windshield sitting in long-term parking. Before they left Cedar Springs, Brodie requested and was granted a warrant to search the van and seize anything incriminating it might contain. After handing the warrant to the security officers, she tried the driver's door and found it unlocked.

"Obviously not worried about anyone stealing this POS," Nicholls said.

Brodie glanced around the interior of the van without touching anything. "It's been hot wired," she said over her shoulder. "Don't see much in the front. The son of a bitch probably didn't leave clue one. Check the back, Maggie."

Maggie opened the doors to the cargo area and used a flashlight to inspect it as closely as possible. "A couple of dark spots that could be blood," she reported. "Looks like something was dragged across the carpet back here from front to back, too."

"How can you tell that?" Nicholls asked as he peered into the cargo area.

"It's a woman thing." Maggie smiled. "The carpet looks relatively new. The fibers in this area are brushed toward the back doors while along the sides the fibers are either straight up and down or brushed toward the front of the van."

"Well, how about that shit!" he said.

"You need to vacuum more often," Brodie said. "Call the plates in to DMV and find out who the lucky owner is."

As Nicholls turned to call in the license plate, she added, "And contact the lab to have this vehicle towed to the impound lot for a closer exam."

Nicholls nodded and trotted to their car. Brodie joined Maggie at the rear of the van. "Good work, Maggie," Brodie said. "Damn good."

Maggie blushed slightly and glanced at her. Royce was finally using her first name. "Thank you."

"Tow truck's on the way, RB," Nicholls said when he rejoined them. "And the owner is listed as none other than Antonio Obregon. He filed a stolen vehicle report last Friday morning."

"Obregon is Brauner's assistant at the university," she said as she squinted at the sky.

"He didn't say anything about his vehicle being stolen when I interviewed him," Maggie said.

"He didn't mention it when I spoke to him either," she frowned. "It's possible he didn't connect his stolen vehicle with Brauner's death. Cars are stolen every day."

"It's possible he reported it stolen to cover himself if he's our perp. We'll need to speak to him again."

"So what's the plan now?" Nicholls asked.

"You wait here. Go to impound and stick with the lab guys when they go over the van. Contact us if anything earthshaking turns up. Maggie, you and I are going back to the university to ask Mr. Obregon a few more questions."

BRODIE SHIFTED THE Camaro into park near the Science Quad. She got out of the car and stopped to lean against the front of the vehicle.

"What did you think about Obregon when you interviewed him the first time?" she asked.

"A little hostile, but no more than anyone else with his background."

"He probably hasn't had many pleasant encounters with the police in the past," Brodie said as she turned her head to look at Maggie. "Tell you what. I want you to go up and interview him again...alone."

Maggie looked puzzled. "What are you going to do?"

"When I talked to him he said his girlfriend worked in payroll. I'll check her out and see what she has to say about the van and about Obregon. She shouldn't be expecting the police and maybe she'll drop something unintentionally."

"You don't really think he killed Brauner, do you?"

"He may have been a gang member, but none of this looks like a gang killing to me. You ever see any Austin gangs try to cover up a killing by burning a body or dissecting it?"

"It wouldn't be your typical gang killing. Most of the gang related deaths I saw were usually over some misguided point of honor and left where Helen Keller could have found them."

"Just feel him out to see if there was something, even something trivial and seemingly unimportant, that he might have noticed about Brauner or Garcia. I'll meet you here in about an hour."

WHEN MAGGIE REACHED Brauner's office, the door was unlocked and she found Obregon sitting at his desk jotting notes onto a legal pad. He looked up when the door opened. Removing his glasses and leaning back in his well-worn chair, he sighed.

"What can I do for you today, Detective? More questions about stuff I don't know nothin' about?"

"Well, I was hoping you would know something about your van," she said as she glanced around the office. The door into Brauner's office was open.

"Mrs. Brauner gave me access to his office and files," he stated before she could ask. "If they expect me to teach this class, I have to be able to get to the doc's files."

"Sounds reasonable." She smiled. "Now about your van..."

"What about it? I reported it stolen already. Not like the Austin PD placed it at the top of their priority list."

"We found it," she said. "It was in long-term parking at the airport."

"No shit!" he laughed.

"When was the last time you saw it?"

"The night Brauner went missing. I was with my old lady and when I left the next morning the hunk of junk was gone."

"Not a safe neighborhood, I gather."

"Some *pendejo* must have been desperate for a ride to want that piece of shit. No self-respecting gang member would be caught dead in it. I figured some kid took it for a joy ride and the damn thing broke down again."

"There were a couple of spots that looked like dried blood in the cargo area. Any thoughts about that?"

"Nope. If there was blood there at some time it coulda been from before I bought it."

"How long have you owned it?"

"Maybe a year, year and a half. It rolled and passed inspection, which was all I cared about."

"How are the classes going?" Maggie asked, changing the subject.

"Pretty hard to believe most of these idiots made it into graduate school."

"Keeping up Brauner's high standards, I presume."

Obregon laughed easily. "Yeah, I guess so. They all thought Brauner was a mean sonuvabitch. Now he's been replaced by an even meaner motherfucker."

Maggie had to smile. "You know, Mr. Obregon, I thought you'd be a little more hostile about answering more questions from the police."

"Why?" he shrugged. Leaning forward and resting his forearms on the desk, he studied his hands for a moment before speaking. "I had a long talk with Helen...Dr. Brauner. She's a real class act, ya know? Told me a lot of stuff I didn't know, about her and the doc. I'll be receiving my Ph.D. in Microbiology in another couple of months. Dr. Brauner, the old man, actually recommended me for a teaching position that's coming vacant at his alma mater. Can you believe that shit?"

"Congratulations," Maggie smiled. "You planning to take it?"

"What kind of fool would turn down a position at Columbia? It's a chance to leave my past behind. A new start."

"I hope you're half the teacher Dr. Brauner was."

"Yeah, me too, Detective," he smiled.

"I'll let you know when you can pick up your van from the impound lot. Looks like you're going to need it since you're planning to move."

Despite the fact she was usually cynical about people, she was glad things were working out for Tony Obregon. He had broken away from the gang mold and his future looked promising.

"If you think of anything you think we should know concerning either the theft of your van or Dr. Brauner's death...," she began.

"I'll give you a call." He smiled slightly. "I hope you catch whoever killed the doc."

"Eventually we will, I'm sure," she said as she left the small office.

Since she had completed her interview fairly quickly, Maggie found a bench in the shade outside the Biology Building and sat down. Pulling her notebook from her shoulder bag, she was glancing over her notes from interviews when her thoughts were interrupted.

"Making any progress, Detective Weston?" a man's voice said.

Looking up and squinting against the sunlight filtering through the trees, she saw Daryll Chambers and a young woman approaching the bench.

"Mr. Chambers," she said. "How are you?"

"Sweatin' the last couple of months," Chambers answered. "Leaving this weekend for a little trip."

"Going to the beach?"

"I wish," he said. "I have to fly back east for a job interview."

Maggie glanced at the young woman with Chambers. She was an attractive blonde with blue eyes. Every college man's dream, she thought.

"Oh, I'm sorry, Detective. This is Karen Dietrick," he said. "Karen, honey, this is one of the detectives working on the Brauner case, Detective Weston."

Maggie stood and shook hands with the young woman. "Are you a student at the university?" she asked.

"I'm in grad school here, but I work over in Admissions," the young woman offered.

"Are you graduating this year, too?"

"I have one more year to go. Hopefully it will go by as quickly as this year has because I'm more than ready to be out of school."

"I can understand that," Maggie smiled. As she looked toward the parking lot, she saw Royce striding toward their car. "Well, it looks like my ride is here," she said. "It was nice to see you again, Mr. Chambers, and good luck with your interview."

She extended her hand to Chambers. He seemed surprised by the gesture and as he took her hand, a set of keys fell to the ground between them. She squatted down and picked them up. Before she handed them back to him, she noticed a bright gold medallion attached to the key ring. Flipping it over, she examined it closely.

"This is beautiful," she said. "I noticed it the first time I interviewed you. Is it a religious medal?"

"Yeah," Chambers laughed lightly as he took the keys. "It was a gift from my mother. She thinks I need all the help I can get."

"Well, it's lovely. Where did your mother find it?"

"I think she picked it up when she was in Costa Rica last summer. Probably just a cheap trinket from some town market," he answered.

"It's supposed to be the thought that counts," she said as she began to walk away. "Have a safe trip."

"HOW DID THE interview with the girlfriend go?" Maggie asked as she buckled her seat beat.

"Actually, she seemed like a very nice lady," Brodie said as she turned the key in the ignition. "Naturally she confirmed everything we already knew about Obregon."

"He's been offered a teaching position at Columbia," Maggie said. "Seems Dr. Brauner had recommended him for an opening before he was killed. He'll be leaving in three or four months."

"Was that Roth's assistant you were talking to?" Brodie asked as she backed the Camaro out of its parking slot.

"Yeah. He's leaving this weekend for a job interview himself."

Brodie pulled a cell phone from her jacket pocket and handed it to Maggie. "Hit the speed dial and get hold of Nicholls. See if we need to pick him up."

BRODIE WAS AWAKENED from a sound sleep by an incessant ringing sound. It was dark outside and at first she thought it was the alarm clock. She turned her head and the red numbers showed one thirty-five. Suddenly she realized it was her telephone. She climbed groggily out of bed and made her way toward the living room, being careful not to trip over Max. She turned the switch on a table lamp near the phone and picked up the receiver.

"Brodie," she croaked, clearing her throat.

"RB, you better get over to Cedar Memorial right away."

"Who the hell is this?" she asked, holding the phone on her shoulder and rubbing her face as she spoke.

"It's Nicholls. Wake up, Brodie."

"What's going down at Cedar Memorial?"

"It already went down. Weston's been hurt. I don't know how serious it is, but an ambulance was dispatched to take her in. I got a call from the desk officer a few minutes ago."

"What..."

"I don't know what happened for sure yet, but the desk sergeant said she was assaulted."

"I'll meet you there," Brodie said.

She dressed quickly, pulling on old jeans and a t-shirt. Max followed her with his eyes without raising his head. He had become accustomed to late night calls.

She jumped in her Camaro and lit a cigarette, holding it tightly between her teeth as she backed out of the driveway and sped toward the hospital. She arrived in less than ten minutes and parked in the emergency room parking lot. They didn't appear to have many customers. She saw an ambulance backed into the emergency bay as she entered the automatic doors and approached the slightly overweight young woman seated at the triage desk. She had an attractive face that would have been more attractive with less makeup and less baby fat.

"You have Margaret Weston here?"

"Are you a relative, ma'am?"

She answered by pulling out her badge and flashing it at the clerk.

"Let me check, officer," the young woman said as she got up. She went to the doors leading to the treatment area and punched numbers into the security lock. In less than a minute she reappeared at the door and motioned for Brodie to enter.

"They brought her in a little while ago. She's in Treatment Room Four, but you won't be able to talk to her. She was unconscious and the doctor is with her now."

"How serious are her injuries?"

"I couldn't say," the clerk said. She looked around the treatment area and pointed. "There's the policeman who came in with the ambulance. You might talk to him."

"Okay, thanks. Listen, my partner should be arriving in a few minutes. Tall, handsome blond surfer type named Nicholls. Send him back, will you?"

The clerk nodded as Brodie crossed the treatment area toward the police officer. She recognized him as Patrolman Carl Adams. He was talking to a cute ambulance attendant who seemed to be hanging on his every word. Brodie had hated hospitals since she had been wounded. The antiseptic smells. The whispering voices. Everyone seemed to be going about their business without a sense of urgency, even when it was urgent. The treatment area had six identical rooms and the ones she passed were full of men, women, and children dressed in ill-fitting hospital gowns. From what she could see, it looked like the usual collection of croup and ear infections that kept parents up at night. Two of the patients looked healthy as horses and she wondered if they just didn't have any other way to kill an evening. Adams ended his conversation with the ambulance attendant when he saw her striding purposefully toward him.

"What're you doin' here, RB?"

"I was called about Maggie Weston. I'm her TO. What's the story?"

"Well, she got the shit beat out of her, that's for sure. I don't know how bad it is."

"Has anyone been arrested?"

"No. She managed to use her cell to dial 9-1-1, but was unconscious when we arrived at the scene."

"She's got parents in Westlake. Tell the desk sergeant to call them. The father's name is Timothy Weston. If he's not in the book, get the number from her personnel file."

Adams walked across the treatment area and pushed the doors open. On his way out he passed Nicholls.

"How is she, RB?"

"Don't know yet."

"What the hell happened?"

"Don't know that either. We won't know much until she's conscious."

The door to Treatment Room Four opened and a doctor came out. His hair was disheveled and he looked like he had been on the job way over eight hours. She estimated his age as younger than Maggie's. He pushed his glasses up and looked at the two staring at him.

"Are either of you a family member?" he asked.

"Police," Brodie said. "But I've sent for her parents. How is she?"

"She'll be all right in a few weeks. We're still waiting for a few tests to come back. She has a concussion and a slew of bruises. Her nose is fractured, as well as her left cheekbone, but they're hairline fractures. She took a pretty good thrashing, but it could have been worse. Lots of defensive injuries on her arms so she obviously put up quite a fight. We had to put in a few stitches, but there shouldn't be any permanent scarring."

"Can we talk to her?"

"Yeah, but not too long. I had to sedate her. Once she regained consciousness, she became pretty agitated."

Brodie turned to her partner. "Tell the clerk at the desk that her parents will be coming."

Nicholls nodded and left as she slipped quietly into the treatment room. Maggie was lying on a gurney with a sheet pulled over her. The fluorescent lighting made her look whiter than normal. It reminded Brodie more of an autopsy room than a treatment room. She felt a shiver run down her spine as she realized she could have lost Maggie again, permanently. A tray near the gurney held a variety of instruments, a bloody green cloth lying under what appeared to be a stitching tray. Maggie's face was puffy and swelling had already begun around her nose and eyes. Her eyes were closed and she was breathing evenly. Brodie noticed the bruising on her arms. An IV line ran into her left arm. As Brodie quietly approached the side of the gurney, she saw a fresh row of five or six stitches running above Maggie's left eyebrow, an inch or so below her older scar.

Brodie gently touched Maggie's forehead to brush a few stray strands of hair away from the sutures. The touch startled Maggie. She raised her arm defensively as her eyes opened and darted them around the room. When she saw Brodie standing over her, her eyes filled with tears. Brodie had seen the same frightened look in Maggie's eyes years earlier when she awoke in another emergency room.

"Don't look at me, Royce," her voice cracked.

"The doc says you're going to be okay," Brodie said. "Your folks will be here soon."

Maggie nodded slightly, grimacing as her head moved. Tears escaped from her eyes and ran down the sides of her face. "I'm so tired," she mumbled.

"Stay with me, Mag," Brodie said, struggling to sound calmer than she felt. "Tell me what happened."

Maggie blinked hard and closed her eyes.

"When I got home I discovered I was out of milk. There's a little convenience store a few blocks from my place and it was a nice night." Maggie paused and her eyes closed.

Brodie shook her shoulder gently. "Maggie. What happened next."

"It was dark. I didn't see anything and don't remember much after being grabbed. I'm sorry, Royce."

"Just rest, Maggie," she said.

Brodie brushed another strand of hair away from Maggie's face and let her hand linger for a moment along her cheek. Maggie's eyelids fluttered as the sedative finally took control. Brodie felt a lump growing in her throat as she leaned down and kissed Maggie on the forehead. Stepping away from the gurney, she turned to leave the room, but before she reached the door it burst open, revealing Tim and Peg Weston along with two of Maggie's brothers. They had all dressed hastily and Peg didn't appear to be fully awake.

"You!" Tim hissed when he saw Brodie. "Wasn't once good enough, you fucking bitch?"

Ignoring his accusations, she pushed past him and continued out the door. Peg Weston went to the side of the gurney and took her daughter's hand, looking shocked at the sight of her battered face. Tim glanced at Maggie and followed Brodie out of the room, grabbing her by the shirt and shoving her forcefully against a wall.

She broke his hold and shoved him away. Sean Weston grabbed Brodie's arm as she advanced toward her former commander, fist clenched. She jerked her arm away and glared at Tim, now being restrained by his son Liam.

"If you ever touch me again, Tim, I'll arrest you for assaulting a police officer."

"What the hell happened, Brodie? Were you drunk again?"

She couldn't blame him for assuming the worst and lowered her voice as she spoke to him. "No. I would never hurt her."

"You're responsible for her training, goddammit!"

"It's not my job to watch her during her off-duty hours!"

"Then find whoever did it! I want to be there when you interrogate the son-of-a-bitch."

"You don't have any jurisdiction here. As a matter of fact, now that you're retired, you don't have jurisdiction anywhere. So why don't you go back in there and take care of your daughter and let us take care of finding the person responsible."

She left Tim Weston and his sons standing in the corridor of the treatment area and pushed open the swinging doors with enough force to slam them against the walls of the waiting area. As soon as she spotted Nicholls, she motioned for him to follow her outside. Leaning against the wall, she lit a cigarette and took a long drag to calm her nerves.

"How is she, RB?" Nicholls frowned.

"Lucky," she said as she exhaled. "I want you to go over to where she was found. Make sure the lab doesn't fuck up the scene. And make sure they cover everything. Tonight! I want preliminary reports on my desk by the time the sun comes up!"

"Roger that," Nicholls said as he turned to leave.

"And Nicholls," she said. "Get an officer over here to guard her room. I'll join you after he arrives."

As soon as she saw Tim and Peg Weston pull away from the hospital parking lot, Brodie re-entered the hospital through the emergency entrance and got Maggie's room number from the emergency room clerk. It was three forty-five in the morning by the time she made her way through the winding hospital corridors toward the elevators. There was still some activity in a few of the labs even in the middle of the night. The walls were lined with framed pictures of the doctors who practiced in the hospital and she wondered why they had been relegated to the basement instead of an area where more people could see them. Colored lines on the floor branched off into the various sections of the hospital. She finally found the public elevators and pushed the button for the fourth floor.

The main hospital was configured in three circles joined by carpeted corridors. Just off the elevator was a bank of pay phones.

Bleary-eyed family members leaned against the wall, explaining the situations of their particular loved ones to someone else. As she proceeded down the hall, she saw a waiting room off the main corridor. She looked inside and found a cluster of vending machines offering candy, cold food and weak coffee. She searched through her pockets and managed to come up with enough change for one cup. She could see the bottom of the cup through the coffee, but at least it was hot. She carried it carefully as she approached the nurse's station in the center of one of the circular wings of the building. A young woman dressed in jeans and a western shirt topped by a navy blue smock greeted her at the desk.

"Can I help you, ma'am?" the clerk asked.

"Which room is Maggie Weston's?" she asked quietly as she glanced around the circle.

"Unless you're a family member, you'll have to come back during regular visiting hours."

She brought out her badge for what seemed like the hundredth time that evening and showed it to the clerk.

"I doubt you'll be able to speak to her, officer. She's been sedated and should be asleep."

"I know. I won't be here long. There'll be a uniformed officer stationed outside her room in a little while."

"Let me check with the charge nurse."

The woman looked around until she spotted an older woman coming out of one of the rooms. She went to the far side of the station and spoke in a low voice to the nurse. The nurse looked around her at Brodie and their conversation continued for a few more seconds.

"You can go in for a few minutes, officer, but please don't try to wake her," the clerk said as she returned.

"Thanks. Which room?"

"Four sixteen. It's a private room."

Brodie walked around the nurse's station. Most of the doors leading into rooms were closed. Nurses were busy waking patients up for blood pressure checks or medication in some of the rooms. The door to Maggie's room was slightly ajar and she pushed it open slowly, just enough to squeeze in. Except for corridor light filtering in through the partially opened door, the room was dark. It took a few minutes for her eyes to completely adjust to the dim lighting. Maggie was asleep and despite the swelling and bruising on her face, she seemed peaceful. A steady drip of clear liquid ran down the IV tubing into her arm, a green light blinking steadily on the machine controlling the drip.

She set her coffee on the rolling tray and put her hand out to touch Maggie, but drew it back, clenching it into a fist before it made contact.

"Don't touch her!" a man's voice ordered. "You've already done enough!"

Brodie looked up and saw Sean and Liam standing in the doorway to the room. She took a step away from the bed.

"We need to talk, Brodie," Sean said, anger in his voice.

"Not in here."

She took a last glance at the sleeping form on the hospital bed and followed Sean out of the room. Liam fell in behind her and her muscles tensed. Sean walked past the elevators and shoved open the door to the stairwell. She hesitated, but Liam's hand on her back forced her forward. They made their way down two flights of stairs before Sean stopped on the cramped landing and whirled around, the back of his hand striking Brodie's face with all the pent up anger inside him. She fell to her knees and tasted blood in her mouth. "You're a gutless bitch, you know that Brodie?" he hissed.

"I didn't...," she started.

"Didn't what? Beat the shit out of my sister again?" His arm came around and struck her a second time. Her glasses flew off her face from the force of the blow. She drew a hand across her mouth and stared at the blood on it. Hands grabbed her from behind and dragged her up. "I didn't hurt Maggie," she managed. "Maybe you should do something about Tim hitting her."

"I'm gonna mess you up, Brodie." Sean was talking through clenched teeth. A strong blow caught her in the abdomen and dropped her back to her knees. She wrapped one arm around her waist and tried to catch her breath.

"You tore our family apart!" he yelled as his foot came up and struck the side of her head. She fell onto her side and covered her body the best she could from further blows. She was gasping for air as a foot caught her in the abdomen.

She didn't know how much time had passed when she heard a voice close to her ear. "I should kill you right now, bitch. If you report this to anyone, we'll both swear you fell down the stairs. It's your word against ours. Am I making myself clear?"

Brodie nodded her head the best she could. She heard heavy footsteps going up the stairwell as tears rolled from her eyes.

Chapter
Ten

"WHAT THE HELL happened to you?" Nicholls asked when he saw Brodie's face the next morning.

"Bar fight," she mumbled, wincing from her split and swollen lip.

"You're too fuckin' old for that shit. What the hell were you..."

"You got the report on Maggie's attack?" she interrupted.

"Yeah. Not much there," he said, shaking his head. "Looks like she was grabbed from behind and dragged behind some bushes. Probably never saw her attacker. Forensics got a few shots of some footprints, but a lot of people have been through there. It's a shortcut to the university."

Brodie flipped through the folder. Blood was found at the scene, but it was probably Maggie's. A few old cigarette butts and candy bars were found and taken for fingerprinting and DNA testing."

"When's Maggie being released from the hospital?" Nicholls asked.

"Probably in a few days. They're running some tests to make sure there wasn't a more serious brain injury than the first scans showed."

A WEEK LATER, Brodie, accompanied by Nicholls, knocked at the door of Maggie's duplex and waited. Maggie had spent four days in the hospital and although she had already been home three days, Brodie had been reluctant to visit her until her own injuries had faded. She had gone to the hospital twice, but only to inquire about her status in an official capacity. She didn't feel like having another confrontation with Tim or any other member of the Weston family. There was nothing to be gained by upsetting Maggie. Other than the lingering soreness to her ribs Brodie appeared to be back to normal except for a couple of small bruises on her jaw. The door finally opened and Maggie's face peeked around the door. When she saw who it was, she opened the door all the way. She was dressed in an oversized velour bathrobe and slippers. Her hair hung loosely around her face.

"Jesus, Weston, you look like a fuckin' raccoon," Nicholls said with a smile.

"Thanks, Nicholls," Maggie said as she attempted a slight smile. "I feel much better now. Come in."

"You and RB could have passed for twins a week ago," he said as he entered the house and kissed her lightly on the cheek.

Brodie waited until she was inside before removing her sunglasses.

Maggie stared at her. "What are you talking about?"

"Brodie hoisted a few after your attack and lost a fist fight," Nicholls said.

"It was nothing," Brodie said. "I've been in worse."

"Please, sit down," Maggie said, continuing to stare at Brodie. "Can I get you something to drink?"

"I'll get it. Where's the kitchen?" Nicholls asked.

Maggie pointed over her shoulder and he followed the direction of her finger. She took a step closer to Brodie and brought her hand up to touch her lieutenant's face. Brodie caught her wrist and stopped Maggie's hand.

"So how're you feeling, Maggie?" Brodie asked, shifting the conversation back to Maggie.

"Sore, but other than that, and a case of humiliation, I'm okay," Maggie answered as she lowered her body slowly onto the couch.

"You're not okay, but you'll survive."

"The beer looked enticing, but unfortunately I remembered we were still on duty," Nicholls said as he came out of the kitchen carrying three glasses.

"It's Sunday," Maggie said.

"RB couldn't quit thinking about the murders, so here we are. Besides, she's driving us all nuts demanding reports and every other damn thing on your case. When are you coming back so we can get a break?"

"The doctors say by next Monday, I hope."

"Give her the files," Brodie ordered.

"What files?" Maggie asked.

"The ones from the Brauner and Garcia cases," Nicholls said as he opened his briefcase and handed her a stack of manila folders. "Since you're just sittin' around all day watchin' your bruises change color, you might as well do a little work to take your mind off your aches and pains."

"We've been over these a thousand times already," she said looking at the stack.

"Well, now it'll be a thousand and one," Brodie said. "There are a few new things. Nicholls and I finished the interviews with everyone we could get hold of. Somewhere in those files is something that's trying to catch our attention, but we just haven't seen it yet. Go over them again and write down anything we might have overlooked. It could be something so obvious that we bypassed it or it could be something more obscure."

"You mean like a gut feeling?"

"Yeah. So far your hunches have been pretty damn good and it's been a few days since you've looked through them so you're more detached than Nicholls and I are right now. You've had other things on your mind besides the cases."

"I'm nearly cross-eyed from reading them," Nicholls said. "I know what's on the next page before I even turn it. I can recite it in my sleep."

"We get the idea, Nicholls," Brodie frowned.

"Okay," Maggie said looking at the folders. "But if you two haven't found anything, I might overlook it, too."

Brodie got up and slid her sunglasses back on. "We better get going."

"Where are you off to now?" Maggie asked.

"Nicholls is going to attempt to show me the value of computers in police work," Brodie smirked.

"Probably going to be like trying to teach a dinosaur to use a litter box," he quipped.

"Ouch!" Maggie laughed. "That's harsh, Nicholls."

"If that's a crack about my age, Nicholls, we could go a few rounds in the gym," Brodie said. "After last week I obviously need some work-out time."

BRODIE LEFT THE office that evening as the sun was setting and drove to a fast food chicken joint. She placed her order and then found herself driving toward Maggie's duplex. At first she drove past, then circled the block and stopped in front, sitting in the car a few minutes finishing a cigarette. As she crushed it out in the ashtray, she took a deep breath, picked up the chicken and walked to the front door, waving at the police car parked across the street.

"Royce," Maggie said when she saw her at the door. "I haven't gone over the files yet. I didn't know you wanted feedback so quickly."

"I don't, but I thought you might not feel like cooking so I picked up some chicken."

"You must have a full-service police department if you make deliveries."

"The sooner I can get you back to work, the better."

"I'm sorry. Come in."

Brodie entered the living room and carried the boxes of chicken into the kitchen. She looked through a couple of cabinets before finding plates, filled two with food, taking soft drinks from the refrigerator before carrying the plates and drinks back into the living room. Maggie was sitting on the couch when she handed her a plate.

"Looks good," Maggie said as she took it. "Thanks."

"Hope you don't mind if I kinda poked around in the kitchen." Brodie said as she sat down in the chair across from Maggie.

"As long as you didn't find my secret stash of drugs."

"You mean those painkillers over the sink?"

"Yeah." Maggie smiled. "They work great."

They ate silently for a few minutes before Maggie broke the silence.

"Did you find anything interesting on the computer?"

"Don't know yet. I had Nicholls put out a search for similar crimes through NCIC. It could be a while before we get a reply, so we decided to call it a day."

"I appreciate you bringing dinner to me. I really didn't feel like cooking and I'm getting a little tired of soup."

"No problem."

The silence between them grew awkward. Brodie began to wish she had dropped dinner off and gone on home. In less than half an hour they had finished their food and she carried their plates back into the kitchen. She cleaned up what little mess there was and turned to go back into the living room and make her excuses about getting home. When she turned, Maggie was standing in the doorway, watching her.

"I think I put everything back where it belonged," she said as she wiped her hands on a dishtowel.

"If I can't find something I'll let you know," Maggie said, her voice soft, almost a whisper.

"Well, I better get going. Give us a call if you find anything in the files."

"I will. And I'm sorry."

"Don't worry. You won't be out long. It won't affect your training."

"I'm scared, Royce. I've never been hurt on the job before."

"There's no evidence your attack was job-related. Probably a junkie looking for money for his next fix." When she looked at Maggie, she saw tears pooling in her eyes. "You'll never forget it happened, Maggie, but I guarantee you'll get over it eventually," she said softly.

"Promise?"

She went to where Maggie was standing and took her in her arms. "I promise."

Maggie cried softly as she held her. When she stopped, she raised her head and looked at Brodie, who wiped away the tears that had run down Maggie's face, being careful not to press too hard against the bruised areas. Letting her hand rest on the side of Maggie's face momentarily, she leaned down and kissed her cheek. As she backed away, Maggie's grip tightened around her arms.

"It sounds stupid, Royce...but I'm afraid to be alone. I know there are police officers outside, but the slightest sound wakes me up."

"It's not stupid. Go lie down. I'll stay until you go to sleep."

"Will you...could you hold me?"

"I don't want to hurt you, Maggie."

"You won't," Maggie said as she took Brodie's hand and led her toward the bedroom.

Turning the bed down, Maggie slipped her robe off, revealing only an Austin Police Academy t-shirt and briefs. Brodie slipped her shoes off and as she leaned back on the pillows, Maggie rolled into her arms. She closed her eyes and held Maggie, lightly stroking her hair and back. In spite of the enormous pleasure she felt holding Maggie in her arms again, a surge of guilt flowed through her. She knew she was on the verge of having to make a difficult decision. At that moment she didn't know what she wanted and desperately wished her life was less complicated.

It was nearly midnight before she woke up. She tried to slide her arm from under Maggie's body and slip out of bed. Maggie mumbled to herself as Brodie moved and it took her nearly ten minutes to extricate herself and sit up on the side of the bed. She needed a cigarette, but before she could stand, she felt Maggie's hand touch her back. When she looked over her shoulder Maggie was awake and looking at her.

"Go back to sleep," Brodie whispered, even though there was no one else in the house.

"Do you have to go?"

"Yeah. Will you be all right?"

"I'm fine," Maggie said as she readjusted herself on the bed.

Brodie stood up and looked around for her shoes. She slipped them on and picked up her jacket. Maggie sat up on the bed and drew her legs up to her chest, wrapping her arms around them.

"Do you need anything before I go?"

"No. I'll finish looking over those files in the morning."

"Take your time. Brauner and Garcia aren't going anywhere."

Maggie leaned against the headboard of the bed and closed her eyes. Brodie moved to her side of the bed and sat down on the edge.

"Will you come back?" Maggie asked, her eyes still closed.

Touching her face lightly with her fingertips, Brodie said, "Probably not."

IT WAS AFTER three in the morning by the time Brodie pulled into her driveway. She was exhausted, but she was almost afraid to go to bed. Three hours sleep wouldn't help and she reminded herself that either way she would undoubtedly be irritable later in the day. She entered her house briefly to let Max outside before leaving again. She drove to an all-night restaurant near the highway leading to Austin, ordered breakfast and downed several cups of coffee. An hour later she entered the police station. The desk officer looked surprised to see her.

"What're you doin' here, Brodie?"

"Couldn't sleep, Don, so I figured I might as well get some paperwork done."

"We're sending out for some food in a little while. Can we get something for you?"

"No, thanks. I already ate. Looks like it was a calm night."

"Pretty boring. Had to slap myself a while ago to stay awake."

As she walked into the squad room the sound of her feet moving across the linoleum floor echoed in the empty room. When she got to Nicholls's desk she saw a stack of computer printouts in the basket behind the ancient dot matrix printer. She picked up the papers and tore them from the paper still feeding into the machine and carried them to her desk.

Halfway through the stack, she began to get drowsy. Functioning on no sleep wasn't so bad when she was involved in something physically active, but now the words and numbers on the printouts were beginning to run together. She put the papers down and went down the hallway to the bathroom. She splashed water on her face and looked at herself in the mirror. A little more than three weeks earlier, her life had been relatively simple. She had a job she liked, a comfortable house, enjoyed the affections of a beautiful woman, and even managed to sleep peacefully at least one night a week. Now she was no longer sure she knew the woman she saw looking back at her.

She grabbed her jacket from the back of her chair and, suddenly wide awake, walked out of the squad room.

"When Nicholls comes in, tell him something came up and I won't be in until around noon."

"Sure thing, Brodie," the desk sergeant nodded without looking up.

THE ILLUMINATED DIAL on her wristwatch showed five thirty-five as Brodie took a long drag on her cigarette and waited. She blinked as the porch light flipped on and the front door opened.

"RB?" Camille said.

"Sorry if I woke you up," she said.

"No, no. I was already up."

Brodie flicked her cigarette into the flowerbed next to the front entry of Camille's townhouse before entering.

"Is something wrong?" Camille asked as she closed the front door. "Did you have the nightmare again?"

"No," Brodie said. "Been up all night thinking, and needed to talk to you."

Camille smiled and pushed her hair back from her face. "Come to the kitchen. I just made a pot of coffee."

"Sounds good," Brodie said as she followed Camille down the main hallway and into the kitchen.

"Is it your cases?"

"We've actually made some progress there. Someone attacked Weston though," Brodie said as she looked at the liquid in her cup and frowned. "We're not sure if it's related to the cases yet."

"Oh, sweetie, I'm sorry. Is she okay?"

"She'll recover."

"Do you feel responsible, RB?"

"There wasn't anything I could have done to prevent it."

"Let's go sit someplace where we can be more comfortable," Camille suggested.

Brodie leaned back on the couch in Camille's office and set her coffee on the end table. Camille sat next to her. "Want to talk about it?"

Brodie sat up quickly when a woman, yawning and wearing a bathrobe, wandered into the room. Her dark hair was disheveled and she coughed lightly to clear her throat. She walked to the couch and leaned down to kiss Camille lightly. Glancing at Brodie, she asked, "Everything all right, darling?"

Smiling up at the woman, Camille pressed her hand against the brunette's cheek.

Brodie looked at the two women. "Maybe I should call your office and make an appointment."

"The coffee's ready. I'll join you in the bedroom in a few minutes," Camille said as the woman bent down to kiss her once again. Brodie thought there was something possessive about the kiss, something telling her she had been replaced.

She watched the woman leave the room and smiled at Camille. "Where did you meet her? She's lovely."

"At the conference I attended in San Diego a few months ago," Camille answered as her eyes followed the departing figure. "We've spoken on the phone a few times since. Then she appeared at my office about a week ago." A wistful smile crossed her lips and she shook her head. "Sorry. Where were we?"

"Actually, I wanted to speak to you about us...but it doesn't seem necessary now."

"Don't you mean about you and Maggie? I don't need a degree in psychology to know you're still attracted to her. What are you looking for, RB? My blessing?"

"Of course not. I never meant to hurt you, but I know I did."

"You're not in love with me. I think, deep inside, I've always known that. I won't lie and say I wasn't a little hurt. I guess I hoped you'd eventually come around, be the one I was looking for, but when Maggie arrived, I knew it was time to move on."

"What were you looking for?"

Camille propped her head against her hand and closed her eyes. When she opened them again, they were crystal clear. "Someone who needs me as much as I need them. Someone who is willing to give themselves to me and our relationship completely."

"I couldn't give you that. I hope you've found it now," Brodie said quietly. "I'm sorry. I never intended to use you."

"I suppose, in a way, we were using each other, although I'd prefer to think we've both been waiting for the real thing to come along. You can't be afraid to commit to someone because you might get hurt again."

"Can we still be friends?"

"Of course. Now why don't you go home and lie down?" Camille asked. "I'm sure the department can get along without you for a few hours."

"Thanks, Camille, but I'll be okay."

"Don't be ridiculous," she said firmly as she stood and pulled Brodie up from the couch. "You're too tired to be of much use to anyone right now. As your psychologist, I'm prescribing rest. So get up and haul your ass out of here." Glancing in the direction the other woman had gone, she added, "And let me get back to entertaining my guest."

Brodie laughed as she hugged her. "Doctor's orders, huh?"

Kissing Brodie's cheek, she said, "Absolutely."

BY ELEVEN FORTY-FIVE, feeling somewhat more refreshed after a short nap and a long shower, Brodie sat down at her desk.

"Long night, RB?" Nicholls asked, looking up from a stack of computer printouts.

"Yeah," she answered. "What're you looking through?"

"We got the print-outs back from NCIC on similar crimes, but so far it's not looking too promising. Beheading is a pretty rare occurrence even among the criminal element."

"Send it through again and narrow the search to murdered

janitorial or maintenance workers at any university. This might have been our guy's first foray into beheading, but I guarantee it's not his first murder."

While Nicholls punched information into his computer, she looked through a stack of case folders on her desk. "Where's the file on Maggie's attack?" she asked.

He picked up a folder on his desk and handed it to her. "Still pretty sketchy," he said as he returned to his computer terminal.

She read the responding officer's report and glanced through the forensic report. Nicholls had been right; there wasn't much new in the report. Without a description from Maggie, the perp could have been anyone. Removing the stack of crime scene photos, she looked over each shot carefully. On her second look through the black and white photos, she paused at a shot of a footprint found at the scene.

"You got a magnifying glass?" she asked.

"I think so," he said as he rummaged through his desk drawers, finally producing a small magnifying glass.

"Get this from a cereal box?" she chuckled as she took it and leaned over the picture.

"You find something?" he asked.

"It's another one of those woman things Maggie's so fond of," she said. "She still has the folder from the Brauner scene, doesn't she?"

"Yeah, why?"

"Let's go see how she's doing," she said as she stood up and closed the file on Maggie's assault.

"LOOK AT THESE two pictures," Brodie said as she set a picture from Maggie's file next to one from the Brauner file. Maggie and Nicholls looked at the pictures, but it was Maggie who saw it first.

"It looks like the same shoe pattern," she said.

"Might not be the same guy, but it's apparently a very popular shoe among the local criminal element," Brodie said.

"Well, I'll be damned," Nicholls breathed. "The attack on Maggie is related to the Brauner and Garcia cases?"

"Maybe. Maggie," Brodie said, "you must have heard or seen something our killer doesn't want you to remember."

"And he thought he'd shut me up before I figured out what it was," she frowned. "I'd feel better if I knew what the hell it was, but I honestly have no idea, Royce."

"Have you found anything in the files that has tripped your trigger?" Nicholls asked.

"No, nothing," Maggie shook her head. "I still have a few more reports and notes to read, but so far I haven't found anything that even remotely makes me want to look elsewhere."

"There has to be something," Brodie said. "The guy was desperate enough to risk attacking a police officer near her own home."

"Think he followed her?" Nicholls asked.

"If he thinks you're a threat because you know something, he could try again," Brodie said as she looked at Maggie. "Maybe you should think about staying with your folks for a while."

"No way in hell! There is a patrol car outside now. He wouldn't risk it."

Unable to convince their trainee to move someplace safer, even temporarily, Brodie and Nicholls left Maggie to continue scouring the files half an hour later. As Brodie settled into the passenger seat Nicholls glanced at her. "What's up with you and Weston?"

"What do you mean?"

"Come on, Brodie. I'm not blind. I see the way you look at each other. You fuckin' her?"

"Yeah. I sneak over here every damn night and grab a fast roll in the hay right under the noses of a couple of our patrolmen, all while I'm trying to avoid the bruises and cracked ribs from her beating. Very hot stuff."

"I'm serious, Brodie. When did she start calling you by your first name? Something no one else is allowed to do."

"Look, Nicholls, you know I knew Maggie years ago. She used my first name back then."

"Straight up. Are you fucking Weston?"

"No. Now drop it!"

MAGGIE'S DOCTOR CLEARED her to return to duty the beginning of the following week, and she would be glad to get back. She could only take so much sitting around the house and the idea that her attacker might know where she lived hadn't helped her sleep pattern much either. She had read the case files a half dozen times without a clue as to what she was looking for. Failing to find anything obvious, she began to concentrate on minor facts. It was easy to skip over small things trying to get the bigger picture. Propping her feet up on her coffee table, she flipped open the file on Cruz Garcia, whom they now believed had been the first victim. There wasn't anything in the forensics reports that she didn't already know. His wallet and keys had never been found and presumably were disposed of by the killer. Through Garcia's cousin, his wife had described the wallet and it contents. The university had provided a list of keys Garcia carried with him while on the job, as well as their serial numbers. The university security office had changed all the locks involved, rendering the keys useless.

In the back of the file were pictures taken when Garcia's various parts had been found. Among the pictures was the family photo she and Brodie had gotten from Garcia's wife when they were still trying to identify him. Garcia, his wife and their children were dressed up. What was it the cousin had said? The picture had been taken the previous Christmas before midnight mass, something like that. They were an attractive family, Maggie thought, as she looked at the picture. They were the picture of health and happiness. It was a shame some maniac had ruined all of that. She slid the picture back into the file and then pulled it out again.

THE NEXT MORNING, Maggie walked purposefully into the squad room.

"What are you doing here?" Brodie asked. "The doc hasn't released you for duty yet."

Maggie slapped the picture of the Garcia family on the desk in front of her training officer. "Daryll Chambers killed Cruz Garcia and Elliott Brauner," she said flatly. "Son of a bitch was probably my attacker, too."

"And how did you determine that?" Brodie asked, picking up the picture.

"Mrs. Garcia's necklace," Maggie said as she pointed to the picture. "There was something familiar about it so I went to see Mrs. Garcia last night. The medallion on the necklace is Our Lady of Guadalupe. Mr. Garcia had the same medallion. The necklaces were wedding gifts and they always wore them."

"So?" Brodie prompted.

"So Mr. Garcia broke his necklace a couple of times at work and finally decided to carry the medallion on his key ring, which is still missing. When I first interviewed Chambers about Brauner, I saw this exact medallion on his key ring. The day before I was attacked I spoke to Chambers and saw the medallion again and asked him about it. He said it had been a gift from his mother. He said she had picked it up in Costa Rica."

"Could be true," Brodie said. "Religious medallions aren't exactly a rarity among Hispanics and Our Lady of Guadalupe is probably the most popular religious figure in Mexico."

"In Mexico, *not* Costa Rica. These two were handmade by Garcia's brother who's a silversmith *in Mexico* and, according to the wife, were a one-of-a-kind matching set. I saw Mrs. Garcia's necklace and the medallion is identical to the one Chambers had. I'm telling you, Royce, He's our guy," she said forcefully.

"Nicholls, do you have that report we just got in from NCIC?"

Brodie asked.

"Yeah, and there was a similar incident at Clarkson University in Potsdam, New York. Janitor killed and keys taken. Perp never apprehended," he answered.

"Chambers is from New York," Brodie said. "When I interviewed him he said so. Call that university and see if Mr. Chambers was a student there at the time their janitor was murdered," she instructed. "How was that one killed?"

"Acid to the face," Nicholls said.

"Charming," she muttered.

Nicholls hung the phone up several minutes later and shrugged, "Daryll Chambers was never a student at Clarkson."

"Shit," Maggie said as she slammed her hand down on Brodie's desk. "It has to be him! We need to see his university records. Wait, his girlfriend, I met her the same day I asked him about the medallion. She works in admissions at the university."

Brodie stood up and slipped her jacket on. "Nicholls, Maggie and I will be at the university. I'll call if we find anything you can follow up on."

Brodie backed her Camaro out of its parking space and shifted into drive. "You're meant for this job, Maggie. Another hunch?" she smiled.

"More like an electrical shock. I was putting the file away when I noticed the picture and thought how sad it was for Mrs. Garcia and her kids. Then I noticed the necklace and remembered Daryll's key ring. I commented about how beautiful it was and that must have spooked him into attacking me before I could put it together."

"Guess we'll have to have another chat with Mr. Chambers, too."

"He's supposed to be out of state for a job interview back east somewhere," Maggie said as she looked out the side window. "Maybe the girlfriend will know when he's supposed to return."

"Depending on what we find out, I'll have Nicholls get a search warrant for his home and work area in Roth's office."

The admissions office was open when they arrived. A clerk at the reception desk announced, "We're not really open. It's spring break, ya know."

"Yeah," Brodie said, holding her badge up to the woman. "We need to see the university file on Daryll Chambers, one of your graduate students."

"It'll take me a few minutes. I'm here alone today trying to catch up on some provisional admission paperwork."

"We can wait."

"Is Karen Dietrick working today?" Maggie asked.

"All of our student workers are off for the break," the woman said as she turned away from the counter.

"We'll need to see her personnel records as well," Maggie said.

Brodie and Maggie cooled their heels for over twenty minutes before the woman re-appeared carrying two files. Chambers' file contained transcripts for his undergraduate work, personal data sheet, letters of recommendation from previous professors and other pieces of 'administrivia'.

"There's nothing from Clarkson University," Brodie said. "According to his records, he did his undergrad at Boston College."

"This can't be right, Royce," Maggie said as she looked over the paperwork. "I know he's our killer."

"Nothing in this folder helps prove that."

"We need to talk to Karen Dietrick," Maggie said. Flipping open Dietrick's personnel file, Maggie jotted down the address. "Maybe she stayed in town over the break."

Brodie closed the files and started to get up when Maggie stopped her. "Wait. Is there a permanent address for Daryll, a home of record, next of kin or anything like that in his file?"

Brodie reopened the file and found the original admission application. "There's a Mildred Chambers in Potsdam, New York. Probably his mother," she noted. Pulling her notebook from her jacket pocket, she wrote down the name and telephone number for Mrs. Chambers.

Smiling, Maggie said, "Potsdam. That's where Clarkson University is."

A grin Maggie remembered spread across Brodie's face. It was almost feral-looking, as if she had her prey in her sights. "You're right. He may not have gone to college there, but he damn sure lived in the town."

"We need a little more to ask for a search warrant," Brodie said as they left the Administration Building and walked to their car. "All we have right now is a bunch of conjecture and coincidences. We need something more tangible."

"We need that medallion. My word that I saw it isn't good enough." Maggie said with a frown. Brodie noticed that she was looking a little deflated.

"Tired?" she asked.

"A little," Maggie smiled. "This is the first exercise I've had in almost two weeks, if you want to call a hundred yard stroll exercise."

"It takes some time to get back in the swing when you've been out for a while," Brodie said as she turned the key in the ignition.

"Your leg still bother you?" Maggie asked, glancing at Brodie's thigh.

"Only when I dance too much. You'll be back in shape before you know it. Call Nicholls and have him contact Boston College.

Let's see if Mr. Chambers was really a student there. If he was, have them fax us a copy of his transcript."

"Did you notice something in his file?" Maggie asked as she punched numbers into her cell phone.

"Maybe." After Maggie finished her call, Brodie handed her notebook to Maggie and said, "Dial this number, then let me have the phone."

"It's ringing," she said, handing the phone to her a few minutes later.

"Mildred Chambers, please," Brodie said to a person at the other end of the line. Holding the phone with her shoulder, she took her notebook back from Maggie and set it on her thigh, pulling a pen from the sun visor.

"Hello? Mrs. Chambers? Ma'am, my name is Regina Bruce. I'm the Director of Personnel for Southeastern Pharmaceuticals in Savannah, Georgia," she lied.

Maggie smiled and shook her head at the fake accent as Brodie continued. "I'm hoping you can assist me, Mrs. Chambers. Your son, Daryll, has applied for a position with our company and I haven't been able to contact him in Texas."

She listened for a moment. "I see. Well, ma'am, we'd be interested in scheduling an interview with him. Would it be possible for you to give me a little information. I'm on the road right now and don't have his file with me at the moment. He did his undergraduate work at Clarkson University near your home, didn't he?" She smiled and nodded as she looked over at Maggie after receiving the answer. "We haven't received a copy of his undergrad transcripts from them yet. I called their admissions office and they didn't seem to have any record of him as a student."

In response to whatever was being said, Brodie began scribbling down information. "Ah, that makes sense, ma'am. When did he do that? Guess he just got used to using your name. After all it has been a few years." She laughed as she continued a congenial conversation with Chambers' mother until she finally said, "You've been very helpful, Mrs. Chambers and I certainly appreciate it. Rest assured that we are extremely interested in Daryll. He's exactly the person we're looking for. We'll keep trying his phone in Texas until we reach him. You have a good day now, ma'am."

Punching the disconnect button to end the call, she handed the cell back to Maggie. "Call Nicholls and have him contact Clarkson again to see if they have a record for a Daryll Griffin, Jr., which they will. Have them fax us whatever they have on him and then contact the Potsdam Police Department for their file on the murder of one of the university janitors during that same time period."

"He changed his name?"

"Took step-daddy's name two or three years ago."

"But all the paperwork at the university here lists him as Chambers," Maggie said as she redialed Nicholls.

"I think the girlfriend can solve that mystery for us. Probably changed the name on incoming transcripts and re-Xeroxed it over another student's transcripts. I'm betting his undergrad grades weren't good enough to get him into Podunk U., let alone our modest little university here. Tell Nicholls to get the paperwork started for another search warrant for the girlfriend's address and workplace."

As Maggie filled Nicholls in, Brodie suddenly felt deliriously happy. This was the best part of her job, putting the pieces of the puzzle together and squeezing the bad guy until he choked. When they walked into the squad room, Nicholls was looking over the faxes he had received and smiling, too.

"Good work, ladies," he beamed. "The warrants will be ready by the time we get to the courthouse."

"Did you fill Donaldson in?" Brodie asked.

"Yep, and needless to say he's relieved the crimes have been solved," Nicholls responded. "It seems that Chambers or Griffin or whatever you want to call him was a well below average student at Clarkson. In fact, I think you'll find this part particularly interesting." He smiled as he handed Brodie the faxed transcript.

Maggie looked over her shoulder as they both glanced over the document. "When was the janitor at Clarkson killed?" she asked.

"During Chambers' senior year," Nicholls said. "I called up there and talked to his old advisor who described him as a pain in the ass. Seems the only reason he graduated was a sudden burst of brilliance on his final exams."

"Probably courtesy of the murdered janitor," Brodie frowned.

"The fax from the Potsdam PD should be coming in any time. I spoke to one of their detectives who also remembered Chambers. He said the packet on him was pretty thick and might take a while to be transmitted."

"But they never considered him a suspect in the killing at the university there?" Maggie asked.

"Most of his shit was petty juvenile stuff plus a few more serious offenses involving dead pets in the area. His daddy was stinkin' rich and most of it got swept under the proverbial rug. They can't send us everything because some of it's in a sealed juvie file. But, the detective gave me a phone number for a retired cop up there who tried unsuccessfully to nab Chambers for a lot."

"A career criminal in the making," Brodie said. "I knew he wasn't a beginner. Grab your coat, Nicholls, and call the lab boys to meet us. Maybe we can turn up something more concrete."

"Who're we gonna hit first?" he asked as he picked up the receiver.

"The girlfriend," she answered. "I want to confront her with the records she falsified and get that part wrapped up. We'll meet you at the car."

Brodie started the car as Maggie slid into the passenger seat. "You know you're not officially back on duty yet," she said.

"Victim's rights. I'd really like to be there when you bust him."

"You will be, Maggie. I promise," Brodie said as she smiled warmly at her. "The bastard almost cost me a very good detective. You're thorough and you know how to work your hunches. You've dealt with my shit better than anyone would have expected."

"I knew there would be issues when I applied for this position, Royce, and sooner or later I knew we had to deal with them. It's hard to plan a future when there's still past unfinished business," Maggie said.

"We'll work on it, Maggie," she said, shifting the car into drive as Nicholls jumped into the back. He passed Maggie a slip of paper as he fastened his seatbelt.

"I already told the backups where to meet us," he said.

"Karen Dietrick lives at the El Dorado Apartments on North Grand," Maggie said. "You know where it is?"

"Yeah," Brodie said. "Not far from the university."

Two black and whites were already in the parking lot of the apartment building when Brodie brought her car to a stop.

"Send a couple of these officers to cover the back and have the other two come with us," she ordered as she walked toward Apartment 128. "Maggie, find the apartment manager in case she isn't home." She and Nicholls drew their service revolvers as they approached the door. He stood to one side of the door while Brodie stopped on the other side.

She struck the door soundly with her fist. "Cedar Springs Police, Miss Dietrick. We have a warrant to search your apartment," she announced loudly.

She had made the announcement twice when Maggie rounded the corner of the building with a stocky man in his mid-sixties. She held her hand up to stop them.

"Maggie, get the key," she ordered.

Maggie took the key from the apartment manager and tossed it to Nicholls. Drawing her revolver, she moved closer to the apartment door and crouched down. Brodie nodded at Nicholls as he slipped the key into the lock and turned it. Turning the knob, he pushed the door open, but it was stopped by a chain lock.

"Fuck it," Brodie said as she stepped in front of the door and landed a solid kick to the door, popping the chain from the doorframe.

She entered the apartment, followed by Nicholls. Within a few seconds of entering, she knew they would need the forensics team and the coroner. Breathing through her mouth, she signaled Nicholls to move to the right and they began checking to make sure no one else was in the apartment. Down a short hallway, the bedroom door was partially closed. Standing to the side, she crouched down and nodded again to Nicholls before cautiously pushing the door open. She swept her gun quickly around the room before reholstering it.

"Jesus Christ," Nicholls breathed.

Karen Dietrick's bloated naked body was spread-eagled on her bed, hands and feet tied to the headboard and footboard, her head encased in a plastic bag. It was obvious she had been dead more than a few hours. More like a few days. Brodie could feel her gag reflex begin to kick in as she and Nicholls backed out of the room.

Walking quickly out of the apartment, she said solemnly to one of the patrol officers, "Call forensics and don't let anyone else near this apartment."

Although she was taking in deep, cleansing breaths, she knew it would be a while before she got the scent of death out of her nose and her mind.

"Are you all right?" Maggie asked, resting her hand on Brodie's shoulder.

"Better than Karen Dietrick," Brodie said as she exhaled. "This fucker's not leaving any loose ends, that's for damn sure."

"He has to know he'll be the primary suspect for her death," Maggie said.

"Didn't you say he was going out of town for a job interview?"

"That's what he said."

"We'll have to wait for the medical examiner to determine her time of death. If he was out of town, then he couldn't have killed her and will be the luckiest fucker on the planet. Have this whole area, front and back, cordoned off until Frank and his guys finish. There's nothing more we can do here for now. Where's Nicholls?"

When Nicholls finally joined them, he was wiping his face with a handkerchief. "Boy, that was nasty, RB," he said softly.

"You okay?"

"Yeah, but I think I'll burn these clothes as soon as I get home," he answered, attempting a weak smile.

"I'm betting we won't find the same thing at Mr. Chambers' residence. Since he knew this victim, I'll take what we have and ask for a warrant. You up for it?"

"Only if we can ride with the windows down," Nicholls said as he pushed his handkerchief into his pocket.

DARYLL CHAMBERS RENTED a small two-bedroom house on

the north side of Austin. Brodie requested back up from Austin PD via a secure frequency to the Austin dispatcher. Parking a block away from Chambers' house, she briefed the patrol officers and instructed them to cover front and back entrances to the house. When no one responded to her call to open the door, a patrol officer broke the door open. It was quickly determined that the house was empty. The three detectives spread out through the small house. The second bedroom had been converted into a study. Brodie looked through the drawers of an old desk without finding much of interest. A desk calendar was filled with scribbles, notes and phone numbers. A calendar entry for the previous Sunday showed what appeared to be a flight number and times and she jotted down the information in her notebook. The airline might be able to tell her when his return flight was scheduled.

"Royce!" Maggie's voice called from another part of the house.

She found Maggie in Chambers' bedroom. "Find something?"

Maggie backed out of the closet and held up a shoe. "Look familiar?"

Moving closer, she examined the pattern on the sole of the shoe. "Looks like a match for the pattern in the pictures we have."

"I'd like to wear these when I kick his ass," Maggie fumed.

"Well, bag them and we'll let the lab determine if they match. Hopefully they won't be the most popular shoe ever sold," Brodie said.

The remainder of their search didn't reveal much to indicate that Daryll Chambers had been involved in any type of criminal activity. If he had the key ring, it was probably with him and it was the only solid evidence they had against him, but he could argue he had found it. Lying to Maggie about where he got it was the only incriminating thing they had. Conveniently, any witnesses to his academic misdeeds were dead. With Daryll Chambers' shoes in hand, the three detectives left Austin and drove back toward Cedar Springs.

"Now what, RB?" Nicholls asked as he seemed to be getting the color back in his face from their earlier discovery. "The only other place covered by the warrant is his work area at the university. Want to try there?"

"Yeah," she said. "Might as well check that and get it out of the way."

Reaching into her jacket pocket, she pulled out her notebook and handed it to Maggie. "See if you can find out what date and time Chambers' flight will return to Austin. There was a lot of doodling on his calendar, but he traced over a couple of things several times to make them bolder. I think he used United Airlines. Either that or he's planning something at the University of Alabama."

"Or Arizona," Nicholls added.

"Or Arkansas," Maggie said.

"Or Alaska," Brodie laughed.

As Maggie called directory assistance for the phone number, they all laughed. It had been a horrendous day, but their laughter broke the tension they were all feeling about the spiraling murder spree in Cedar Springs.

PRESSING THE WARRANT into the campus security guard's chest, Brodie took the master key from him and entered the outer office belonging to Malcolm Roth. "Unlock the inner door," she ordered Nicholls as she began rummaging through the desk used by Daryll Chambers while Maggie pulled open the top drawer of the first of six four-drawer file cabinets.

"I'll have to contact Dr. Roth about this," the security guard said.

"Knock yourself out," Maggie answered, thumbing through a row of horizontal files marked examinations. "What are we looking for specifically?" she asked.

"No clue," Brodie muttered. "Maybe we'll get lucky and find a stolen copy of Brauner's exam."

"You've been watching too much Perry Mason."

"Waiting for the one piece of evidence to fall in her lap always worked for Nancy Drew," Brodie chuckled. "You find anything in there, Nicholls?"

"Just remnants of some pot smoking," he called back. "What do you want me to do with it?"

"Leave it. It's not listed on the warrant."

As Maggie moved to the second file cabinet, Brodie got her knees and felt along the bottom of the desk drawers, but found nothing more than cobwebs. Standing, she joined Maggie. "I'll start on this end and meet you in the middle. This is probably a waste of time anyway."

"About half of what we do is a waste of time," Maggie said. "But you never know until you look, right?"

"You shouldn't even be here, Maggie."

"It beats watching my bruises turn a lighter shade of green and purple."

Half an hour dragged by and the three detectives had nothing more to show for their efforts than they had when they began the search. By the time she reached the final file cabinet, Brodie's back was beginning to tire from bending over. Kneeling in front of the bottom drawer, she tried to pull it open, but something inside caught and stopped it less than half way open. "Well, damn," she mumbled.

The drawer rested at a slight angle.

"What's wrong?" Maggie asked.

"The drawer came off the roller and there's too much damn weight in it."

"If you can lift it while I pull, maybe we can get it back on track," Maggie said, joining Brodie on the floor.

Rising to her knees, Brodie put her hands under the drawer and lifted slightly. Maggie put a foot against the adjoining file and tugged at the drawer. It inched forward accompanied by the screech of metal against metal.

"Well, hell," Brodie fumed. "Scoot over." Sitting in front of the drawer, she placed a foot on the cabinets on either side of the stubborn drawer. Jerking it up and toward her, they heard a loud pop as the drawer broke loose and off the rollers, landing in front of Brodie.

A quick look through the files revealed nothing of interest. "Okay," Brodie said, taking a deep breathe. "You grab your side and I'll take mine. We'll lift it onto the rollers and hopefully it will close."

Maggie nodded and on the count of three they lifted the drawer. After three tries, Brodie gave up. "Nicholls! Give us a hand out here!"

Grinning as he knelt in front of the drawer, he said, "Finally needed a little manly muscle, huh girls?"

"Whatever," Maggie laughed. "Watch your fingers."

Two tries later, Nicholls said, "Check the rollers. It feels like it catching on something."

"So much for Mr. Manly," Brodie said. She took her penlight from her inside jacket pocket and shined the light under the cabinet. "What the hell? Looks like a piece of plactic that has lodged on the track. Move the file cabinets away from the wall," she said as she stood up.

"What?"

"Just move the damn thing," she ordered. When Nicholls was out of the way she went to the end file cabinet and, with Maggie's help, walked it away from the wall.

Three file cabinets later they were looking at what appeared to be a utility door hidden behind the file cabinets. Brodie flipped the latch and pulled the door open, using her back to move the file cabinet farther away from the wall. Clicking on the pen light, she peered into the opening. "Call the lab," she said.

"What is it?" Maggie asked.

"An entrance into the tunnels," Brodie said as she stuck her head into the opening. "The original entrance used to be in this hallway. I can see where it was bricked up." Pulling her head back, she said, "Get the Mag-Lites from the car and bring some gloves."

"IT'S AN OLD utility entrance for the wiring in this part of the building," a university maintenance worker said as he wiped his hands on his pant legs.

"How many more of these are there?" Brodie asked.

"Probably one on each floor."

"We searched those tunnels. I didn't see any evidence of these then," she groused.

"If you go inside the tunnel and close the door, you can barely see the seam. It's just cut into the plaster. Over the years and about twenty-odd coats of paint it sort of blended in. I doubt anyone would be looking for a way out of the tunnels now, only in, for maintenance," he explained.

"These weren't on the original blueprints we were given," Nicholls said.

"They wouldn't have been on the originals," the technician said. "They were more than likely added after the tunnels were shut down in case they needed to get to the wiring inside."

"Get some people over to the other original buildings. Tell them to look for openings near the original entrances for the tunnels. Then padlock the damn things," Brodie said.

Chapter
Eleven

IT WAS FINALLY the weekend and Brodie was exhausted and wired at the same time. They discovered Daryll Chambers was booked on a flight scheduled to arrive in Austin at 1:42 Sunday afternoon. The forensics lab hadn't been able to contribute much to their investigation. Bruising on her body indicated Karen Dietrick had been sexually assaulted. Deep bruises and bite marks around her breasts and thighs suggested it had been more than rough sex and had taken place over a period of time. Her exact time of death was difficult to determine due to the condition of her body. The best guess they could make on the preliminary report was she had been dead between four and six days at the time her body was found. Six was good for their case because Chambers would have still been in town at the time of her death. Four was bad because, according to the airline, he would have been out of town. All they could hope for was that he would still be carrying that damned key ring.

Assuming he was the killer of three people in less than a month, leaving virtually no evidence pointing directly to him, she was sure he wouldn't suddenly become careless or arrogant enough to keep physical evidence as a trophy. Like Maggie, she was absolutely certain Daryll Chambers was their killer. She just couldn't prove it conclusively...yet.

Maggie wouldn't officially be back on duty until Monday, but Brodie promised she could be at the airport when Chambers would be arrested the minute he stepped off the plane. What she really needed was a mindless day off.

Getting up early, she kept a promise she made to Max and the two of them set off for a run through the woods not far from her house. It was two miles to a nearby small lake and she soon fell into a comfortable rhythm as she maneuvered through the trees and light brush that were beginning to leaf out. Occasionally Max would discover a hapless squirrel and chase the small animal up a tree, barking exuberantly before racing to catch up with his owner. Once they reached the lake, she sat down to catch her breath before making the return trip, watching as Max dove into the lake to retrieve sticks she threw for him. She loved spending quiet time with the long-suffering Labrador. He never judged her and always forgave her when she neglected him due to a new case.

In spite of the still cool spring air, by the time her house came into view, sweat soaked her t-shirt. Max collapsed on the back deck and she smiled as the big dog's eyes drooped, indicating the beginning of a nap. Stripping off her damp shirt and sweatpants, she tossed them into the clothes hamper and slipped into drawstring shorts and a white t-shirt. Fifteen minutes later she was spraying water over the Camaro's hood. Besides Max, the vintage vehicle was the only other thing she loved. It had begun as a project car before she moved to Cedar Springs and she'd invested hundreds of hours of her time and a considerable chunk of her savings into restoring it. Except for the engine, most of the vehicle was original. She had been forced to replace the engine two years earlier and enjoyed tinkering with the vehicle, which ran better than many newer cars she'd driven. She had been offered fairly serious money for it, but couldn't bring herself to part with it.

Brodie was chamoising the top of the vehicle when Maggie's Subaru pulled into the driveway. She was surprised as she watched Maggie step out of the vehicle.

"What's up?" Brodie asked.

"Nothing much," Maggie said, shoving her hands into the back pockets of her jeans. "Just got tired of sitting around the house waiting for tomorrow to get here."

"You're looking better. How are you feeling?"

"Fine, thanks. Need help?"

"I'm about finished with the outside. You can clean the windows if you feel up to it."

Grabbing a roll of paper towels and a bottle of glass cleaner, Maggie opened the driver's side door and began spraying cleaner on the windshield, watching the muscles in Brodie's arms flex and relax as she moved the chamois over the hood of the Camaro. Working silently, the two women cleaned the vehicle until it sparkled inside and out.

An hour later Maggie followed Brodie into the house. "Would you mind getting some coffee started?" Brodie asked. "Everything's in the bottom cabinet. I'll be right back."

"No problem."

Brodie returned to the kitchen barefoot, wearing jeans and a UT t-shirt, her dark hair still damp from the shower, as the coffeemaker beeped. When Maggie glanced at her, she smiled to herself. It was obvious from the outline of hardened nipples under the t-shirt that Brodie hadn't bothered with underwear before dressing.

"Sorry, but I had to get cleaned up," Brodie said as she took a deep relaxing breath and pulled a mug from the cabinet next to the sink. "Been a long day."

Maggie looked at her watch. "I should get going and let you get some rest. Big day tomorrow."

"I wasn't hinting for you to leave, Maggie," she said.

"Royce...," Maggie started. Staring at the ceiling and clearing her throat, she said, "I...um...I wanted to thank you."

"For what?"

"For believing me about Chambers."

"The medallion started us looking in the right direction, and you found it," Brodie said, reaching out and placing her hand on Maggie's shoulder. "You're going to be a good detective. I've already told Donaldson that so start thinking about who you'd like to work with as a partner."

"I wish I could work with you."

"I've got my hands full with Nicholls. You might get lucky and get Romero."

Maggie laughed, "Is he always such a Don Juan wannabe?"

"Yeah, but he's a good investigator."

Maggie turned and rinsed her mug out. "Are we going to be friends, Royce?"

"I hope so. I'd like that."

"Me too. Well, I'd better shove off. I need to hit the grocery store before I go home."

As Maggie walked by her, Brodie brought her hand to rest in the small of her back and escorted her to her car. She reached around Maggie to open the car door. Stopping before she got in, Maggie asked, "Would you pick me up tomorrow?"

Brodie was partially bent at the waist. When she turned her head toward Maggie she found their faces were within inches of one another. There had been a time when being that close to Maggie's lips would have been more temptation than she could handle.

"Around noon," Brodie nodded as she straightened and stepped away from the Subaru.

CHECKING HER WATCH, Brodie turned onto Highway 71 and headed south toward the Austin airport. Hitting the speed dial on her cell, she had to wait only two rings before she heard Nicholls's voice.

"Where are you?" she asked.

"I'm at the gate waiting for Chambers' plane," he answered cheerfully.

"Maggie and I will be there in about fifteen minutes," she said. "Is the flight on time?"

"The arrival/departure board says it is. See you in a few," he said as he disconnected.

Nearly ten minutes later, Brodie brought the Camaro to a stop behind a Cedar Springs patrol car parked in front of the terminal. Another glance at her wristwatch told her it was one twenty-five. Another fifteen or twenty minutes and Daryll Chambers would be out of circulation and the citizens of Cedar Springs could fall asleep safely in their beds again. Even though she doubted the events on the university campus had kept many of them awake, she knew the student body had been edgy since the first two murders and they wouldn't know about the third until the next day when classes resumed.

Brodie and Maggie flashed their badges at the security gate leading to the arrival and departure gates for United Airlines. An airport security officer met them and escorted them to the waiting area where Nicholls was seated, watching planes take off and land.

"I just checked with air traffic control," he said as Brodie sat down next to him. "He's on the passenger manifest. The flight is on final approach, actually a couple of minutes early."

"Let's try not to scare the other passengers to death as they deplane," she said. "We'll just meet and greet him when he enters the waiting area and escort him to airport security for the actual arrest. Understand?"

"Between us and the additional security guards, I don't think he'll put up much of a struggle," Nicholls smiled.

The walkie-talkie held by one of the security guards squawked briefly. The man touched Brodie on the shoulder. "They're on the ground and it should take about ten minutes to taxi to this gate."

The three detectives stood up. "Maggie, I want you to stand here in the waiting area where Chambers will see you. Nicholls and I will stand on either side of the ramp entrance. Give us a signal when you see him. Hopefully when he sees you, he'll be distracted long enough for us to grab him."

Maggie nodded as they watched the plane roll slowly toward the exit portal. Brodie winked at Maggie as they moved to assume their positions. Just in case things didn't go as planned, Maggie unsnapped her holster and took the safety off her revolver, resting her hand on the butt of the gun.

Slowly, passengers began making their way up the ramp, some pulling carry-ons, others carrying laptops and briefcases. Periodically, there would be a large space between one group of passengers and the next. Maggie tensed every time she caught a glimpse of a younger man, only to be disappointed when the man looked up or came closer to the entrance to the lobby. After nearly fifteen minutes of deplaning passengers, three stewardesses pulling rolling airline luggage walked through the door. Brodie reached out and stopped them before they made it to the waiting area.

"Are there any other passengers on the plane?" she asked as she produced her badge.

"No," one of the women answered. "There's no one left except the cockpit crew."

She thanked the women and she and Nicholls rejoined Maggie to ponder their problem.

"What the hell happened, Royce?" Maggie asked, clearly disappointed.

"Beats me," she shrugged. "Let's check with the airline and see what we can find out. Maybe he changed to a later flight at the last moment."

At the main terminal for United Airlines, the detectives explained their problem and the missing passenger. The ticket clerk called for her supervisor, who escorted them to his office. After introductions, Brodie explained their situation again.

"We're here to apprehend a suspect who was scheduled to arrive in Austin on your 1:42 flight from Boston. He was confirmed on the passenger list. Is it possible he changed to another flight?"

"He could have missed the flight. I can check our passenger lists to see if he's on a later flight," the supervisor offered. "What's the name?"

"Daryll Chambers," she said.

The man punched information into a computer terminal at his desk and checked all flights arriving in Austin the remainder of Sunday and until Monday evening.

"I'm sorry, Detective, but we don't have a passenger with that name listed on any incoming flight for the next forty-eight hours."

"How about earlier flights? Maybe last Friday?" she asked.

More information went into the computer and the supervisor watched as previous passengers manifests ran past his eyes. Finally, he shook his head and said, "Sorry. No Daryll Chambers or D. Chambers listed on earlier flights going back forty-eight hours either."

"Can you check other airlines from your terminal?" Nicholls asked.

"The ones flying in and out of Austin? Sure," the man said. Minutes dragged by as the man accessed the other airlines one at a time.

"Why do you think he changed his travel plans, RB?" Nicholls asked.

"Who knows? Maybe he's clairvoyant," she said with a frown.

"Maybe he talked to his mother," Maggie suggested, "and she told him about Ms. Bruce's call."

"I'm sorry, Detectives, but none of the airlines servicing Austin has had a passenger named Chambers on any of their past flights or have one listed for any incoming flights."

Brodie rubbed her eyes and looked at Maggie and Nicholls. "I hate to ask you to go over the passenger lists again, sir, but how about Griffin?" Shrugging, she said, "It's a long shot, but then this guy is slicker than a greased pig."

"If he did talk to his mother," Maggie observed, "then maybe he won't come back here at all and head off for parts unknown."

Brodie smiled, "No, I'm betting he's too arrogant to leave. After all, we don't have much on him except hunches and suppositions. Without the key ring, it's only your word against his. Pretty hard to base a conviction on that."

"Detective Brodie," the supervisor said as he stared at his computer screen.

"Yes, sir," she said.

"A D. Griffin was listed as a passenger on an American flight that came in Friday evening," the man said.

"What time did the flight land?"

"A little behind schedule. About 8:50."

"Where did the flight originate?" Brodie asked.

"Looks like a one-way, non-stop from LaGuardia."

"That's him!" Maggie said excitedly. "It has to be."

"What the hell is this asshole up to?" Nicholls asked. "He obviously knows we're onto him. This is just a sick fuckin' game for him."

"Guess we'll have to regroup," Brodie said as they walked out of the airline terminal toward their cars. "It's a head game now. I hope the three of us are smarter and quicker than he is. Put out an APB on him and make sure they have as recent a picture of him as we can find. Nothing more we can do right now. We'll start fresh Monday morning and hope no one else dies."

Once Brodie pulled away from the terminal, she cleared her throat and said, "I think you should stay at my place tonight, Maggie."

Maggie laughed. "Why?"

"Chambers is back in town and knows where you live. He was probably your attacker and I don't want to take a chance on an encore."

"If he's been back since Friday night he could have already tried again."

"Humor me. I have kind of a hinky feeling about this whole thing and I don't like it. I think he knows we're after him. That makes him extremely unpredictable."

"I'll have to go back to my place and pack a few things. And I need to call Carrie."

"How's that working out for you?" Brodie could have slapped

herself for asking such a personal question about something that was none of her business. "Sorry. I shouldn't have asked that."

"It's okay. I've known Carrie a long time. She's been a good friend, but I'm sure she wants more than friendship."

"If you have a chance to be happy, you should grab it," Brodie said as she kept her eyes glued to the road. "A very smart woman told me that recently."

"WHAT THE HELL do you mean you're staying at Brodie's house tonight?" Carrie demanded. "If you need a place to stay, you can stay with me."

Maggie took a deep breath and carried the cordless phone into her bedroom. She smiled briefly at Brodie as she left the room. When she closed the door to her bedroom she said, "You live in Austin, Carrie. Traffic back to Cedar Springs would be hell in the morning."

"Is she coming on to you, Mag?"

"No!"

"You're my girlfriend now. Surely you can understand why I'd be a little upset. I don't trust Brodie now any more than I did eight years ago."

"I suppose that means you don't trust me then," Maggie said as she rubbed her forehead.

"I do trust you, baby. I just don't trust her."

"Look, can we talk about this later? I have to pack a few things before we leave."

"What if I told you not to go? I can stay at your place with you."

"We're dating, Carrie, we're not married. Get a grip, for Christ's sake. There's nohting going on between me and Brodie. You can't give me orders. You sound like my fucking father."

"He was right the last time, or don't you remember that?"

"Of course I remember it. I'll tell you, just like I told my father. What happened eight years ago was an accident. An avoidable one, but still an accident. I have to go," she said quickly and disconnected.

Maggie was fuming as she threw clothing and toiletries into a small rolling suitcase. Who the hell did Carrie think she was? Sure, they had been dating a while, but no matter how hard she tried, Maggie couldn't see them as a couple. The sex was good, but not enough to build a relationship on. They didn't have the kind of relationship Maggie wanted. She knew what she wanted. She looked in the mirror over her dresser and ran her hands through her hair. She knew exactly what she wanted.

ROYCE AND MAGGIE spent the remainder of the day together. Before dark Brodie grilled steaks on the barbecue and they spent a relaxing evening talking, laughing and getting reacquainted. After dinner Maggie volunteered to wash their dishes and ran Brodie out of the kitchen.

She lit a cigarette and filled her lungs with the welcome rush of nicotine as she rested her forearms on the deck railing. It was a beautiful early spring evening. She hated the idea of it ending. She felt surprisingly at peace for the first time in a long time.

"You really should stop smoking, you know?" Maggie said as she stepped up to the railing next to Brodie.

"Yeah. I know."

"I want to run by the university before I go to work in the morning."

"Why?"

"I want see if there's an entrance to the tunnels in the Biology Building we missed."

"I'll agree only if you take another officer with you."

"I don't think Chambers would be stupid enough to return to the university. He knows we're looking for him."

"Promise you'll take a campus security guard with you or I'll go over there myself."

"All right. I promise. Thanks."

"It's been a long day. Ready to call it a night?"

"Royce…" Maggie started. She stopped and looked out over the back yard.

"What?"

"Nothing really," Maggie chuckled. "Today just reminded me of old times. Good times."

Brodie looked at Maggie's profile in the moonlight. It had been like old times. Having Maggie with her at the end of the day was something she had never gotten over. She probably never would. She wanted that feeling back in her life. Without Maggie she was only living half a life. She blinked hard when she discovered Maggie staring back at her. Not sure what she saw in her eyes, she reached out tentatively and stroked her hair. Maggie leaned into the touch for a moment before straightening and stepping into Brodie's arms. She closed her eyes and wrapped her arms around Brodie's neck.

"I've missed you so much," Maggie said, her voice a soft sigh against Brodie's neck.

Slipping her hands under Maggie's shirt, enjoying the feel of her skin, warm and smooth beneath her fingers, Brodie felt her stomach clench. "I've missed touching you."

She kissed Maggie tenderly and without hurry, content with the intimacy of the moment. Slowly pulling Maggie's shirt over her head, Brodie could sense Maggie's growing arousal as her eyes took in her body and her hands continued to explore the once familiar and sensitive areas of Maggie's body.

"Maggie...," Brodie began softly.

Maggie kissed her again before she could finish what she was going to say. Her lips parted, allowing Brodie's tongue to probe her mouth. Maggie knew she could not get enough of that touch. Her need for Brodie to make love to her again became unbearable and she felt herself being lowered onto the chaise lounge on the deck, Brodie's thigh pressing between her legs. Brodie had never spoken much when they made love, letting her hands and mouth tell Maggie everything she felt.

With her mind numbed by the delicious feel of Brodie's mouth taking her, Maggie pressed against her, seeking more, awed by the gentleness their foreplay.

"Please, Royce...I...," Maggie managed as her hips fell into the rhythm of Brodie's mouth moving against her, pushing her body closer and closer to the edge of explosive pleasure. Maggie's thoughts were brief as Brodie thrust into her, suddenly hard and demanding. The feeling was so unexpectedly intense that Maggie bucked violently toward the inevitable release her body demanded. Their kisses became passionate and frantic.

"I've been waiting for you....so long," Maggie gasped. Finally overtaken by the pleasurable feelings, Maggie could hold back no longer, her body exploding with the orgasm that took control of her body. Brodie pulled Maggie into her arms and held her tightly as a series of smaller shudders coursed through her until her body relaxed. They were both physically exhausted.

"That was...incredible, Royce," Maggie said as she began to regain control of her breathing.

"We should talk, Mag."

"I couldn't think straight if I had to right now. Can we just go to bed?"

Brodie pulled Maggie up and led her into her bedroom where she continued to hold her until they both fell asleep. A few hours later Brodie was awakened by Maggie's lips on her back and they continued their lovemaking through the night. Neither could get enough of the other and Maggie seemed to never run out of ways to excite and satisfy her.

When Maggie awoke the next morning, Brodie was dressed and holding two mugs of coffee. She leaned down and kissed her lightly before handing her a cup.

"I hope it's all right," Brodie smiled as she handed her a mug and sat on the edge of the bed.

Maggie smiled back as she took a sip. "Have you been up long?

Brodie sat down on the edge of the bed next to her.

"About an hour," Brodie said as she reached over and smoothed Maggie's hair. "How are you feeling?"

Maggie smiled at her and set the cup down on the nightstand. Turning to face Brodie, she took her face in her hands and kissed her deeply.

"Maggie...," Brodie began.

Maggie silenced her by placing her fingers on Brodie's lips. Brodie took her hand and kissed the fingertips. "Did we make a mistake, Maggie?"

"I made a mistake eight years ago, but not now. I'm in love with you, Royce," Maggie finally managed to get out as she leaned toward her and took her in her arms. "I always have been. I always will be."

Brodie glanced at the clock on the nightstand. "Once we have our guy in custody, we have a lot to talk about," she said as she kissed Maggie lightly.

Chapter
Twelve

SOMETHING NAGGED AT the back of Maggie's brain, but she couldn't quite come up with what it was. She smiled as she stepped out of the shower, remembering the feel of Royce's body against hers the night before. She'd given Royce up once and was determined not to lose her again. She had finally taken control of her life and while she might go to hell the way her father predicted, she would enjoy every step along the path. She should have left Austin when Royce did. She had been a coward and didn't realize what she had lost until it was gone. Not this time. She would prove to Royce she loved her and to her father that she deserved to be a detective. She picked up her cell phone and punched in a number.

"Brodie," a voice answered.

"Good morning," Maggie said.

"We already said that about fifteen minutes ago," Brodie laughed.

"Just wanted you to know I meant it. I just got out of the shower."

"Wish I'd been there for that," Brodie said.

"Next time. Now I'm going to get dressed and head to the university."

"Call me if you find anything and remember your promise. And hey, Maggie?"

"Yeah."

"In case I didn't say it last night, I love you."

"You told me in several ways," Maggie said with a smile. "I love you too, Royce."

BRODIE WAS IN a good mood when she arrived at the squad room. For the first time in longer than she cared to think about, she had something to look forward to when she returned home at night.

"Anything new?" she asked cheerfully as she sat down at her desk.

"No one else has been killed...yet," Nicholls said, not quite as cheerfully. "Maggie's late."

"She'll be here later," Brodie shrugged. "She wanted to take another look at something at the university. Anything from the APB?"

"Well, we know he's in the area," Nicholls said. "It's not like he's the Invisible Man, for God's sake. We've put campus security on alert and I asked Romero and a couple of others to stroll around the campus in plain clothes. We have an unmarked unit keeping an eye on his house."

"It sounds like we've done all we can for now unless we want to spend the day driving around hoping to trip over him," Brodie shrugged. "Let's put together everything we know so far and see if we can get a feel for what he might do next."

"Do you think it's possible he might have other victims in mind?" Nicholls asked.

"Well, so far everyone he's killed has been for a purpose," Brodie said. "He needed Garcia's keys, Brauner showed up unexpectedly, Maggie saw the key ring and so did the girlfriend who probably also doctored his academic records. Maggie's the only one who survived. I don't think he'd really planned on that one," Brodie said. "If she hadn't seen the key ring it wouldn't have happened. And maybe he just didn't want to take the chance that the girlfriend would put it all together. One thing for sure, though, is that his whole game plan has gone out the window. He could easily move on to another job or another college, cozy up to another unsuspecting woman and continue on his merry way. Once he knew we were on his trail, he should have disappeared to parts unknown."

"Could be he's pissed at us for ruining his little scam," Nicholls said. "If he's back here to seek revenge against any of us, then he's probably gone completely around the bend."

"Don't worry. He can't stay hidden for long. He needs the attention," Brodie stated.

"What do you mean?" Nicholls asked.

"Everything he's done in the past and his most recent actions seem to indicate that he's seeking attention and apparently trying to prove to us and himself that his intelligence is greater than ours."

"A giant in his own mind," Nicholls said.

"Possibly."

MAGGIE WALKED DOWN the steps to the basement of the Biology Building. She had searched the interior of the building again and found nothing that would pass as an entrance into the old tunnel system. She looked through a set of keys she had picked up from the University Police. She tried two or three before finding one that unlocked the padlock on the outside door into the basement. She looked around the area nearest the building as she removed the padlock and opened the door. Now that it was officially spring, the grounds crews were busy making the large gardens that dotted the campus ready to receive new plants. The fresh scent of newly turned earth made her smile. Spring was a time for new beginnings.

She entered the basement and switched on the weak overhead light. She had promised Royce she'd take a security guard with her, but would prove she could handle it alone. "There's another door into the tunnels behind these old file cabinets," she muttered to herself as she walked across the room. She peered over the top of the cabinets and located the door. She heard a muffled sound and glanced over her shoulder. She spun quickly around and reached for her service revolver. A fist to her jaw stopped her immediately and she fell to the floor.

OVER THE NEXT two or three hours, the two detectives put together a detailed timeline of Chambers' actions and movements along with a timeline of their responses. It was nearly noon by the time Brodie rubbed her eyes and stretched.

"I don't know about you, but I'm thinking I need to rejuvenate with a little chicken fried steak. How about it?"

"Sounds like a winner to me," Nicholls said. "Give Maggie a shout and have her join us."

Brodie stood up and began pulling her jacket on. As she was waiting for Nicholls to return from the men's room, she called Maggie's cell number. The phone switched over to voicemail as the desk officer came into the squad room.

"This came for you a little while ago, Lieutenant," he said as he handed Brodie a small manila envelope.

"Thanks," Brodie said with a smile and flipped her cell closed. Looking down the hall, she muttered to herself, "What's taking him so long? And where the hell is Maggie?" Absently, she tore open the end of the envelope and looked inside.

"Oh, fuck," she breathed as Nicholls finally walked up beside her.

"What is it, RB?" he asked.

Brodie looked at him as she dumped the contents of the envelope onto her desk.

"Where the hell did that come from?" Nicholls asked as he stared at the religious medallion.

"Someone left it here for me. The fucker was right here in the station!" Brodie exclaimed, moving quickly to the front desk and trying to remain calm. When the desk officer saw her, he smiled," What's up, Loo?"

"Were you at the desk when this envelope was left for me?"

Brodie asked.

"Yeah. I would have gotten it to you sooner, but it was left at the same time a patrol unit brought a guy in for booking," the officer answered.

"Can you describe the person who left it?"

"I think so, but I wasn't paying total attention. It was a man, probably in his late twenties or early thirties," the officer started.

"Five ten, around 180 pounds with blue eyes and short black hair?" Brodie continued for him.

"Yeah," the officer smiled, "that sounds about right."

"Then I guess," Brodie seethed as she reached onto the counter and grabbed a copy of their APB, "you didn't notice that he matched this description of a triple murderer we're looking for?"

"Shit!" the desk officer hissed.

"How long ago did he leave the envelope?"

"Ten or fifteen minutes ago. I'm sorry, Lieutenant."

"Did you notice whether he was in a vehicle?"

"Sorry, he just asked that I get it to you and left," the officer apologized. "He was only here less than a minute."

"Okay," Brodie sighed.

"He's playing with us," Nicholls said.

"And he's winning," Brodie retorted, walking toward the front entrance of the station.

Nicholls followed her and they both stepped outside and looked up and down the street.

"He could be anywhere," Nicholls sighed, placing his hands on his hips and squinting up into the sun.

"Do the reports on him tell us anything about his habits, likes and dislikes?" Brodie asked.

"Not much. Except for Karen Dietrick he seems to have pretty much been a loner."

As Brodie turned to reenter the station, her cell phone chirped. Pulling it out of its holster, she flipped it open. "Brodie!" she barked.

"Lieutenant Brodie, this is Sheriff Cantrell."

"What's up, Sheriff?"

"I'm over here at your house. We received an anonymous phone call about twenty minutes ago that a crime had been committed. There's a bod...," the Sheriff started.

"No!" she shouted as she bolted down the steps and raced toward her car, fumbling to get the keys out of her pocket.

"Brodie!" Nicholls called as he ran after her. By the time he reached her car and jerked the passenger door open, the Camaro was already in reverse. Just as she threw the gear into drive, he managed to jump in. "What the hell's going on?"

"He's been in my house," she said through gritted teeth.

"Maggie was there when I left for work." Glancing from side to side at intersections, she gunned the engine and flew through red lights, barely avoiding other vehicles that had the right of way. Turning sharply to the right, the Camaro sailed over a rise on the road leading to her home ten miles outside Cedar Springs. Five minutes later, she slowed as she approached the driveway of the house. Maggie's Subaru was parked in front of the detached garage.

She skidded to a stop and flew out of the vehicle, Nicholls close behind her. She ran toward the front porch, but was stopped by a Sheriff's Deputy.

"Get out of my way," she growled menacingly. "This is my house."

"It's a crime scene and you'll have to wait out here until we're finished and the body is removed," the deputy said.

Brodie shoved the deputy away and started for the front door again. He grabbed her and spun her around, just in time to take the full force of her fist.

"Cedar Springs Police," Nicholls yelled, flashing his badge.

"Let them through, Doyle," the Sheriff called out from the porch.

Brodie's legs felt like melting Jell-O as she made her way up the front steps. She looked numbly at Sheriff Cantrell, not sure what to say. He placed a big hand on her shoulder. "It's ugly in there, Brodie. Maybe you should wait outside. We're waiting for your forensic people to arrive."

She shook her head and stepped into the living room. Nothing looked disturbed as she walked slowly through the front rooms. Turning down the hallway she stopped in front of the bathroom, the room where she had last seen Maggie. Her heart stopped as she looked into the room. A pool of blood surrounded the black body on the white tiled floor. She blinked back tears as she saw smeared blood on the floor leading out of the room.

She stepped back and looked at Nicholls. Her eyes shifted toward the room at the end of the hallway, her bedroom, the scene of so much joy just a few hours earlier. She could see bloody footprints leading to it. Nicholls moved ahead of her and glanced into the bedroom. Four sets of eyes turned toward him, momentarily stopping their work. Nicholls swallowed hard before facing Brodie to prevent her from seeing the scene.

"No! No! No! No!" Brodie screamed as she tried to push past him. "Maggie! Oh, God! Maggie! Please!"

"Brodie!" Nicholls yelled as he grabbed her and wrapped his arms around her to keep her out of the room. She fought against him, but grief had sapped the energy out of her and she collapsed to the floor, rubbing her face and burying her head in her hands. She sobbed uncontrollably and barely heard Nicholls calling Donaldson. As he slipped his cell phone back into his pocket he knelt next to Brodie and helped her to her feet, guiding her down the hallway toward the living room.

BRODIE STARED AT the wall in her living room without acknowledging the activity around her. Frank Cardona and his men walked past her without their usual banter. Just a few short hours ago Maggie had been vibrantly alive in her arms, laughing. Now she was gone, her laughter silenced...forever. She drew a shaky breath as tears burned down her cheeks unnoticed.

"Brodie?" She looked up into the eyes of Fred Donaldson. "Can I get you anything?"

She shook her head and closed her eyes, forcing more wetness onto her face. "Have they found anything useful?" she asked.

"It doesn't matter. I'm taking you off the case," he said quietly.

"No!" she said forcefully, anger and hatred flashing in her eyes. "He's mine."

"You can't..." he started.

"I'll work it on my own even I have to resign to do it!"

She stood and walked down the hallway on wobbly legs. When she entered her bedroom, Nicholls was at her side in an instant to turn her around. "You don't want to see this, RB," he said quietly.

"I have to," she said grimly. Pushing past him, she took a deep breath and inhaled the unwelcome scent of death around her. As she approached the bed, she patted Frank on the back. He turned away from the body on her bed and stared at her.

"Jesus, Brodie! You shouldn't be in here."

"It's okay, Frank. I just need a minute," she said. "You got an extra pair of gloves?"

As she pulled the gloves on, she forced herself to look at the body. The woman's pale body had begun to take on a gray, ashen look. Slowly scanning the victim, her eyes traveled up well defined legs, over the auburn mound of her crotch, and along the flat abdomen. The breasts had large bruises and bite marks resembling those on Karen Dietrick's body. She shuddered involuntarily at the pain Maggie had endured. Standing to the side of the bed, she looked at the disfigured face, partially covered by auburn hair. She used her gloved fingers to tenderly lift the hair away from the ruined face. Bending over slightly, she saw the gold hoop of a pierced earring resting against the woman's neck. Standing up, she pulled the gloves from her hands and tossed them in the wastebasket next to the bed. "Thanks, Frank," she said, turning to leave the room quickly.

In the hallway she stopped and let her body slide down the wall.

Resting her elbows on her bent knees she covered her face with her hands as the tears began flowing once again. She felt a hand on her shoulder and looked up into Nicholls' worried eyes.

"It's...it's not Maggie," she managed.

"How the hell you know that? Without a face..." He stopped and said, "I'm sorry, RB."

"It's not Maggie, Nicholls. Maggie doesn't have pierced ears," she said tersely.

"Jesus," Nicholls breathed. "Then who's in there?"

"Her name is Kara. I don't know her last name. Kara might not be her first name. I only met her once, but it was enough to cause her death."

"What?"

"She was a call girl I met."

Nicholls frowned. "You're a sick bitch, Brodie."

Brodie held her hand out and Nicholls pulled her up. "Have they removed my dog yet?" she asked.

"Yeah, they took him away a little while ago."

She walked into the bathroom, avoiding the pool of blood, and closed the door before she turned and vomited into the toilet. She was overcome with fear. Chambers had to have followed her to know about Kara. But that had been weeks ago. She splashed water on her face and slowly dried her hands and face before stepping out of the bathroom.

"What are you going to do now, Brodie?" Donaldson asked as soon as she joined him and Nicholls in the living room.

"Try to think," she said as she walked onto the front porch. She slipped on her sunglasses and looked around her yard which was now full of police cars and vehicles from the crime lab. She caught something out of the corner of her eyes and said, "He's got Maggie!"

Chapter
Thirteen

MAGGIE GROANED AND tried to touch her face. It was dark and damp and her hands were handcuffed behind her back. She heard what sounded like water dripping somewhere in the distance. She tried to remember what had happened and shook her head. She had been in the basement. She squeezed her eyes closed. She remembered seeing a man wearing a brown grounds crew uniform and sunglasses. She remembered catching a glimpse of a smile as a fist made contact with her jaw. The hint of a smile was familiar. Chambers! He was here...in the tunnels. Her breathing increased and she began to feel sick. She was trapped, probably alone with a killer.

"WHAT DO YOU mean, he's got Maggie?" Donaldson demanded.

"Her car is here and it shouldn't be. We have to get to the university," Brodie said as she tried to restrain the near-panic she felt inside.

"Maggie went to the university?" Donaldson asked. "You chewed her ass out once before for going somewhere alone."

"She called me on my way to work this morning. I told her she could go as long as she took a security guard with her. Chambers must have attacked her again. He used her car to transport the body here." Brodie rubbed her forehead, trying to draw together the scanty facts she knew, all the while wondering how Chambers had managed to pull off another possible double murder.

"Call some patrol units and get them over to the university," Donaldson ordered. "Where was she going?"

"The Biology Building. Call campus security and see if the guard with her has checked in yet." Brodie pulled out her cell and punched in Maggie's number, praying she would answer. Four rings later the phone switched to voice mail. "I'm going to the university," she announced as she ran down the steps of her home.

Nicholls sprinted after her and got in the Camaro. Brodie backed out of the driveway and swung the vehicle onto the main road into Cedar Springs. Nicholls stared at her across the front seat for a few minutes. "So why would Chambers bring Maggie's car to your house, Brodie?"

"He must have seen us and is using it as a mind game."

"Seen what?"

She looked across the car at him. "You don't want to know."

"Know what? That you're fuckin' your trainee?"

"Something like that. Make sure you include that in your report to Donaldson," she said bitterly.

"Not my business," he said, looking out the passenger window.

"Look, Nicholls. I know how you feel about gays so let's not tip-toe around it anymore."

"You're right. I think it's sick. Up until now we've been able to work around it, but now, in my opinion, it's interfering with your ability to do the job. Your personal life is intruding too much into your professional life. You can't do your job when you're busy looking at a piece of ass all the time."

"Is that what you think I've been doing?"

"You are now."

"Chambers has made it personal. I need you to back me up professionally. Can you do that?"

"I know my job," he snapped. "We'll discuss the rest when Weston is safe."

Brodie pulled into a parking slot in front of the University police office. She and Nicholls walked quickly into the office and showed their badges.

"Well, you're the second and third Cedar Springs detectives to grace us with your presence today," the officer at the reception desk said.

"Has the security guard who accompanied Detective Weston returned yet?" Brodie asked.

"No one went with her. She just waltzed in here and asked for the master keys to the Biology Building and left."

"An officer didn't go with her?" Brodie asked again.

"She said she just wanted to look the building over. Didn't request any further assistance."

"Fuck!" Brodie exclaimed. "She promised!"

Nicholls grabbed Brodie's arm. "Let's go. Donaldson's sending some patrol units and we already have Romero and a couple of others watching for Chambers."

Brodie peeled away from the police office and drove as fast as she could toward the Science Quadrangle. When she stopped in front of the building she and Nicholls looked around. A few minutes later Nicholls spotted Romero.

"You seen Weston?" he asked as they approached him.

"She was here earlier. She and I practically crawled over every inch of this building. Didn't find anything new and exciting,"

Romero said with a shrug.

"Well, where the hell is she now?" Brodie demanded.

"She told me she was going to the office. Her car's gone so I figured she was enjoying coffee and doughnuts while we're out here watching for the phantom."

"Did you see her leave?" Brodie pressed.

"I went inside for a few minutes to cool off. Her car was gone when I came back outside. What's the deal?"

"She's missing," Nicholls said. "Did you see anyone suspicious hanging around? Anyone at all?"

"Shit! There's people all over the damn place including a bunch of groundskeepers who've been working around here since I arrived."

Four patrol cars came to a halt in the middle of the Science Quadrangle. Two officers climbed out of each vehicle and looked around the area.

"Take two officers and go through the building again," Brodie ordered. "Nicholls, have the others cordon off the building. You go around the outside to the right and I'll take the left. Take a walkie talkie and let me know if you find anything."

Brodie and Nicholls each grabbed a walkie talkie and began their search around the exterior of the building. She searched behind every bush and stopped to ask a few of the groundskeepers questions, without success. When she turned the corner of the building, she glanced down at the door to the basement. The padlock was closed and she started to move away when she decided to double check the padlock. On the last step she saw that the padlock was locked, but wasn't through the hasp attached to the door. She grabbed her walkie talkie to call Nicholls. She pressed the transmit button and heard only static. She smacked the device with the flat of her hand, but was still unable to transmit.

"Fuck!" She dropped the walkie talkie and pulled her revolver from its holster, holding it down as she quietly opened the door. With a final shove the door flew open and she knelt as she visually swept the room. She moved to the second door. Old rusting file cabinets no longer obstructed the entrance into the tunnel system. She took a deep breath to calm herself as she reached out and turned the doorknob.

A HARSH BEAM of light struck Maggie's eyes. She turned her head away from the light, hoping her eyes would adjust quickly.

"I've been watching you. I could have killed you any time I wanted to," Chambers' voice rasped.

"Then why am I still alive?" Maggie managed.

"I was curious how long it would take you to put together what you'd seen." He squatted down beside her and turned her head to face him. She winced from the dull pain along her jawline.

"Now what are you going to do? Finish the job?" she asked.

"Soon. You've already spilled the beans, so to speak."

"If you knew that why would you be stupid enough to come back here?" Maggie asked.

Her question was answered by a slap across the face. "Never call me stupid!"

She ran her tongue over her teeth and was glad to feel they were all there despite the taste of blood in her mouth.

"I didn't mean you were stupid, Darryl, but coming back may not have been the best move," she said, trying to remain calm.

"The game isn't over yet," he sighed.

"What game? Three innocent people dead isn't a game, dammit."

"Survival of the fittest, or the smartest, has always been a game, Detective."

"Since I'll probably end up another loser in your game maybe you'll answer a question for me."

"What's that?"

"How the hell did you get in and out of these tunnels without being seen? I've searched this entire building two or three times and never found anything but the maintenance openings."

"Then you found the answer."

"You couldn't have carried those men's bodies down that vertical ladder."

"They were dead when they hit the bottom," Chambers said matter-of-factly.

Maggie closed her eyes and swallowed hard.

"I felt bad about Garcia. He trusted me, but had what I needed."

"His keys."

"Yes. Brauner walked in on me in his office and didn't leave me any choice."

"And Karen?"

"Also a means to an end, but she was beginning to ask too many questions. I can't leave witnesses behind. I'm sure you understand that. Now, unfortunately, you've put yourself into that category. You saw the medallion. You can place it in my possession. Only you can do that. Everything else is nothing more than conjecture, despite what you've told others. I no longer have it."

Chambers reached behind Maggie and jerked her to her feet. The sudden movement shot a jolt of pain through her shoulders and she couldn't suppress crying out.

THE DOOR INTO the tunnel was unlocked when Brodie turned the knob and stood to the side to push the door open. She reached inside and flipped the light switch next to the door, but no lights came on. She stepped inside and scanned the walls and ceiling while her eyes adjusted to the dim light that made its way through the overhead grates.

Holding her revolver in front of her, she inched into the tunnel, listening carefully for any sound that might guide her toward Maggie and Chambers. It was damp and musty in the old tunnel, but beads of sweat began forming on her forehead, every muscle in her body tense. Her eyes swept along the checkerboard of light as she slowly moved forward, staying as close to the wall as possible. She was well past the scene of Garcia's murder before she heard anything except the sound of dripping water and the pounding of her own heart.

"Fuck," she breathed when she spotted a rat scratching along the tunnel floor. There were no more sounds as Brodie continued down the tunnel. She stopped at an intersection that apparently led to other buildings. Ahead she could no longer see light from the grates. Thinking she must be under the building itself, she stood still for three or four minutes hoping her eyes would adjust to the darkness, but it didn't help. There was nothing but black for her eyes to adjust to. Using her free hand to feel along the damp wall, she moved as fast as she felt comfortable moving, sliding her feet along the floor in case it had been booby-trapped. There was a slight curve in the wall and halfway around the curve her eyes picked up an extremely dim light and the sound of low voices. She estimated she had moved about a hundred feet into the tunnel and stepped back from the curve and gripped her revolver down in front of her with both hands.

She rested against the damp tunnel wall, attempting to bring he erratic breathing under control before cautiously moving again. The farther she moved the more light she saw, although it was extremely weak. She paused every few steps to listen for sounds that might indicate she wasn't alone. What she wouldn't give for a team of S.W.A.T. officers watching her back right now.

She had gone only a few feet when she heard a woman's voice cry out. *Maggie!* She increased her speed until she came to what appeared to be a small room off the main tunnel and the source of the light. She stepped into the entrance of the room and brought her gun up quickly. Maggie's hands were secured behind her back and Chambers' arm was wrapped around her neck, forcing her closely against his body.

"Step away from Detective Weston and put your hands behind your head, Chambers," Brodie ordered, leveling her revolver at his head. "This doesn't have to go any further."

"Royce...," Maggie started as Chambers swung the beam of the flashlight up into her eyes. Brodie raised one hand to block the light and saw the glint of a knife blade in his right hand held against Maggie's neck.

"I think it would be a better idea for you to lay the gun down and kick it away. Don't you think so, Detective Brodie?" Chambers grinned.

"Don't...do...it," Maggie managed as the blade pressed into her neck with each word.

"Shut up!" Chambers ordered, pressing the sharp tip of the knife blade into the soft skin under Maggie's chin. Turning his attention back to Brodie, he said, "I'd like to think you came alone, Brodie, but I'm not stupid."

Looking around, she answered, "You don't see anyone with me, do you?"

"Lay the fucking gun down and kick it away," Chambers ordered. Brodie saw the knife tip push into Maggie's neck, drawing blood.

Squatting down, she kept her eyes on Chambers as she lowered the gun to the floor. As soon as she stood up, she pushed it away and watched it slide across the cement floor.

"Now what?" she asked. "You know there's no way out of here."

"That would seem to present a problem, wouldn't it?" Chambers hissed slowly.

"Well, the floor is all yours, Daryll, and you seem to be holding all the cards. What's your next play going to be?" Brodie challenged.

Chambers smiled, allowing his left hand to slide idly up Maggie's body. Watching Brodie's face for her reaction, his fingers enclosed Maggie's breast, causing her to gasp as he caressed it. Closing his eyes briefly, he said, "Very nice. I can see why you couldn't resist yourself. That was quite an entertaining display I witnessed on your deck."

Hands clenching in a desire to kill, Brodie hoped she could keep her voice calm. "How long have you been following me?"

"From the beginning. It pays to know who you're playing the game against."

"You've already killed four people, but if you don't harm anyone else, maybe a jury will see that you're just a garden variety whack-o," Brodie smiled.

"You think I'm a whack-o, Detective?" Chambers snapped. "Didn't you like the present I left for you in your bed?" he taunted.

"She didn't deserve to die that way. You didn't even know her," Brodie snarled.

"But you knew her, didn't you, Detective? Does Maggie know

how intimately you knew Kara?" He watched Brodie's eyes shift toward Maggie. "Tell me, Brodie, on a scale from one to ten, who turned you on more?"

Chambers was goading her, pushing what he knew could be an advantage in his favor. She would explain everything to Maggie if they both survived. She forced her body to relax and smiled. "You're pretty good, Daryll. But you're still certifiable."

She noticed a slight change in Chambers' demeanor and knew she needed to push him harder. She needed to draw his attention away from Maggie. "You know, Daryll, I'm really getting tired of this game. You left clues a Boy Scout could follow and once we found the first one, you were already a goner. Your planning was mediocre at best. You know what they say about prior planning preventing piss-poor performance," Brodie pushed, taking a step forward. "That's what Brauner thought of your work, wasn't it? It was only mediocre. That's why you had to steal one of his exams. Without it you didn't have a fucking prayer of graduating without cheating!"

Chambers frowned as Brodie stared intently at Maggie and saw the fear in her eyes replaced by trust. Taking another step forward, she spat derisively, "You're still the same fucking loser you've always been, Daryll."

"I won't be the only loser here, Brodie," Chambers seethed. He grabbed Maggie's hair and pulled her head back sharply to expose her neck

Maggie brought her foot up and slammed it down into the arch of his foot, allowing her body to become dead weight as Chambers howled in pain, unable to continue holding her up. In an instant, Brodie attacked him, grabbing his right arm to prevent him from using the knife. He had difficulty standing on his injured foot as he and Brodie grappled. He finally managed to use his arm strength to shove her against the wall of the tunnel, dazing her slightly as her head struck the stone wall. He lunged at her with the knife, drawing blood as she barely managed to sidestep him to avoid more serious injury. The knife slashed through the air, backing her up as she felt a trickle of blood run down her arm.

There wasn't much maneuvering room in the tunnel, but she had to keep Chambers away from Maggie. In the second it took for her to glance toward where Maggie was struggling to get to her feet again, she felt the blade of the knife cut into her cheek and saw Chambers smiling. He was toying with her to drag out his game for as long as possible. Feeling all the rage she had kept bottled up inside explode, she launched her body into his, knocking him backward. His back struck the tunnel wall with a thud that she thought had surely knocked the breath from his lungs. She watched as he fell and slid halfway down the wall, then grabbed Maggie, quickly pushing her behind her own body for protection as she looked around for her revolver. Feeling blood running down her face, she set herself to meet the attack she knew was coming as she watched Chambers push himself away from the tunnel wall.

"Freeze! Drop the knife!" Nicholls' voice yelled as he stepped into the tunnel and aimed an assault rifle at Chambers. Allowing herself to relax slightly, Brodie turned her attention to Maggie. Her nightmare was over at last, she thought as she heard the knife clatter on the cement floor. Glancing at Nicholls, she said, "I'll cuff him."

While Nicholls covered her, she pulled handcuffs from her belt and walked toward Chambers. "You don't look like the bondage type to me, Detective Brodie," he laughed as she turned him around and grabbed his left arm. In a move she never saw coming, he bent his right arm and drove his elbow into her abdomen, knocking the breath out of her. Nicholls hesitated before firing and Chambers dove toward the flashlight and plunged them into darkness.

"Shoot!" Brodie ordered. She heard the sound of footsteps running, but couldn't see a damn thing. She groped for the flashlight and a minute later blinked as light lit up the walls once again.

"I'm sorry, RB," Nicholls said. "It happened too fast. I could have hit you or Weston. He can't get far." Brodie stopped herself before she snapped the same sentiment Tim Weston had said to her after Wheeler was killed. *Everything we do is fast.*

"Get these things off me," Maggie said. "Hurry!"

Pulling his handcuff keys out, Nicholls unlocked the handcuffs restraining Maggie's hands. She rubbed her wrists and quickly examined the cut on Brodie's cheek.

"I'm fine," Brodie muttered. "I hope you like your women scarred."

"I like my women alive," Maggie said. "Let's get you to a paramedic."

Moving quickly, the three detectives made their way out of the tunnel. "Send the S.W.A.T. team down there. I want every inch of those damn tunnels searched," Brodie ordered. "Anyone searching the building see him?" she asked.

"No one's reported anything unusual," Nicholls said.

"Well, fuck! He didn't just disappear into thin air. He couldn't have gone far."

"He told me he used the maintenance openings," Maggie said as she looked around. "Call a paramedic to check out Detective Brodie's injuries."

"I'm fine, Maggie," she snapped.

Running an arm around Brodie's waist, Maggie said, "Humor me."

"I'm sorry, baby," Brodie said with an attempt at a smile. "Oow!"

AS SHE LET a paramedic clean the cuts on her face and arm, Brodie listened to the com chatter between the S.W.A.T. team and Nicholls' walkie talkie. She visually made sure Maggie hadn't been injured and felt drained of energy. Maggie was alive and that was all that mattered at that moment.

"He left a woman's body in my house," Brodie said, wincing at the antiseptic stinging her cheek. "When I thought he had killed you I was out of my mind, baby."

She relaxed into Maggie's arms and scanned the small groups that were being held well behind the newly formed police lines. Suddenly she stood up. "It's him," she said. He was walking nonchalantly away from the Science Quadrangle.

As if he sensed he had been seen, Chambers glanced over his shoulder and saw Brodie pushing her way through a group of spectators. Quickly he stepped into the road and was almost hit by a compact car. The squeal of brakes was followed by Chambers opening the driver's door and pulling a woman out, shoving her toward the curb as he got in the car and put it in reverse.

Brodie stopped when she saw what was happening and ran toward the nearest police car, keeping her eyes on the vehicle as it picked up speed. She grabbed the open door of the patrol car and swung her body behind the wheel. She turned the key dangling in the ignition as Maggie jerked open the passenger door. Flipping on the lights and siren, Brodie sped after the dark-green Toyota. She was concentrating so hard on keeping him in sight she wasn't paying attention to whether other cars were following her.

The radio crackled and she heard Nicholls' voice. "We're not far behind you, RB. Don't lose him."

Not a chance in hell, she thought. Chambers wove the small car through early evening traffic, turning abruptly across lanes in his attempt to escape. As she gained on him, she slid past the street he had turned onto and had to back up. If he made it to the Interstate, he would be stuck in the congestion of commuters trying to get home. She floored the patrol car and frowned. If she didn't stop him before it got much darker, she could lose the dark car. He was driving dangerously fast now through suburban streets. She glanced in the rearview mirror, but didn't see another police car behind her. "Report our location," she ordered. Maggie grabbed the patrol car mic and keyed it. "We're moving down Southerland traveling southeast. Where are you?"

"Running parallel to you. Missed a turn," Nicholls reported.

"Garland curves back into Southerland a few blocks ahead," Brodie said.

Chambers swung the Toyota into another turn. "Turning on Westerfield," Maggie broadcast.

"Where the hell you going, asshole," Brodie muttered to herself. Westerfield was the curviest road in Cedar Springs and the scene of numerous accidents caused by drunks taking the curves too fast. She had to slow to keep from running her vehicle off the road. The smaller car had a shorter turning radius and was more maneuverable. Chambers was maintaining his speed, but was all over the road. He crossed the center line around another curve and Brodie saw headlights approaching and swerved back into her lane. Ahead of her she saw the Toyota lean and go up on two wheels for a few seconds before it dropped back onto road and began to skid as Chambers tried to bring it under control before the next curve. He didn't make it and the little vehicle left the road and sailed over a small drainage ditch before slamming into a wrought iron fence and stopping.

The patrol car slid to a stop as Chambers ran from the compact car. Brodie jumped out of the vehicle. "Wait for back-up!" she shouted to Maggie over her shoulder.

"He's out of the vehicle! Brodie's in foot pursuit near the old county cemetery!" Maggie reported, anxious to sprint after Chambers and Brodie.

It was getting dark, but Brodie could still see him ahead of her. Maggie was right, she thought. I need to quit smoking. Her lungs were bursting and her legs throbbed, but she let her anger drive her on. She heard sirens behind her in a distance, but couldn't risk stopping to wait for more officers to arrive. Long shadows from the trees in the cemetery were making it difficult to see and she slowed, looking around her. Old, ornate tombstones loomed before her and he could be hiding behind any of them. Moving forward in a low crouch, she drew her weapon, swinging it down each row of stones.

She stopped to listen and glanced behind her. The beams from several Mag-lites bounced in the closing darkness as other rushed to join her. They would be there in a few minutes. She listened for the sound of footsteps, but heard nothing. Working her way cautiously forward, she heard the sound of a cracking twig to her left and turned her weapon toward it. Light burst behind her eyes as she was struck from behind and fell to her knees. Before she could react, a blow across her ribs and abdomen forced the air from her lungs. As she gasped to breathe and call out her location, an arm wrapped around her throat and tightened. She struggled to get her feet under her and threw herself back toward her attacker, knocking him off his feet. He released her as he fell, but quickly scrambled up. Standing, she held an arm around her ribs. It was hard to breathe. She saw the flash of metal as it swung toward her.

Backing away, she tripped over a footstone and fell. Chambers stood over her, grinning. "Looks like the end of the line for you, Brodie," he said, breathing heavily.

Raising his foot, he brought it down over her chest. Mustering the last of her strength, she rolled away and only took a glancing blow to her side. A hand rolled her onto her back and she grunted as she felt the blade of his knife blade sink into her upper chest near her right arm. Suddenly blood exploded from Chambers' head and Stan Wheeler's face floated briefly through her mind. She brought her hand to the handle of the knife protruding from her body as she heard the call. "Brodie's down, get a paramedic here now!"

She smiled weakly as she saw Maggie's worried face leaning over her. Placing her hand over Brodie's, Maggie said quietly, "Leave it there, Royce. Let the doctors remove it."

"I'm tired, Maggie," Brodie said flatly.

"I know," Maggie said softly as she stroked a hand through Brodie's hair. "Don't you think about leaving me now."

FIFTEEN MINUTES LATER paramedics carried Brodie on a litter away from the cemetery. Maggie held her hand as the paramedics lifted the gurney quickly into the waiting ambulance.

She could barely keep her eyes open as the paramedic started an IV line in her left arm. She pulled Maggie down to her. "I was terrified that I'd lost you again, baby," she whispered.

"Never again, my love," Maggie smiled.

Brodie suddenly couldn't keep her eyes open. As her eyelids fluttered, she heard Maggie's voice calling her from somewhere in the distance. "Royce! Stay with me, baby."

Suddenly, the paramedic slapped the wall of the ambulance behind the driver. "Blood pressure's dropping fast. Let's go!"

"What's wrong?" Maggie demanded, feeling Brodie's hand go limp in her hand.

"Not sure," the paramedic said quickly as he grabbed the radio connecting him to Cedar Springs Memorial.

"Hang on, baby," Maggie pleaded as she spoke softly into Brodie's ear and squeezed her hand. "I love you."

Chapter
Fourteen

MAGGIE JERKED HER head up quickly when she felt a hand on her shoulder.

"Go home, Detective," a deep male voice said calmly.

Bringing her eyes into focus, Maggie saw Captain Donaldson standing over her, his face serious. Realizing she was still holding Royce's hand, she released her grip and stood, her body stiff from lack of movement.

"I'm okay, sir," she said, clearing her voice. "I'd like to stay."

"There's nothing you can do right now, Weston. Go home, get some rest."

"Please, Captain, I can't go until I know she'll be all right."

"That's not a request, Detective," Donaldson said firmly. "Someone will be with her until you return."

"Then I'd like to request a few days off," Maggie said.

"Request denied. Regardless of Detective Brodie's current situation, I need your report to wrap this case up. Nicholls told me you were invaluable in nailing Chambers. You can have a couple of days after your paperwork is completed."

It crossed Maggie's mind to resign on the spot as she looked down at Royce. As if reading her mind, Donaldson placed his big hand on her shoulder once again and looked at her closely. "She's going to be fine, Maggie," he said softly. "As your training officer, what would she tell you to do? She'll be expecting to see you here when the drugs wear off and she wakes up. So I'd move my ass if I were you."

"Thank you, Captain Donaldson," Maggie half smiled.

Briefly touching Royce's hand, Maggie turned to leave. "And bring me another cup of coffee when you come back," Donaldson ordered as he sat down heavily in a chair near Brodie's bed.

As the elevator descended to the main lobby of the hospital, Maggie finally realized how tired she was. Hailing a taxi, she closed her eyes during the short trip to her duplex and was startled when the driver tapped her on the leg. "We're here, lady."

Paying the driver, she struggled out of the back seat and trudged into her home. She didn't remember the last time she had eaten, but decided that a shower was more important. Stripping out of her clothes, she noticed for the first time that there was blood on her shirt and slacks, Brodie's blood. Shivering slightly, she threw them in the trash before stepping under the spray of water to wash away the fear that had gripped her heart for the last two days. Chambers' knife had done more damage to Brodie's body than the doctors originally believed, glancing off a bone and nicking the aortic arch. Brodie nearly bled to death internally before she was rushed into surgery. It was the middle of the night before she was finally taken to intensive care. Nicholls arrived at the hospital nearly an hour after she had been brought in and tried to convince Maggie to go home. She suspected he had been responsible for Donaldson's unexpected appearance that morning.

Drying her hair and quickly pulling on tan khakis and a polo shirt, Maggie grabbed her car keys and headed for the police department. The paperwork wouldn't take her more than an hour, she mentally estimated as she swung into a parking space. Nicholls looked up, surprised, when he saw her pull the chair away from her desk.

"What are you doing here?" he asked. "Is she..."

"She's not awake yet. Donaldson ordered me to leave and finish my paperwork for the case. Do I have you to thank for that?" she asked coldly.

"I haven't seen Donaldson, Maggie. I swear."

"As soon as I finish this, I'll be taking a few days off," she said matter-of-factly.

Reaching across her desk, Nicholls took her hand. "Is there anything I can do?"

Finally smiling, Maggie took a deep breath. "I'll let you know when you can visit. I know she'll want to see you, Nicholls."

His face darkened as he said, "I don't know what happened, Maggie. I...."

"It wasn't your fault. Royce and I both know that. Don't second guess yourself."

By noon Maggie was back in the hospital elevator carrying the promised cup of coffee for Donaldson. As she approached the ICU, she saw a flurry of activity around Brodie's area and her heart stopped. Rushing toward the room, she grabbed a male nurse. "What's wrong?" she asked.

Seeing the panic in Maggie's eyes, he patted her hand lightly. "Nothing. We're just getting everything ready to move her to a regular room."

Maggie felt as if her legs might collapse under her from the sudden relief. "Is she awake?"

"Still a little groggy from painkillers," he grinned. "You must be Maggie."

When Maggie nodded, he added, "Then you better get in there. She's been asking for you."

Maggie pushed her way into the room and her eyes found Royce's. Her mouth formed a half smile as Maggie made her way to the side of the hospital bed, taking the hand Royce held up for her. Setting the Styrofoam cup on a rolling table near the bed, Maggie leaned down. "I'm sorry I wasn't here when you woke up."

"Donaldson told me he ordered you out. You look great," Brodie said hoarsely.

"Where is he anyway? He promised to stay with you until I got back," Maggie said with a frown.

"He got a call on his cell and had to leave."

"I took the next couple of days off, so you're stuck with me now," Maggie smiled.

"I think I can endure it," Brodie said as she coughed. "Ouch! Remind me not to do that for a while."

"Excuse me, ma'am," the male nurse said. "We're ready to move her now. You can follow us."

"How about if I walk beside the bed while you move it?"

Seeing Maggie's grip on his patient's hand, he smiled. "I guess that would work, too." Looking at the orderly who would be helping with the transfer, he said, "Let's rock and roll, Leon."

By the time she received her hospital dinner tray Brodie and Maggie had talked and napped through the afternoon. After she ate the skimpy meal the hospital nutritionist provided for her, Brodie couldn't stop herself from going to sleep again. Maggie used the opportunity to leave for an hour to grab some dinner. She was hungrier than she thought and even the hospital cafeteria food tasted good. She finally pushed her tray away and leaned back to finish drinking a glass of tea.

Maggie stepped off the elevator on the fifth floor and nodded and smiled at hospital workers she passed in the hall as she walked back to Brodie's room. Pushing open the door to the room, Maggie stopped immediately. She would have recognized the back of the person standing next to the bed anywhere. Tim Weston turned his head toward her when he heard the door open. She glanced at Brodie, who was still sleeping peacefully.

"What are you doing here?" Maggie hissed.

"Just came to pay my respects to an injured officer," Weston said as he joined her at the door.

"I'll tell her you were here," she said, holding the door open for him.

"Can we talk?"

"Not here. There's a waiting room down the hall. I'll meet you there."

Tim left the room quietly while Maggie went to Brodie's side. Gently brushing dark hair away from her forehead, she leaned down and kissed her. She was almost to the door when she heard her voice. "Don't be too hard on him, Maggie."

Returning to the bed, she took Brodie's hand and smiled. "I didn't mean to wake you up."

"It's all right. Go talk to him, Mag."

"What's the point, Royce? I already know what he's going to say. I've heard it all before. He's not going to convince me to leave this time."

"Is that what happened eight years ago?" Brodie frowned.

"He threatened to ruin your career and could have gotten you killed. I...I couldn't let that happen to you."

"There's nothing he can do to me now. He's your father. I can't blame him for wanting to protect you from getting hurt."

"He hurt us both."

MAGGIE SHOVED HER hands into her jeans pockets as she walked into the waiting room. Tim Weston stood up when he saw her. He still carried himself ramrod straight, a habit he hadn't managed to break even in retirement.

"What do you want, Dad?"

"Just to talk. How is Brodie?"

"Not that you give a shit." She took a deep breath and cast her eyes down to the floor. "She has broken ribs and nearly bled to death from the shoulder wound. I'm sure you'll be disappointed to know she will survive."

Looking uncomfortable, Tim motioned toward a chair. "Can we sit? Please."

Maggie shrugged and sat down, stretching her legs in front of her, crossing them at the ankles and waited for her father to make the first move.

"Fred Donaldson called me yesterday," Weston began awkwardly. Clearing his throat, he continued, "We had a long talk."

"About what? Getting me re-assigned? I won't accept that."

"No, it wasn't about your training. Brodie is doing a...fine job with that," he said looking at his hands.

"She's an excellent officer and always has been," Maggie said flatly.

"Yes, yes she is. Listen, Maggie, I'm sorry about what happened, you know...before."

"I'm not the one you need to apologize to. You didn't try to destroy my career."

"You're my daughter, Maggie. Stan Wheeler was my best friend.

I was angry when he died because of a stupid mistake. And I was angry because I couldn't...accept who you were. I had to blame someone."

"And Royce just got in the way both times, I suppose."

"Look, Mag, I won't try to say I understand the choices you've made about your life. I probably never will. But you were only twenty-three. I'd heard lots of rumors about Brodie during the ten years I was her commander, not all of them good. She was fifteen years older than you and had, well...been around. Of course, I questioned her motives. I didn't want my daughter to wind up another notch on her belt."

"She's still fifteen years older, Dad. She has never treated me with anything but respect. When I was hurt eight years ago, you were the one who pushed her into it with the way you were riding her," Maggie said forcefully. "She almost lost her life to save me and bring a killer in. She would have done the same for Stan if she could have."

Maggie stood up and straightened her jeans. Tim looked at his daughter and pushed himself out of his chair. "Donaldson also told me you're going to make an excellent detective."

"I hope so," Maggie smiled slightly in spite of herself.

"Just pay attention to what your training officer tells you," Tim said as they began walking out of the waiting room.

Stopping him, Maggie looked at Tim. "I don't expect you to understand me or my life, Dad. I'm sorry if I've disappointed you and Mom, but this is who I am."

"You're a strong woman, Maggie," he nodded. "Always have been. I want you to be happy. I'm proud of what you've accomplished in spite of my interference."

When they reached Brodie's room, Tim turned to Maggie. "I'd like to speak to her alone, if you wouldn't mind."

Maggie frowned, but finally shrugged and leaned against the wall outside the room. "She knows how to take care of herself."

Fifteen minutes later, Tim left the room and kissed Maggie on the forehead. "I better get home before your mother reports me as a missing person."

Maggie found Brodie lying partially inclined on the bed. She smiled when she saw Maggie, "I'm glad you're back. I missed you," she said, extending her hand.

Maggie stepped forward and took Brodie's hand, lifting it to her lips. "I was only gone an hour."

"It was an eternity."

Leaning closer, Maggie's fingers caressed Brodie's face.

"Maggie, I...," Brodie began softly.

"Don't talk, baby," Maggie said as their lips met. Deepening their kiss longingly, they were both breathless when their lips finally parted.

"You're in some serious trouble when I get out of here," Brodie said huskily.

"I think I can handle it, Lieutenant," Maggie grinned. "Right after you tell me about Kara."

More Brenda Adcock titles to look for:

Pipeline

What do you do when the mistakes you made in the past come back to slap you in the face with a vengeance? Joanna Carlisle, a fifty-seven year old photojournalist, has only begun to adjust to retirement on her small ranch outside Kerrville, Texas, when she finds herself unwillingly sucked into an investigation of illegal aliens being smuggled into the United States to fill the ranks of cheap labor needed to increase corporate profits.

Joanna is a woman who has always lived life her way and on her own terms, enjoying a career that had given her everything she thought she ever wanted or needed. An unexpected visit by her former lover, Cate Hammond, and the attempted murder of their son, forces Jo to finally face what she had given up. Although she hasn't seen Cate or their son for fifteen years, she finds that the feelings she had for Cate had only been dormant, but had never died. No matter how much she fights her attraction to Cate, Jo cannot help but wonder whether she had made the right decision when she chose career and independence over love.

Jo comes to understand the true meaning of friendship and love only when her investigation endangers not only her life, but also the lives of the people around her.

ISBN 1-932300-64-3
978-1-932300-64-2

Reiko's Garden

Hatred...like love...knows no boundaries.

How much impact can one person have on a life?

When sixty-five-year old Callie Owen returns to her rural childhood home in Eastern Tennessee to attend the funeral of a woman she hasn't seen in twenty years, she's forced to face the fears, heartache, and turbulent events that scarred both her body and her mind. Drawing strength from Jean, her partner of thirty years, and from their two grown children, Callie stays in the valley longer than she had anticipated and relives the years that changed her life forever.

In 1949, Japanese war bride Reiko Sanders came to Frost Valley, Tennessee with her soldier husband and infant son. Callie Owen was an inquisitive ten-year-old whose curiosity about the stranger drove her to disobey her father for just one peek at the woman who had become the subject of so much speculation. Despite Callie's fears, she soon finds that the exotic-looking woman is kind and caring, and the two forge a tentative, but secret friendship.

When Callie and her five brothers and sisters were left orphaned, Reiko provided emotional support to Callie. The bond between them continued to grow stronger until Callie left Frost Valley as a teenager, emotionally and physically scarred, vowing never to return and never to forgive.

It's not until Callie goes "home" that she allows herself to remember how Reiko influenced her life. Once and for all, can she face the terrible events of her past? Or will they come back to destroy all that she loves?

ISBN 978-1-932300-77-2
1-932300-77-5

Redress of Grievances

In the first of a series of psychological thrillers, Harriett Markham is a defense attorney in Austin, Texas, who lost everything eleven years earlier. She had been an associate with a Dallas firm and involved in an affair with a senior partner, Alexis Dunne. Harriett represented a rape/murder client named Jared Wilkes and got the charges dismissed on a technicality. When Wilkes committed a rape and murder after his release, Harriett was devastated. She resigned and moved to Austin, leaving everything behind, including her lover.

Despite lingering feelings for Alexis, Harriet becomes involved with a sex-offense investigator, Jessie Rains, a woman struggling with secrets of her own. Harriet thinks she might finally be happy, but then Alexis re-enters her life. She refers a case of multiple homicide allegedly committed by Sharon Taggart, a woman with no motive for the crimes. Harriett is creeped out by the brutal murders, but reluctantly agrees to handle the defense.

As Harriett's team prepares for trial, disturbing information comes to light. Sharon denies any involvement in the crimes, but the evidence against her seems overwhelming. Harriett is plunged into a case rife with twisty psychological motives, questionable sanity, and a client with a complex and disturbing life. Is she guilty or not? And will Harriet's legal defense bring about justice—or another Wilkes case?

Recipient of a 2008 award from the Golden Crown Literary Society, the premiere organization for the support and nourishment of quality lesbian literature. Redress of Grievances won in the category of Lesbian Mystery.

ISBN 978-1-932300-86-4
1-932300-86-4

The Sea Hawk

Dr. Julia Blanchard, a marine archaeologist, and her team of divers have spent almost eighteen months excavating the remains of a ship found a few miles off the coast of Georgia. Although they learn quite a bit about the nineteenth century sailing vessel, they have found nothing that would reveal the identity of the ship they have nicknamed "The Georgia Peach."

Consumed by the excavation of the mysterious ship, Julia's relationship with her partner, Amy, has deteriorated. When she forgets Amy's birthday and finds her celebrating in the arms of another woman, Julia returns alone to the Peach site. Caught in a violent storm, she finds herself separated from her boat and adrift on the vast Atlantic Ocean.

Her rescue at sea leads her on an unexpected journey into the true identity of the Peach and the captain and crew who called it their home. Her travels take her to the island of Martinique, the eastern Caribbean islands, the Louisiana German Coast and New Orleans at the close of the War of 1812.

How had the Peach come to rest in the waters off the Georgia coast? What had become of her alluring and enigmatic captain, Simone Moreau? Can love conquer everything, even time? On a voyage that lifts her spirits and eventually breaks her heart, Julia discovers the identity of the ship she had been excavating and the fate of its crew. Along the way she also discovers the true meaning of love which can be as boundless and unpredictable as the ocean itself.

ISBN 978-1-935053-10-1
1-935053-10-8

Another Quest title you might enjoy:

Hanging Offense
by Cleo Dare

Mandy Barnes, her trust betrayed by her husband Jay, needs a summer away to think about her marriage. She opts for a seasonal job at Bryce Canyon National Park in remote southern Utah and there meets Jo Reynolds, a lesbian park ranger from California. Mandy is attracted to Jo, but uncertain of her own sexuality.

On a hike into the wilderness, Mandy chances upon some vintage coins in a rusted can and is then plagued by violent dreams of a murder from the past. Are the coins connected to the dreams? Will deciphering the mystery of the past help her unravel the tangled knot of the present? Can she overcome her fears to find renewed trust and true love in Jo's arms?

ISBN 978-1-935053-11-8
1-935053-11-6

Coming Soon from Quest Books:

Ties That Bind
by Andi Marquette

When the Albuquerque Journal reports that a white man was found dead along a remote stretch of road on the Navajo Reservation in northwestern New Mexico, UNM sociology professor K.C. Fontero thinks she might be able to use the case as an example of culture and jurisdiction in one of her classes. But it's soon apparent that this dead man has something to do with a mysterious letter that River Crandall, brother of K.C.'s partner Sage, recently received from the siblings' estranged father, Bill. What does the letter and Bill Crandall's link to a natural gas drilling company have to do with the dead man? And why would Bill try to contact his son and daughter now, after a decade of silence? From the streets of Albuquerque to the gas fields of northwestern New Mexico and the vast expanse of the Navajo Reservation, K.C. and Sage try to unravel the secrets of a dead man while Sage confronts a past she thought she'd left behind. But someone or something wants to keep those secrets buried, and as K.C. soon discovers, sometimes beliefs of one culture jump the boundaries of another, and challenge her logical and analytical mindset, threatening to drive a wedge into the relationship she's building with Sage.

Joined by K.C.'s younger sister Kara and Sage's brother River and aided by best friend and police detective Chris Gutierrez and Chris's partner Dayna Carson, K.C. and Sage are drawn into the life of a dead man, the embittered past of an estranged father, and dark, inexplicable forces whose origins are rooted in Navajo culture and traditions. Whatever happened out there along that road is inextricably linked to Sage and River, and K.C. knows that in order to help them, she has to change her very way of thinking or she could lose the woman who's come to mean the most in her life.

Available November 2009

OTHER QUEST PUBLICATIONS

About the Author

A product of the Appalachian region of Eastern Tennessee, Brenda now lives in Central Texas, near Austin. She began writing in junior high school where she wrote an admittedly hokey western serial to entertain her friends. Completing her graduate studies in Eastern European history in 1971 with the intention of teaching at the college level, she worked as a graphic artist, a public relations specialist for the military and a display advertising specialist until she finally had to admit that her mother might have been right and earned her public school teaching certification. For the last twenty-plus years she has taught world history and political science. Brenda and her partner of twelve years, Cheryl, are the parents of four grown children and grandparents of three. Rounding out their home are three temperamental cats, a poodle mix, and a Blue Heeler mix puppy. When she is not writing, Brenda creates stained glass and shoots pool at her favorite bar. She is the recipient of the 2007 Alice B. Lavender Award for new author, a finalist for a 2007 Golden Crown Literary Award for Debut Author, and the recipient of the Goldie Award in the mystery category in 2008.

VISIT US ONLINE AT

www.regalcrest.biz

At the Regal Crest Website You'll Find

- The latest news about forthcoming titles and new releases

- Our complete backlist of romance, mystery, thriller and adventure titles

- Information about your favorite authors

- Current bestsellers

Regal Crest titles are available from all progressive booksellers and online at StarCrossed Productions, (www.scp-inc.biz), Bella Distribution and many others.

LaVergne, TN USA
22 December 2010
209785LV00002B/103/P